Images of Devotion

A Blossom Hills Romance, Volume 2

Kate Alexander

Published by Kate Alexander, 2020.

IMAGES OF DEVOTION

First edition. September 22, 2020.

Written by Kate Alexander.

This book is dedicated to all the family and friends
who suffered through my hundred levels of crazy
while trying to write and edit this book.

Prologue

Sixteen years ago

Dixie lifted her head through the open doors of the gym and found her date, Mike Nestor, still dancing with another girl. Sitting on the stairs of her high school dressed in her purple flowing dress, Dixie stared down at her hands that held a battered purple and white corsage attached to her wrist. She was doing her best not to burst into tears. Crying in public was something that she never did. Growing up, if she cried in front of others her father would lecture her about how tears have no purpose and was not something their family indulged in. Her older sister, Elena, never cried. Dixie wasn't even sure that her sister had feelings. Elena was a certified genius and had no time for trivial things like boys, friends or even sisters.

The cold concrete of the stairs worked its way through, giving her an additional chill to add to the one in her heart. She thought that she should just be happy that someone even asked her to the dance, but shouldn't that person spend all their time with her too? She wasn't one of the popular girls and originally wasn't even going to attend the dance, at least until Mike had asked her to be his date.

The day that Mike asked her to the dance, she thought that he was coming to talk to someone else at the table. Boys never came to talk to her, especially the cute ones. She had been sitting in the cafeteria with her best friend Summer and a couple of other girls who had nowhere else to sit. They were the outcast table. Dixie's brown curly hair was always a bit of a mess so she had it in her usual style sweeping it up in a loose pony tail. Her black-rimmed glasses kept slipping off her nose as Mike approached her, making her feel even more inadequate.

At first, Dixie looked down, waiting for Mike to talk to Summer. Summer was very pretty with her sunshine blonde hair and emerald eyes, but was also socially awkward. The two girls had immediately grown close when Dixie moved to Blossom Hills to live with her grandparents. Summer's shyness had put off most boys from asking her out. Then when Mike said Dixie's name, she had to shake her head and look up to make sure he was talking to her.

After awkwardly clearing his throat, he gave a crooked grin and asked her to the homecoming dance. Dixie quietly sat there dumbfounded. She thought for sure that if he was going to ask her something, it would be to tutor him in English or maybe something about the school paper where she worked as the photographer. Blinking and staring wide eyed through her glasses that were yet again slipping down her nose, she could only give a small squeak of a reply. Finally, Mike repeated his question and Summer took over and answered, "She would love to go."

Mike smiled and asked Dixie for her phone number to set up the date. Dixie finally managed to gather her wits enough to scribble her number on a piece of paper and slid it over to Mike. Summer was ecstatic for her friend and talked animatedly while Dixie sat quietly for the remainder of the lunch.

Summer seemed more excited about Dixie's date than she did. She even insisted on letting her help Dixie with a makeover. Dixie didn't really want to get a makeover. She liked being comfortable in her jeans, t-shirts and sweatshirts. She never really found it necessary to get all dressed up like the other girls, but a date with Mike Nestor was a big deal. After a couple of days of Summer's insistence, Dixie finally agreed to suffer through a makeover day the night before the dance as long as Summer would do everything with her.

That Friday after school, Dixie and Summer went to the salon with the money that Dixie's grandmother had given her to get the works done. Dixie felt like a science experiment between the highlights put in her hair, the waxing of her eyebrows, and the mani-pedis she got with Summer.

The day of the dance, Dixie went across the street to Summer's house to get ready. Summer fixed her hair in a partial updo and allowed some curls to stray from the upswept hair to frame her face. Then she applied Dixie's makeup with a light touch and added some glitter to her chest that was just above the cleavage of her new dress.

Putting her glasses back on, Dixie looked in the mirror and couldn't believe what she saw. She didn't look like herself. This girl in the mirror was much prettier and couldn't be her. Summer was beaming behind her and then pulled a small box from a bag on her bed.

"Your Grandma gave me these for you to wear tonight." She pulled out a box of new contacts.

Dixie looked at her friend, confused. "I don't own contacts."

"Your Grandma ordered them after I told her about the makeover day. The doctor had measured your eyes for contacts when you got your exam last time, and had written the prescription, but you refused it. So, we thought you might like them for tonight. You can go back to the glasses after the dance if you really want to."

It took Dixie about five minutes to get the contacts in, and once she did, Summer smiled with tears in her eyes. "You look so beautiful. Mike is going to have a heart attack."

The girls made their way downstairs to find Summer's parents and her big brother Chase sitting in the living room. Chase was in a button-down shirt and tie, waiting to also pick up his date for the dance. He was three years older and a freshman at UNC, but had come back for the weekend to take out an old friend, Amy, who was still a senior, to the dance. Her boyfriend had gotten appendicitis and was still recovering from the surgery. Amy wanted to attend her last senior homecoming dance and had asked Chase to go with her as a favor. Chase was already going to be attending the festivities since he was the homecoming King the previous year and had to crown the current year's King in the ceremony. After getting Amy's boyfriend's permission, he was happy to take his friend to the dance.

Chase looked a bit shocked when he turned around to see Dixie. He stared at her not moving. Was there something wrong with her dress? Her hair? For once in their ten years of being friends she couldn't read him. They first met when she would come for visits with her grandparents, and then six years ago when she moved in with her grandparents to attend school in Blossom Hills. She watched him shake his head. He did look stunning but she knew not to get lost in him. He was nineteen, and she was only sixteen. He finally gave a grin to Dixie and said, "You look amazing Dixie. Mike is a lucky guy."

Dixie looked down and blushed. "You really think I look okay?"

Chase came over and gave her a hug. "You look more than okay. You are going to have a great night."

Chase's parents, Carrie and Jeff, both nodded in agreement and also came to give Dixie a hug. She loved them both. They were like surrogate parents. They watched out for Dixie just as if she was their own child.

After posing for several pictures, she walked across the street to wait for her date. Mike showed up a few minutes later with corsage in hand. His eyes widened as Dixie greeted him at the door. He complimented her and placed the corsage around her wrist. They posed for pictures for her grandparents and left for the dance.

Once they reached the school Mike politely opened the door for Dixie and held her hand as they walked into the dance together. Dixie felt incredibly light and happy. This was her first date. She had never even been kissed before, and this cute guy was walking hand in hand with her to the dance. Once they arrived, they sat at a table by the dance floor and Mike nervously looked around the room. Dixie tried to keep his attention and talk to him about things that she knew he liked. He was a basketball player and was active in the yearbook committee where she also helped with pictures. He was still distracted and looking around the room. Finally, Dixie asked him if he would like to dance. He agreed and led her to the dancefloor.

Dixie tried to enjoy the dance and had even leaned her body close to his, but he seemed to stiffen when she got closer. She caught the eye of Chase who was dancing with Amy just a few feet away. At first, he smiled at her but then frowned when looking over at Mike. Dixie couldn't understand why Chase looked mad at her, and she tried to shake it off while finishing the dance with Mike's arms wrapped around her.

CHASE WAS GETTING ANGRY. Dixie's date wasn't paying any attention to her. In fact, he kept looking around the room, especially over at one corner where another girl was sitting alone. He leaned over and whispered in Amy's ear, "What do you know about Dixie's date?"

Amy spun with Chase to get a better look at Dixie dancing with Mike. "Oh, you mean Mike Nestor?"

"Yeah."

"Not much. He is a basketball player and I thought he was dating Amber, but I guess not since he came here with Dixie."

"Is Amber that girl sitting over at the corner table?"

Spinning again, Amy looked at the corner and confirmed it was indeed Amber.

Chase shook his head. "Dammit. Guys are such assholes."

Amy laughed. "You do realize that you are a guy too."

"Yeah, I can be an asshole too."

Amy shook her head. "No, you can't. Are you planning on doing something about that?" she asked while nodding her head over to Dixie and Mike.

"Not unless I need to."

Amy nodded. "Well let me know if I can help."

The dance carried on and things seemed like they were going to be okay until Dixie left to use the restroom. When she finally returned everything had gone wrong. Chase saw her stop in the doorway and stare into the middle of the crowd. He followed her gaze and found Mike with his arms wrapped around Amber, kissing her right in the middle of the floor. Chase wanted to punch the guy, but he knew that he was older and bigger and couldn't punish the guy physically.

Chase watched Dixie turn to leave the gym, only to sit on the stairs just outside the entrance. He wanted to give Dixie a few minutes alone before going to her. Searching the room, he finally found his best friend's younger brother Kyle, talking to Derek over at the drink stand. He knew a bunch of the guys had gone stag to the dance and went over to talk to them. After explaining what happened, he made his way through the dancefloor and tapped Mike on the shoulder.

"We need to have a talk."

Startled, Mike looked at Chase and said, "Chase, hey. What's going on?"

"I think that you would like this talk to happen alone."

Mike looked from Chase back to Amy and back at Chase again. "Okay."

Chase led Mike out the other exit from the gym and into the parking lot. Rubbing his head with his hand, he turned and took a deep breath. "You are a stupid asshole. I should beat the shit out of you right now."

"What? Why?" Mike was looking a little nervous. Even as Chase was asking the questions, Mike was taking a couple steps back.

"Did you or did you not ask Dixie to come to this dance?"

"Uh, yeah. I brought her here."

"So, you asked the girl out, brought her to the dance and then decided it was okay to go stick your tongue down some other girl's throat?"

"I didn't plan it... it just happened."

"You just happened to stare at Amber all night? You just happened to ignore your date all night? You just happened to embarrass Dixie by kissing another girl?"

"Amber said she was sorry. She has been my girlfriend for the past six months. I had to take her back now or she wouldn't take me back at all."

"That just makes both of you assholes. You couldn't give that amazing girl a nice night and wait to get back together with Amber?"

"Dixie is nice, but she is a nerd. Yeah, she cleaned up good tonight, but she is still not someone you really date."

Wow, this guy really is a special kind of stupid. Chase stepped closer and growled. "You better watch what you say from here. I may not be able to touch you, but I have several friends in there who are your age who would gladly show you the errors of your ways. She is sweet, smart and funny and you definitely do not deserve to be in the same room as her. Now you are going to take your little girlfriend and you both are going to leave the dance. I will make sure that Dixie gets home safely. You have ten minutes." Chase looked down at his watch and continued, "Starting now."

It took Mike about thirty seconds before deciding that it was in his best interest to gather Amber and hurry back home. Satisfied that Mike was leaving, Chase made his way back to the school to find Dixie. He walked up to her surprised to find her not crying but just looking down at her corsage peeling off the petals one by one.

Chase sat down next to Dixie and put his arm around her shoulders. Dixie sighed and said, "So I guess you saw what happened with Mike."

Chase nodded. "Yeah. Don't pay any attention to him. Any guy who would choose some other girl over you is an idiot."

"You have to say that because you are my best friend's big brother."

Chase leaned his head onto hers and took a deep breath of her hair that smelled like cherry blossoms. His heart skipped a beat as he said, "No, I shouldn't say that because I am your best friend's big brother."

Dixie looked up with her chocolate brown eyes and Chase got lost looking at her for just a minute. He had to avert his gaze, so he drifted his eyes down only to find her chest shimmering with the glitter that Summer had given her. His heart skipped yet another beat. It wasn't long before he found himself mindlessly stroking her back in small circles with his hand as her head dropped back on his chest. He leaned down inhaling her cherry scent again and without thought kissed her on top of her head. "Come on, dance with me."

"What about Amy?"

"She is fine. She was dancing with Derek while I came to check on you."

"She won't mind?"

"Nah. I was just here to keep her company since her boyfriend couldn't make it."

Dixie smiled and let Chase lead her by the hand back to the gym to dance. Dixie and Chase danced with ease across the dance floor. Amy and Derek danced close by as Amy smiled at the two of them. She finally leaned over, winked and said, "Dixie you look incredible tonight. I am glad you found a better dance partner."

Derek smiled and said, "Amy, you are right. I think I need to trade partners. Chase, do you mind?"

Chase shook his head and took Amy back as his dance partner while Derek spun Dixie around the floor. Soon Dixie was dancing with Kyle, and then a few other guys too. Chase could hear them all tell Dixie how pretty she looked and how stupid Mike was. Chase hoped that he was able to turn her bad night into an amazing night. She talked with the guys, all of whom seemed to take a great interest in her. She was laughing and seemed to feel more comfortable as the night progressed. By the night's end, Dixie was surrounded by Chase, Amy, Derek, and Kyle. They all went out to the overlook, where they made a fire and talked until nearly 1 am.

Chase and Dixie dropped Amy off at her house, where her boyfriend was waiting on the porch for her to arrive. Chase and Dixie smiled as the pair greeted each other in a long, passionate kiss. Once they broke for air, the pair waved to Chase as he pulled them out of the drive.

"Amy really likes that guy, doesn't she?"

Chase nodded. "She loves him. There is no doubt about it. I know they talk about getting married already. Normally I would say they are too young, but I have never seen another couple like them except my parents and Tyler's parents."

Dixie nodded. "My parents have never been affectionate with each other. I am surprised that me and my sister were even born. It just seems like they thought 'Hey, we are both really smart, let's just get married and create smart babies to be like us.' I have never even seen them kiss."

Chase shook his head. "I couldn't even image having parents like that. Mine can't keep their hands off each other."

Dixie giggled. "I know."

They finally arrived home and Chase got out of the car to walk Dixie to the door. She placed her hand on the doorknob and turned back to Chase. "I want to thank you again. I know that the other guys only paid attention to me because of you."

Chase took his hand and placed it on her chin to force her to look at him. "Believe me when I say that they noticed you long before I talked to them. When you came down the stairs with Summer, you took my breath away, and I know that you did the same to a lot of the other guys."

"I took your breath away?" Dixie asked in a whisper.

Chase's hand was now cradling her face, and he was leaning in so close the he could feel the heat radiating from her flushed face. Chase didn't say anything. He only slowly nodded his head in confirmation. He wasn't letting her go. He knew he needed to turn around and leave before he did something stupid like kissing her, but his eyes were locked with hers and their breathing had paced to match each other. Dixie gazed at Chase confused and in a barely audible voice asked, "Chase?"

"Yeah?"

He could see that she wanted him to kiss her. He even knew this would be her first kiss if he allowed it to happen. He couldn't do it though. He was too old for her, and he was the person who had always protected her. He made her laugh when her family would let her down. He just held still and allowed her to lean in. Then as if God himself was intervening he felt a blinding light come from their right side. It broke the spell, and the door swung open to find Dixie's grandma, Rose Milani, smiling at them.

"So glad you are back home sweetheart. Did you have a good time?"

Shaking her head Dixie said, "Yes, I did, thank you."

Rose looked at Chase and patted him on the cheek, "Thank you for walking our girl to the door. You are such a nice boy."

Chase gave a small grin. Rose wouldn't think he was such a nice boy if she could have read his mind just two minutes ago. He wanted to back Dixie up against the wall and kiss her until she melted in his arms. He stepped back and said,

"It was my pleasure, Mrs. Milani." He turned to Dixie and said, "I hope you had a good time. I will see you later."

Chase watched Dixie close the door, and then he turned to walk back across to his parent's house. Shaking his head, he knew that he needed to keep some distance from his little sister's best friend. As he walked up on his porch, he found Summer leaning against the door frame with a questioning look on her face. "Not now Summer, I am going to bed." He walked past her as she shook her head and closed the door.

Chapter 1

Present Day

Dixie sat on the gazebo bench, blinking in disbelief. *This can't be right. Jay couldn't be dumping her just a week and a half before their trip.* She looked down at her hands as Jay continued to talk.

"Dixie, it isn't that you aren't great, because believe me you are incredible, but I can't be with someone who doesn't want to be with me as much as I want to be with them."

Dixie started to open her mouth to protest, but Jay put his fingers to her lips to stop her from talking and continued, "I have no doubt that you like me, but if you haven't fallen in love with me by now, I know that it isn't going to happen."

He was right. The poor guy had told her he loved her almost two months ago, and she never said it back. She was never one of those girls who could just throw out those words without the true meaning behind them. She wanted to be in love with him. He was a very nice man. He was attentive and generous to everyone, but she never felt the heat with him. She didn't melt under his touch, but she thought maybe it would just happen over time. Ariel had once told her that when Dixie talked about Jay, she sounded like she

14

was just reading off a grocery list. Dixie knew that Ariel was right, but really had wanted to make this work.

Dixie's eyes lowered to her lap where her hands were twisting together and said, "I'm sorry."

Jay brought his hands to hers, trying to calm them, and said, "It's okay. I'm not mad. I just realized that we both deserve the chance to find someone who loves us the way we deserve."

Dixie couldn't answer. She simply nodded in understanding. Jay wrapped an arm around her and gave her a side hug. She gave a slight laugh as he kissed her on her temple.

He whispered into her ear, "I wish you all the best Dixie."

Dixie let out a deep sigh and said, "You too, Jay."

"Do you want me to walk you home?"

"No. I think I want to just sit here for a few minutes. I can walk the whole block alone when I am ready to go."

"Okay. I guess I'll see you around."

Well, that was a true statement. He worked at Tank's Garage, the only mechanic in town. So, of course she would see him. Her little beater of a car was always getting fixed for one thing or another. At least when she was dating Jay, he kept the dumb thing purring like a contented kitten. Was it sad that she thought her car would miss him more than she did?

Dixie watched him walk around the corner toward his house. Her dating life for the past few years had been such a spectacular mess. Half of the men she went out on dates with were so lackluster that she never even bothered to try and remember their names. Jay had been the longest relationship she'd had since she was twenty-two, and with it only lasting about four months, that wasn't saying much. She knew that she didn't have that soul stirring need for him like she saw with her friends Tyler and Zoey, but she felt that they had a good foundation for a relationship and maybe things would develop over time.

She had only felt a needful longing for two men in her life and both ended with crushing her heart. The first, Chase, started when she was in junior high. Being the older brother of her best friend, she tried to fight how she felt about him, but when she had kissed him so long ago just before he left to go back to college, he rejected her with a simple statement saying he was sorry and it was a mistake.

Then she had fallen for Chris Masterson. They dated for a couple years and once he graduated, she thought that he would ask her to move to New York with him to start a new life, but he simply told her a week before he left that he needed to start fresh and to concentrate on his career. He said that he wouldn't have time for a relationship. Then to make things worse, she found out a year later through mutual friends that he got engaged to a Broadway actress and couldn't have been happier.

Dixie sighed and then felt traitorous tears falling down her face. That just pissed her off. She was so frustrated, and she knew the tears weren't for the loss of Jay as it should have been, but instead it was for just a general lost and alone feeling. How long could she continue this game of trying to make a connection, but never feeling that force that pulls you in, drowning in some kind of devotion, of love?

Breaking her out of her thoughts, she heard the solid pounding of footsteps on the pavement behind her, and then a deep voice that followed, "Dix, what's going on?"

Wiping her eyes, she turned, knowing it was Chase standing behind her. He looked strong and confident standing at his full 6'3" height. He was dressed in his sheriff's uniform and looked so commanding. Dixie always felt so small and delicate next to him, even though she wasn't short. She was a decent 5'6" and had an average, almost athletic build that she knew how to dress to her advantage. She cleared her throat and finally responded. "Hey Chase. I was just taking a minute before heading home."

Chase frowned. Crap. She told him that Jay was taking her out tonight. They had talked about it this morning when they met everyone for breakfast at Sweet Dreams Bakery. She knew it was way too early for their date to be over, and Chase would definitely have questions.

Chase looked around and asked, "Where's Jay?"

Yup. There it was. Dang it.

Dixie lifted one shoulder and said, "Home... I guess. I don't really know."

Chase strode over to her and sat beside her. "I thought you guys had a date tonight."

"Oh, we did, but then we came here to talk and he dumped me."

Dixie watched Chase's fists clinch back and forth. He looked like he was going to search the man out and punch him. His nostrils flared and he finally said, "What the hell? Was he cheating on you?"

Dixie shook her head. "No. He was really nice about it. Honest. Don't go giving him a bunch of tickets for no reason, or try to raid his shop."

Chase raised his hands in defense. "Hey, I would never do that."

Dixie shot him a look. "So that ticket you gave Chris when he came back to visit his family was just a coincidence?"

Chase quirked up a smile. "I did do that, but I was just doing my normal patrol, and he was speeding. Not my fault, I was just lucky enough to be the one who happened to catch him."

"And just how many times did you happen to *patrol* by his house?"

Chase scratched the back of his head, pretending to think. "Just a few extra times, but I was trying to help look for that poor little lost dog in his neighborhood too."

"Uh-huh."

Chase groaned. "He was an ass, and it was just Karma coming back to bite him there."

Dixie sighed and grabbed him by his chin so he was looking directly in her eyes. "Understand this Montgomery, Jay is not to get any tickets from you or from your staff anytime soon or I won't bring you any more food."

Dixie felt a tingling of warning. Chase's eyes seemed to be getting lost in thought. Wanting to bring him back from where his mind was going, she grasped his chin with her hand. "Chase! Tell me you understand."

"Okay, okay. No speeding tickets, but if he does something serious, I will still arrest him."

"Fine. If you find him over a dead body with a gun in his hand, by all means arrest the guy."

Chuckling Chase said, "I wasn't going for that serious, but yes I would definitely arrest him." He wrapped an arm around her shoulders and gave a slight squeeze as she rested her head on his shoulder. "So, do you want to tell me what happened?"

Dixie shook her head. "Can I tell you later? I just want it to settle in a little bit okay?"

Chase squeezed her and said, "Okay, how about we meet for breakfast tomorrow morning? I am off all day and could use some of Zoey's delicious baking." Zoey owned Sweet Dreams Bakery, and was engaged to Chase's best friend, Tyler. Dixie had never seen two people so in love before. They glowed when they were near each other. Dixie and Chase always talked about how they were genuinely happy for them, and they were proud of Tyler for turning his life around after he went through a man-whore phase.

"That sounds good. I am supposed to meet up with Ariel there anyway. We will be there at 7:30 to go over Zoey's wedding stuff. So, how about we meet at 7:00?"

"Okay, see you then." He picked her up off the bench and gave her one more big bear hug. "I still have an hour left on my shift so I need to go. I will see you tomorrow, okay?"

Dixie nodded and waved as she watched Chase leave.

When Dixie walked through her apartment door, she was exhausted. She ambled over to her couch, picked up her throw pillow and then brought it to her face to release a scream in the pillow. She was mad, but not mad at Jay. Jay had never been anything but kind to her, but she was mad at herself. What was wrong with her? Why couldn't she fall in love with a perfectly nice safe guy?

Sighing, she began to take off her shoes. She found herself looking at a picture that was on top of the fireplace mantle. It was a picture of her, Chase, and Summer when Dixie was about fifteen. Dixie and Summer had their arms around each other as Chase was poking his head in between the two girls with a wide grin. She loved that picture. She missed Summer so much. Absentmindedly, she began rubbing her hip where a long jagged scar ran nearly two feet down her leg. She took a deep breath and said, "He is still trying to take care of me Summer. You would be so proud of him."

As she fell asleep that night, her mind was flooded with memories of past relationships, Summer, Chase and how her life never seemed to fit into place.

DIXIE AWOKE THE NEXT morning from the sound of her text message tone. Half expecting it to be Chase, she rolled over with a slight smile. When the screen came into focus, she frowned. Instead of her big bear of a friend, it was her sister Elena. Her perfect, smart and gorgeous sister. It wasn't that she didn't love her, because she did, but when Elena or parents would talk to her, she felt so far from adequate. Her parents were research specialists and highly regarded in their fields. Her sister also followed in her parents' footsteps and worked in Georgia under a grant in neuroscience. Elena was a classified genius and had married a neurosurgeon. She met her husband, Charles while he worked with her on a breakthrough surgery to assist in recovering memory from traumatic head injuries. Their wedding was the only time she had truly seen her sister happy and even slightly emotional, but still no tears.

Her sister had one son, Martin, an adorable little guy who loved to chat it up on Skype with his Aunt Dixie. Elena and Charles had tested him for his IQ at an early age, and when the results came in, they immediately enrolled him into an elite preschool. Dixie's family never failed to mention their disappointment in her life choices, starting with the fact that she did not attend college, and on up to her professional and dating life. It didn't matter to them that her business was a success or even that some of her photography was getting noticed by the local art scene.

When she was in grade school her parents tested her and Elena's IQ. Elena scored very high and their parents were thrilled and immediately enrolled Elena in a local boarding school and started paying less and less attention to Dixie. Dixie's grandparents hated to see how alone Dixie was, and that her parents had ignored her. They asked Dixie if she would like to live with them in North Carolina, and she happily welcomed the idea. Her grandmother, who was a master of manipulation, convinced her daughter that Dixie would benefit with the good local public school, and would be a great help to her and Dixie's grandfather since they were getting older. This would allow them to focus on Elena, who could benefit from their attention. Finally, when Dixie turned ten, she moved to Blossom Hills and only saw her parents and sister once every few years. Her parents continually provided excuses of pressures from work or school events that Elena had to prevent them from coming to see her.

Dixie wiped her eyes, groaned, and swiped the screen to read the text.

Elena: Coming in a day early. Make sure to have the room ready when I get there.

Dixie rolled her eyes and talked to herself. "Really? No asking if it is okay for you to come early, or even a hi, how are you?" Dixie growled and started to type out a response.

Dixie: No, it isn't okay. I want to see you for the least amount of time as possible. Backspace.... Backspace... backspace.

Dixie: Okay, do I ever get a choice when it comes to you people? Backspace... backspace... backspace.

Growling, she typed out the politest response she could muster.

Dixie: O*kay*

Dixie knew Elena was coming into town to help with driving Grams and Gramps to the beach. Originally, she and Jay were driving together to bring a lot of the supplies and their luggage. This didn't leave much room for more people. Elena had also taken over for some of the event planning because she didn't trust that Dixie could handle the responsibility of such a large family gathering.

Her grandparents were celebrating sixty years of marriage, and family from both Grams and Gramps side were coming into town. She loved Gramps side of the family. They were large, boisterous and fun. Most of them still resided in Hawaii, where Gramps was from. Grams side was much smaller and quiet, like Dixie's parents and Elena.

Noticing the time, she quickly rolled out of bed so she could meet Chase for breakfast. She primped in the mirror and started to put on makeup but then put the bag away after only putting on a little mascara and gloss. It was just Chase and Ariel. There was no need to get all dressed up for the two of them.

Dixie heard the small jingle of the bell on the door as she walked into Zoey's bakery. Zoey was helping another customer, but gave a bright smile when she saw Dixie enter the bakery. Dixie gave a small wave and stood in line as she looked over the selections. She smiled at the hand drawn chalk sign that indicated that the special of the day was Berry Goodness Muffins. She loved how Zoey's mood always showed in her daily specials. Her favorite so far was the broken heart brownies, which while it was sad that her friend was going through a bad time, the name was cute and the brownies were amazing. They were heart shaped triple chocolate with a ripple of fudge in the middle that looked as if it was where the heart was breaking.

"Good morning, Zoey."

Zoey beamed at her friend. Being in love looked good on her. Her eyes were sparkling bright blue, and she wore her usual mixture of sugar and flour on her face and apron. "Hey Dixie. How you doing?"

Dixie gave a little shrug. "Okay, could be better."

Zoey frowned with concern for her friend. "What's wrong, sweetie?"

"Jay and I broke up last night."

Zoey immediately came from behind the counter and gave her friend a big hug. "Oh, I am so sorry. Are you okay?"

"It is kind of weird but I think I am a little too okay with it. If that makes any sense."

Zoey gave a sad, knowing little smile. "Yes, it does. Jay was nice, but we all knew you weren't head over heels in love with the guy."

"Why was it so obvious to everyone?"

Zoey tilted her head and walked back to the other side of the counter to gather some treats for her friend. "You can always tell when someone is completely crazy about another person. Jay was crazy about you. We could all see that, but you didn't let go with him."

Dixie winced a little. "Wow, I am not so sure I like this much honesty this early in the morning."

"Maybe, but at least I soften the blow with yummy treats," Zoey said as she handed a small box of pastries over to Dixie.

Dixie looked at the small box and shook her head. "I need more than this."

Frowning Zoey said, "Oh, sweetie, you are more upset than I thought."

Dixie gave a slight laugh and replied, "No, not really. Chase is joining me for breakfast."

Laughing Zoey grabbed the bigger box and filled it with more pastries and handed over two iced coffees to Dixie. "My treat today. Enjoy and don't let Chase eat your portions."

CHASE ENTERED THE BAKERY and watched as Dixie had just sat down and opened the box for her breakfast. He had to appreciate his good timing. Dixie had a donut in her hand that she was getting ready to eat when Chase leaned over and took a bite out it.

"Hey, I was going to eat that," she exclaimed.

"You still can. I only took one bite."

"I got you your own food you know," she said with a small pout.

Grinning and patting his stomach, Chase replied, "Your food always tastes better."

Dixie grabbed a sticky bun from Chase's box and shoved it in his mouth before he could say another word.

With food still in his mouth he said, "I love it when you feed me."

"You are such a dork."

"True, but not a big enough dork to dump you. What happened?"

Chase refused to waste any more time to get information about what happened with Jay. If she thought she could delay the conversation with food, she was sorely mistaken. Dixie set down her donut and told Chase the whole story. He sat quietly listening to every word. Once Dixie was done, he sat back in his chair and thought for just a minute before speaking. "Guess I can't pound the guy for breaking your heart, huh?"

Dixie looked at him wide-eyed. "No. You can't. Honestly, I half expect his sister to come and give me a piece of her mind for breaking his heart. He was right, though. I wasn't in love with him. Sure, I liked him a lot, but there was no fire. My heart didn't skip a beat when I was with him. I didn't melt when he touched me."

Chase held up his hand. "Stop right there. Please don't go any deeper than that. I don't want to hear about how you felt when he touched you."

Tilting her head Dixie asked, "Why not?"

Chase stopped for a second. *Yeah, dummy why not?* "Uh... because you are my friend and I don't want to hear about details of your sex life."

"You and Tyler talk about your sex lives all the time."

"Yeah, but he is a guy and I don't feel protective of him." *Or possessive* he thought. "Besides, when he met Zoey, he stopped talking to me about his sex life."

"Really? Why?"

"Because that is what guys do when they fall in love. They don't share the dirty details with their buddies."

"Well that is sweet."

Chase shrugged. "For what it's worth I am glad Jay broke it off if you weren't in love with him. You deserve so much more than just settling for what's comfortable. You need to feel passion." He moved closer to her. "You need to feel like hearing that person's voice affects you to the very core. That when they are close to you, you feel like you might die if you don't feel their touch in that very moment." Chase was now leaning closer to Dixie with each sentence until he was nearly whispering in her ear. "And when your bodies are only inches apart, you can hear their heartbeat faster to match yours. Inside you are dying just waiting for their warming caress on your body."

Dixie didn't move, but Chase could feel her heart beating faster with each whispered word. She didn't move, and she seemed to be frozen to her seat. Was he freaking her out?

Was he pushing too hard too quick? He was no good at this relationship stuff. If he moved another inch his lips could touch her neck. The last time he was close like this they had kissed, and he screwed it all up with his own insecurities. He had told her it was a mistake and ran out like the coward he was, but no more. They were going to move forward, and he just had to figure out how best to make that happen. She opened her heart first last time and he was the one who broke it, but he swore if she would give him a chance it would never be broken again. Not on his watch. He desperately wanted to put his lips onto hers. She turned to see him looking and her dilated eyes told him she wanted this too, even if her mind was struggling with it.

Then a loud clang broke their attention from each other. Zoey had dropped a tray of donuts and was staring at the two of them. Dixie jumped away from Chase, seemingly embarrassed. Zoey mouthed the word sorry to them just as Phil, her part-time assistant, came over to help her clean up. Dixie looked away from Zoey back to him who had already locked his eyes back on to her.

"Chase," Dixie said questioningly.

He moved his hand to the small of her back and asked, "Yeah?"

Then a soft voice came from the side of them and said, "Geez Dixie, didn't you feed the bear yet?"

Chase slowly moved away and looked over to find Ariel staring at the two of them. Smiling he said, "Yeah she fed me."

"Chase, are you here to help plan stuff for Zoey's wedding? We have lots to talk about like dresses, lingerie, party favors and bridal shower activities," Ariel asked in a sarcastic innocent tone.

Chase grimaced. "Guess that is my cue to run away while I can. Dixie I will see you later. Bye Ariel." He turned to leave only to find Tyler standing in the doorway with his arms crossed and shaking his head at Chase. He walked past Tyler and onto the outside sidewalk. Tyler followed him outside. "What? Thought you were there to see your woman."

Tyler laughed. "My woman texted me to get my ass downstairs to talk to you before you did something stupid." Tyler and Zoey lived in the apartment above the bakery. The guys all gave Tyler crap about being at Zoey's beck and call, but he never seemed to mind. All he ever did was grin and nod.

Chase shook his head. "Stupid about what?"

"Seriously, you don't have a clue?"

The two continued over to the park where Chase stopped to lean on a tree. "No, what were you beckoned down here for?"

"Wow. Okay, you are being dumb today."

Chase quirked an eye so Tyler dug out his phone and handed it to Chase so he could read a text message.

Zoey: You need to get your ass down here. Chase looks like he is going to screw it up with Dixie.

Chase grunted and handed the phone back to Tyler. Tyler put it away and said, "Did you seriously try to kiss Dixie in the bakery?"

Chase clenched his jaw. "No, I didn't try to kiss her."

"Okay, so what were you doing?"

"I don't know. I got a little close in her personal space."

"Have you lost your mind? She is with Jay. You can't just do stuff like that especially in this town."

"She isn't with Jay anymore."

"Wait... What? When did that happen?"

"Last night."

"And you thought it was appropriate to 'get in her personal space' a day after they broke up? She is probably upset that they broke up."

"She isn't upset about losing Jay," Chase said defensively.

"She said that?"

"Yeah. He broke up with her because she couldn't give him all of her."

Tyler rubbed the back of his head. He didn't look surprised. Everyone knew that Dixie wasn't that into Jay. For as long as they had known Dixie her dating life was always a little removed. When she started dating Jay, none of them expected it to last as long as it did. He finally stopped rubbing his head and asked, "So, what were you doing with Dixie?"

"Shit, I don't know. Just lost my head for a minute."

"Planning on losing your head again any time soon?"

"No. I can't, not with her. I need to make sure if we do this, it is done right."

"Okay then, focus and don't mess it up with her. Look, I know all about what happened back then with your mom, Summer and Dixie. If you remember I was there with you. I still think that holding back with her is a mistake, but you made up your mind years ago. You said you couldn't go there, and if you aren't going to change it, don't mess with her head. If you have changed your mind, don't fuck it up."

"You're an asshole."

"True, but I am the asshole that you chose for a best friend."

ARIEL WAS TAPPING HER pen on the pink notepad waiting for Dixie to say something. The girls had watched Tyler and Chase walk over to the park across the street and Dixie's eyes were fixed on Chase. Ariel's normally soft voice was a bit louder as she finally asked, "Dixie, are you going to tell me what the heck is going on?"

Dixie broke her focus from Chase and looked at her friend. Ariel looked amazing as always. She was wearing a spaghetti strap sundress and had her blonde hair in a loose updo. "Why do you always look so perfect?"

Ariel shook her head. "As much as I love a compliment, which thank you by the way, you can't change the subject. Why did it look like Chase was going to maul you in the middle of the bakery? He knows you are with Jay."

Dixie shook her head and then thumped it on the table into her arms. She mumbled down at the table. "I don't know, and Jay and I broke up."

"What?" Ariel shrieked. "When did you guys break up? And pick up your head off the table before answering that."

Dixie sighed and looked her friend in the eyes. "He broke up with me because I couldn't love him the way he wanted, and honestly the way he deserved."

"Oh. I wish I could say that I was surprised."

"So why is it that I seem to be the only one who is surprised by this turn of events?"

"Well, to be honest I thought this would happen, but I really thought it would take longer."

"That is not reassuring or any better."

"Sweetie, since when have I sugar coated anything for you?"

Dixie sighed. "Never, but at least you say it nicer that Josie does."

Ariel laughed. "Josie has no filter." Ariel played with the edge of her dress before continuing. "So why did Chase make a move on you?"

"It wasn't a move."

"Oh, it was a move. If Kyle looked at me like that or had his lips that close to my neck there would have been no turning back."

The girls had long ago bonded over the two men who they loved but didn't seem to love them back. There were times that being so close to the men and not having what they wanted was crushing, but both women had decided that having their friendship was worth the heartbreak it brought not having them.

"Chase made his choice a long time ago. I won't put it out there again. I can't."

Ariel put her hand over Dixie's and looked up at her. "Are you sure he hasn't changed his mind?"

"Fairly certain."

"I think you two should talk."

"I have too much going on right now. The studio is busy, I have that God-awful family trip coming up, and now I have to face it without a boyfriend buffer. Then to top it all off I got a text from Elena that she is coming into town a day early."

Ariel winced. "Sorry, I know how she pushes your buttons."

Dixie laughed. "More like she pulverizes them with a hammer."

Chapter 2

Dixie came home that night exhausted. She had three toddler shoots at the studio, one engagement photo shoot and a consultation with a bridezilla. The bridezilla came armed with four binders of photographs from Pinterest, google searches and bridal websites. She even wanted to demand that Dixie buy a dress that would be specially matched to the bridesmaids' colors. Really? It wasn't like Dixie didn't already have a closet full of wedding appropriate attire, and if she was behind the camera, it wasn't like she was going to clash with the wedding party. Of course, the bride couldn't even pick a style of photography she wanted for her wedding. At first, she said that she wanted photojournalism, but then wanted posed pictures to match those that she found online exactly. So much for originality.

Dixie walked over to Ansel's cage and scooped him out. Ansel was her pet hedgehog that she had somehow adopted after doing a photoshoot with a ten-year boy who had just gotten the pet. The boy had let out an ear-piercing scream about how he hated the animal after a quill poked him in the hand when he squeezed it too hard. The father of the boy said that he would dump the animal on the side of the road if the boy didn't want him anymore. Dixie was outraged. This animal was obviously domesticated and wouldn't survive in the wild. She offered to take the hedgehog if they didn't want him. The father gruffly agreed and then informed her that they wouldn't give the animal's cage to her because it cost too much money. Dixie didn't care about that and told the man that she would take care of finding her own habitat for him. For the remainder of that day the hedgehog curled up with a stuffed chameleon by the poster of an Ansel Adams photograph in her office. Seeing him snuggled up looking so adorable by the poster gave her the idea of his new name, Ansel.

Dixie plopped down on the couch as she placed Ansel on her shoulder. She always enjoyed when Ansel would nuzzle on her neck. "Hey boy, I missed you too. Did you have fun on your wheel today?"

Ansel answered by scurrying down her chest and up to her other shoulder. Dixie grabbed her laptop and opened her photo editing software to go over her day's work. It wasn't long before she heard a knock on her door. She looked over at Ansel to make sure he was secure before standing to go to answer the door. She was surprised to open it and find Chase standing with a couple of carryout boxes and some beer.

Chase made a small grin and walked past her into the entryway.

Dixie rolled her eyes. "Hi Chase. Gee, how about you come right on in? Did you lose your key?" Dixie had long ago given him a key to help take care of Ansel or in case of emergencies. They had gotten to the point where he would just use it at will and make surprise visits, but when she was dating Jay that stopped.

"I brought dinner, and my hands were full. It is good for you to get off the couch once in a while."

Dixie gave a small laugh. "How do you know I haven't had dinner already?"

Chase raised an eyebrow. "And did you?"

Sighing, Dixie shook her head and said, "No."

"Great. I didn't feel like eating alone tonight, so I brought us food." He set the dinner on the counter and noticed Ansel. He took his hand to Dixie's shoulder and rubbed his finger under Ansel's chin. "Hey Ansel. Did you run laps on mom's body yet?"

"No, he hasn't. He is a little cuddly today. He can tell I had a bad day at work."

Chase grabbed the silverware from the drawer and a couple of the beers while putting the others in the fridge. "Yeah? What happened?"

Dixie gave the rundown of her day as they both ate dinner. Chase shook his head after she finished telling him about all the disasters. "I don't know how you can do your job. I would have shot someone by the end of the day."

Laughing Dixie said, "That doesn't bode well for you as a police officer."

"I can tolerate criminals before lazy parenting or immature people throwing tantrums."

"So, no kids for you then."

"No. I want kids, but I will not let my kids act like some of these spoiled little demons I see at the grocery store. My mom would have kicked my ass if I acted like these kids do."

"Yes, she would have. I always thought your dad was softer on you than your mom."

"Dad definitely had his moments, but he stayed out of the little stuff. We knew we were in deep if he got involved."

"Summer got away with everything."

Chase looked out the window and paused. "Yeah, she did."

Wanting to change the subject from Summer, Chase looked back to Dixie and asked, "Has Jay called you?"

"No. It is definitely over. I think he waited as long as he could before breaking up with me, and the sad part is I don't even miss him. I feel like a horrible person. I mean here is this nice guy pouring his heart into a relationship with me and I couldn't give mine back."

"Don't beat yourself up about it. Either you fall in love or you don't. You never gave him any false promises did you?"

"No. I never said I loved him. He told me a few times and I would just either act like I didn't hear him or change the subject."

"You have always been the expert at changing the subject."

Dixie looked at Chase and softly said, "There have been a lot of things in my life that I don't like talking about."

Chase laid his hand just above Dixie's knee and squeezed. "I know."

Dixie abruptly stood up and began to gather the remnants from dinner to clean up. "Anyway, and now I have this stupid family thing next week and I lost my date."

Chase frowned and began to help Dixie finish cleaning up. "Can you get someone else to go?"

"It was supposed to be my boyfriend, not just a random person."

Knowing that Dixie never talked to her family for more than three to five minutes at a time Chase asked, "Did they even know Jay's name?"

Dixie thought for a minute. "Oh my god. No. I just simply said I had a boyfriend and I that I would be bringing him with me. They never even asked anything about him." She shook her head. "They don't even care enough to find out about the man dating me. After I told them I had a boyfriend, they just said 'that's nice' and moved the conversation back to them for the next couple of minutes."

Chase stepped a little closer. "You could always just bring someone else. They would never know the difference."

"Grams and Gramps would know."

"Do you really think they would rat you out?"

Giving a small laugh she said, "No. They would probably encourage me to bring a replacement."

Chase leaned against the counter. "Well just try to have a good time. At least for your grandparent's sake."

"I will." Dixie thought for a minute and finally said, "Hey, I have some cookies from Zoey. Do you want to have dessert and watch a movie?"

"Sure. My choice of movie though."

"Hey. I am the dumpee here. Aren't you supposed to let me pick?"

"If you were broken hearted about it yeah, but since you aren't, the guest gets to pick. So, it is my choice tonight."

Dixie grabbed a white box from the counter and began to walk into the living room with Chase following her. Just before they got to the couch Chase leaned over and whispered, "Besides you never could resist my charming ways."

Dixie rolled her eyes and grabbed a cookie from the box and shoved it in his mouth. "Ugh. Hush you little monster."

Chase chewed the cookie with a wide grin as Dixie sat on the couch and then said, "Nothing little about me babe."

Dixie threw a pillow from the couch at his head. "Eww, please stop while you're ahead." Chase started to opened his mouth to say something just as Dixie stopped him, "Not a word Montgomery."

"You love me."

"And God only knows why."

Chase grabbed the remote from the coffee table and sat next to Dixie. He was scrolling through the choices from Netflix and was taunting Dixie. "Let's see what to watch.... horror? A war movie? Or I know—how about creepy killer clown movie?"

"Do you ever want me to feed you again?"

"Okay. I will take mercy on you. How about this?" Chase selected *50 First Dates*.

Dixie knew that it wasn't too much of a compromise. Adam Sandler movies were his favorites, and he always had a huge crush on Drew Barrymore. He once told her that he thought she was beautiful in a non-traditional way, fearless and disarming with charm. He always said he was never interested in the skinny women who wore too much makeup, even though she knew he picked up that type all the time at the bar in the neighboring town.

Dixie smiled and leaned against Chase as they watched the movie. About half way through she sighed and said, "It's a nice idea but not realistic."

Confused Chase looked down at her. "What isn't realistic?"

"Loving someone so much that you would be willing to make them fall in love with you every day. I don't think that kind of love really exists."

Chase frowned. "You're wrong. I have seen it."

Dixie sat fully up and looked him in the eyes. "You have seen a couple who had some weird amnesia disease where they forgot everything each day?"

Chase draped his arm on the back of the couch closer to her. "Not exactly like that, but you know my grandma had Alzheimer's and couldn't remember who we were most days." Realization slowly crept in Dixie's face before Chase continued. "Grandpa would introduce himself to her every day and let her fall in love all over again. When they first met, they both told me that it was love at first sight. He always said it was like an electric storm in the air and he knew they could light the whole town with the power that surged between them. I watched Grandma fall in love at first sight with him so many times before she died, it was... incredible."

Dixie placed her hand on Chase's arm and immediately felt sorry for her words. She knew how much he loved his grandparents. His Grandmother had died just a year ago and his Grandfather still missed her each day. "You're right. I never really thought about it that way. Maybe it is just me—maybe I can't love anyone that way."

"You know I don't believe that. That kind of love is out there waiting on you, maybe it is just waiting for some things to work themselves out first."

Dixie tilted her head with questioning eyes. They both looked at each other for what seemed like minutes when Chase's cell phone suddenly broke their gazes. Chase stood up and began frowning. He advised the caller he would be there in fifteen minutes and disconnected the call. "There was an accident with fatalities. I have to go."

Dixie stood up and began to put on her shoes.

Chase eyed her cautiously and asked, "What are you doing?"

"I'm coming with you. You are going to need pictures." She did this for them all the time. This shouldn't be a surprise to him.

"You don't have to come for this one."

"Why not? I do this for the department all the time."

Chase clenched his jaw. "Not this one Dix."

Dixie narrowed her eyes and lowered her voice. "Why not?"

"You need your rest. I can have one of..." Chase was stopped mid-sentence by Dixie punching him in the arm. "Ow."

"What aren't you telling me?"

Chase sighed and closed his eyes. "It is on 421, where..."

"Where the accident happened."

"Yeah." Chase went to hug Dixie thinking that would be the end of the discussion only to find her duck out of his embrace and grab her camera.

"I am not afraid to go back there. Let's go." She cocked her hip, placing one arm there and gave him that look of determination, that look she always gave when she wasn't backing down.

"Jesus woman, you are stubborn."

"You love me that way, so get a move on it."

Dixie and Chase got into his car and began the drive back to the bend of the road that haunted them both. Dixie watched out the passenger window as she began to hear sounds that echoed from the past.

DIXIE AND SUMMER WERE at the field of sunflowers. Dixie had just gotten a new camera and had wanted to take some pictures at the field while the sunflowers were still in bloom. Dixie's Grandmother had dropped them off, and they were expecting Chase to pick them in up in two hours since he was on his way home from college. Dixie had the camera held to her face while she focused on her friend standing next to a large sunflower that had a butterfly perched on the petal just inches from Summer's nose.

"Can you print some of these so I can get one framed to give to mom for her birthday?"

"Of course. The light is amazing and I can't wait to get these added to my portfolio."

Dixie looked at her cell phone and frowned. "Chase should be here in about fifteen minutes. Are there any other kind of shots you want before we leave?"

"No. Anything that you think will look good is fine with me."

The girls walked as Dixie wrapped up a few more pictures until it began to get dark. After looking at the time again Summer said, "I am going to call Chase. He should have been here by now."

Dixie nodded while she packed her gear.

Summer sighed. "I don't have reception to get a call out."

Dixie pulled her phone out from her pocket and said, "Me either." The two girls had just gotten cell phones. Dixie considered them lucky, since most of their friends didn't have them yet, but cellular reception in small town America was spotty even on a good day.

"Well lets head towards the road so we don't miss him."

About twenty minutes later Summer's mom pulled up in her well-loved minivan. "Hi girls. Sorry, Chase got delayed at school and is on his way so I had to come and get you."

"No problem Mom. Is he okay?"

"Yes, of course. He just had an appointment with his advisor that ran over. He will be home soon."

Summer climbed into the front of the minivan while Dixie placed her tripod and camera bag in the back seat with her. Dixie listened as Summer and her mom chatted quickly about their days and she began resting her head on the window of the back seat listening to the rhythmic humming of the pavement. Her eyes grew heavy as the lights glowed past quickly in time with the humming and she drifted off to sleep.

Dixie jolted awake as her head ripped to the side and then crashed on the window. Did they hit a bump? Then she felt a sense of weightlessness as her eyes tried to adjust to her surroundings. She heard screaming and then felt a huge jolt followed by a stabbing pain in her right hip. Her eyes went blurry and the blood rushing through her ears drowned out all remaining sounds. Her head was spinning, and she was fighting to keep her eyes open. It took a minute for her to realize that she was hanging upside down and being held in by her seat belt. She coughed and her nose burned with the acid smell of burned rubber and what seemed like melted plastic.

"Summer? Are you okay? Carrie?" Dixie's voice was quiet and hoarse as she kept calling for them through her sobs. Dixie tried to reach for the seat belt but found that she couldn't move her arm to push the button. Then she gasped as she saw the leg from her tripod embedded into her hip and down her leg. Blood was flowing onto the seat and she was beginning to feel cold to her core. An orange light began to glow from the front of the car, and that is when she saw them. Summer's head was bleeding and her eyes were closed. Her body had been twisted to the side so that her front was facing back at Dixie. Dixie began screaming for help and then looked over at Summer's mom. She wasn't moving either and was slumped in an awkward position over the steering wheel and dashboard. "Oh God. Someone help me please!"

The orange light began to glow brighter. She looked over to see another car on its side and it was on fire. Dixie continued her cries and pleas for help, praying for someone to find her. After what seemed like hours but was probably only ten minutes, she heard a male's voice trying to tell her that everything was going to be okay. "Please help my friend. She won't wake up."

"I need to help you first."

"No, please. Help her."

"Shit, okay."

The man went over to the passenger side of the vehicle and started to pull Summer from the car. Dixie's tears continued to flow as she felt the salt and metallic blood taste in her mouth. "Carrie... please wake up. We need you."

Then Dixie could hear another male's voice screaming but couldn't make out what was being said. The first man was pulling Carrie out of the car when the second man began to pull at Dixie's door. Then she heard him calling her name. "Dixie. Oh God hon. I am getting you out of here."

Dixie turned to see a blurry vision of Chase. "Chase? I'm scared."

"I've got you. You are going to be okay." Chase bent over and was finally able to unsecure the seatbelt. Dixie fell into his arms as gravity released from her upside-down position. She screamed out in pain as the tripod moved with her and twisted in her hip and leg. "Hang on Dix. I need to get that thing out of your leg."

Chase pulled on the tripod and watched in horror as more blood came flowing out from her side. "Shit. Hang on!" He pulled her from the wreckage to the side of the road. He laid her down on the gravel as he took off his shirt and balled it up to apply pressure to her wound.

Dixie raised her good arm up and reached for Chase's face as she whispered, "I'm so sorry." She felt her breathing shallow and she started to close her eyes.

"No, no no... don't you do that. You have to stay here with me. You understand? Stay with me." Those were the last words Dixie heard before she lost consciousness.

Dixie began to wake up from the noise of constant beeping. She tried to sit up and felt a stabbing pain shooting down her spine twisting to her hip and down her leg. Her heart began to increase in speed as she tried to move her arm. Then she felt another hand grip hers tightly as she heard a voice gently saying something. She shook her head and struggled to open her eyes. After blinking a few times, she saw Chase sitting next to her looking pale with reddened eyes.

"Calm down Dix. You are okay." Chase was now stroking her forearm with his free hand.

Dixie tried to speak but as she opened her mouth nothing came out.

"Here, have some water." Chase grabbed a small paper cup with a straw and brought it to Dixie's lips. She took a sip and began to cough.

She finally was able to clear her throat to speak. "Where am I?"

"You are in the hospital." Chase began to choke on his sobs as he continued, "There was an accident and we brought you here."

Memories began flashing though Dixie's mind. The jolting of the car, the feeling of weightlessness as the car flipped, Summer and her mom not waking up, and Chase pulling her out of the car. Tears began falling quickly down her face. "Where's Summer? Where's your mom?"

Chase began brushing hair away from Dixie's face and said, "Shhh... don't worry about it right now. We need to make sure that you are okay now."

Dixie's chest began to shake and tears grew even faster. "Chase please tell me. Where are they?"

Chase stiffened and tears began to fall from his eyes now too. "Dixie..."

"God Chase, please just tell me." As Dixie said these words she knew. She knew to the pit of her stomach that they were both gone. She knew it as she hung upside down in the car crying and screaming for help.

Chase took a deep breath. He glanced in the hallway looking for something, maybe someone and then back to her. He looked into Dixie's eyes and she saw so much pain, but it wasn't until he finally spoke that she let it sink in. "They're gone Dix."

"Gone? They're dead?"

Chase began crying and nodded his head.

Dixie began to struggle in the bed and attempted to get up. Chase stood and gently took her shoulders. "What are you doing?"

"I need to see Summer."

"She isn't here Dixie."

"They wouldn't have taken her away that quickly. I want to see her."

Chase shook his head. "Quickly?"

"We just had the accident. Don't they let us visit before..."

He finally seemed to understand, and he took Dixie's face in his hands. "The accident was two days ago."

"What?"

"It was two days ago." Chase began crying again. "We thought we were going to lose you too. You weren't waking up."

"Are they really gone?"

Chase nodded.

"Oh my God, Chase I am so sorry. This is all my fault. I'm so sorry. Please don't hate me. I'm so…"

Chase was shaking his head. "Dixie, please stop. You're breaking my heart. Listen to me, this isn't your fault. You were hit by a drunk driver. This wasn't your fault."

Dixie's chest began to heave as her sobs grew steadily. "But we were out at the fields because of me. I wanted to…"

Chase took Dixie's face into his hands. "Stop it. No one blames you. We blame that guy who got drunk before fucking driving his car. This has nothing to do with you. If we use your logic, then I am also at fault because I was supposed to pick you up, and not Mom."

Dixie stared into Chase's determined eyes and saw his resolve. She searched for blame or anger and took a breath as she found nothing but concern and caring looking back at her. "It wasn't your fault."

"And it wasn't yours either. Understand?"

Dixie sighed and nodded. She closed her eyes and allowed her tears to flow and tried to process what she had just been told. "I lost my best friend. God, my only friend."

Chase wrapped his two hands around Dixie's one hand and kissed her fingers. "Not your only friend. You have me."

"Promise?"

"Always."

Chapter 3

Chase and Dixie arrived at that fateful bend in the road and pulled off to the side. Dixie grabbed her camera and got out of the car to follow Chase to the wreckage. One car was in the ditch and the other car's front was crumpled to half its original size. Dixie walked over to the car in the ditch to begin taking pictures. It didn't take long while looking through the lens that she found it, resting next to two white crosses embedded into the ground. She stood motionless as she looked at the crosses and felt magnetized to the ground until she felt a hand on her shoulder.

Chase leaned down and whispered in her ear. "You don't have to be here."

Now staring at the two crosses without her camera lens she shook her head. "I'm fine. You don't have to be here either."

"It was a fatal accident in my jurisdiction. Yes, I have to be here."

Dixie narrowed her eyes and stiffened her spine. "And I take critical pictures for your department in cases of fatalities, so yes, I have to be here too."

Over the next thirty minutes Dixie continued to take pictures while Chase spoke with the other officers and witnesses that were not involved with the accident. The driver at fault was texting while driving and a mother and son died in the car that was hit by the young man who caused the accident. Dixie could see his frustration and anger over everything from that fateful night. His biggest trigger was people who were irresponsible and disregarded the safety of others, like the man who drove drunk killing his mother and sister.

Dixie watched as Chase walked over to the car and pulled out his jacket. The night breeze had grown a little colder, and he walked over to Dixie. She was standing by the wreckage of the car that the mother was driving and realized that she was rubbing her hip where her long scar was. Chase leaned over her shoulder and asked, "Is your hip bothering you? I thought you weren't having problems anymore."

"It's fine. It just has small flare-ups now and then."

"Okay. But you let me know if it starts acting up again."

"I can take care of myself you know."

Chase wiped a hand down his face. "I know." Shaking his head, he held out his jacket to her. "I thought you might be cold."

"Oh. It is getting colder. Thanks." She took the jacket and put it on looking back at Chase lost in thought.

"Do you have all the pictures we need?"

"Yes, I think so. Are you done?"

"Yeah. They can finish the clean-up," Chase said as he nodded to the other officers.

The drive back home was quiet. Dixie could feel Chase watching her as she stared absently out the window. After about five minutes he took his hand and placed it on the nape of her neck and started rubbing in slow circles. Dixie tilted her head into his hand and gave him a small smile of assurance. Once Chase parked in front of Dixie's apartment, he put the car in park and turned to her. "Do you want me to walk you up?"

Dixie shook her head. "No, I am okay. It has been a long couple of days. I am just going to go upstairs and get some sleep."

Chase didn't respond for a minute and just gazed at her. "Okay. Call me if you need anything." He leaned over and gave her a kiss on her forehead and she could feel him watching her as she walked up to her apartment. She went to the window and noticed that he didn't leave until she turned her lights on.

THE NEXT DAY CHASE was sitting at his desk going over reports from his deputies that needed his attention when a white plastic bag was dropped on his desk with a dramatic thud. Chase looked up to find Derek standing over him. Derek was the owner of McKenna's bar and one of his closest friends.

"Please tell me that all this food you ordered is not just for you."

Chase shrugged. "I didn't make it to Zoey's this morning for breakfast, so I am hungry."

Derek shook his head and sat across from Chase. "I can't believe you don't weigh three hundred pounds."

Chase replied through a mouthful of burger, "That's because I don't slack off like you and Kyle." Chase took a swig of his soda and continued. "Tyler and I go running all the time. You slackers hardly ever join us."

"You changed the running time."

"Had to."

"And why was that?"

"Tyler and Zoey can't pry their bodies apart from each other long enough—"

Derek put up a hand. "Okay stop there. I don't want to hear about your best friend mauling my best friend."

With a smirk Chase continued, "Josie said that her picture fell off their adjoining wall the other day because they were—"

THUD! Before he could finish Derek launched a stress ball and hit Chase on the forehead.

"Not cool."

"Geez you act like I was talking about Ariel's sex life."

Derek grew pale at the mention of his sister's name and her sex life and then started looking around on Chase's desk for something else to throw at him. Chase saw his intent and said jokingly, "Careful I would hate to arrest you for assaulting a police officer."

"You're an ass."

"Yup, I have been told that several times," Chase said as he then went back to eating his lunch.

"You coming to my place tonight?"

Chase stopped eating and looked confused. "I thought we were all meeting at your bar tonight?"

Derek shook his head. "Nope. The girls decided they needed a girl's only night to cheer up Dixie."

Chase's stomach dropped, and he silently cursed himself for letting Dixie go to the accident last night. "Dixie needed cheering up?"

Derek looked at him with confusion in his eyes. "Yeah, you know because Jay broke up with her."

Taking a deep breath in relief Chase said, "Oh yeah. The break up."

"Yeah... anyway Tyler is bringing dessert, I have the wings, Kyle is bringing drinks, so do you want to bring pizza?"

"Sure, I can do that, and please tell me that he is bringing Zoey's desserts and not his."

"God yes. We can't ever let him try to bake her recipes again. That was awful." They both laughed remembering how Tyler had tried to make cookies and didn't know there was a difference in granulated and powdered sugar in the recipe and couldn't measure teaspoons vs tablespoons. Zoey tried to tell him he was doing it wrong but he wouldn't let her help him and wanted to prove he could do it. The cookies were so awful even Chase couldn't eat them.

Derek soon left to return to the bar and Chase continued his work. Just before he was set to leave for the day, he got a phone call from the director at the retirement village, Whispering Oaks, where his grandfather lived requesting him to come and speak to her. After confirming that his grandfather was okay, he told her that he would meet her at five after his shift.

Chase stepped into the office of Mrs. Madigan. Several awards hung on a wall behind her desk and pictures of her family lined the table and desk. She gave Chase a warm smile and asked him to sit down.

Chase fidgeted in his seat and said, "What is going on? Is Grandpa okay?"

Mrs. Madigan folded her hands on the desk and gave a small smile. "His health is okay Chase no need to worry for that, but there have been some issues coming up that we hoped you could provide some assistance on."

Confused he replied, "Okay. What?"

"Well let me just start first with saying that he is a nice man to our staff and we truly appreciate that."

"But..."

"But, he has been misbehaving with some of the residents."

Suddenly his stomach roiled, and he thought he was going to fall out of his seat. "Are you saying he has been uh... you know... with the ladies?"

She stared at him with a blank face for just a minute and then realized what he was saying and gave a short loud laugh. "Oh god no. Not that. At least not that we know of." She seemed to do a small cringe and shudder. "We do have our resident playboys, but your grandfather thankfully is not one of them. No, your grandfather has been hustling some of the other residents at poker."

"He is taking their money?" Well that's not good. These people often didn't have much money to begin with and his grandfather certainly wasn't hurting for money.

She shook her head. "No. But he has been gambling for other things. Petty little bets like giving up their dessert to him for a week, or making them detail his car, and he made Mr. Mellott scrub his toilet with his toothbrush."

Chase was trying to hold back a laugh. He knew how much his grandfather and Mr. Mellott did not get along. They were rivals in school and rivals for his grandmother's affection back in the day, and Mr. Mellott never accepted losing her well. He was constantly trying to irritate his grandfather.

"Are you telling me you would be okay if he hustled their money instead?"

"No, that isn't what I am saying. If they want to play cards, they need to stick to winning for bragging rights and not money or humiliating dares."

Chase was trying not to smile, he really was, but the humiliation bets were growing as an idea for him and the guys that night for their own card game. "Okay. I will talk to him about it."

Chase walked out of the office shaking his head. He knew that his grandpa was a card shark and was probably cheating all his friends during the poker games. Chase once tried to get his grandfather to teach him how to cheat at cards, but he refused saying that he wanted his grandson to be a better man than him. As he rounded the corner, he saw Dixie coming out of her grandparent's apartment. Smiling he said, "Hey there."

"Hi. What are you doing here?"

"Grandpa got in trouble for swindling at cards."

Dixie snickered. "Everyone in town knows not to play him at cards, and it is their own fault if they do."

"I would love to see him play against Zoey." Zoey had been kicking all the guys' butts at poker from the minute she arrived. It was almost as if she had some voodoo magic with cards.

"Ooo... That would be interesting."

"How are your grandparents?"

"They're good and looking forward to getting away. I brought over their beach stuff from storage so they can pack it for the trip. Grams threatened to wear a bikini the whole trip if I didn't bring something from the bakery with me too. I also broke the news that Elena is going to drive them and I am bringing all the luggage and supplies in my car."

Chase grimaced. "And they were okay with that?"

"Grams tried to hide her disappointment, but it still showed. She would rather spend a couple hours in the car with me than my sister. They love her, but her lack of affection can be very upsetting to them sometimes."

"And to you as well."

Dixie shrugged. "We will never be close. I accepted that a long time ago. I have my family here with Gram and Gramps and you guys. I'm okay."

Chase hugged her. "Yes, you are."

"Oh, and Elena is coming in a day early too, and staying with me."

"I thought she was going to stay at the B&B?"

"Nope. She felt that it was a waste of money. Since I am family, I should make her as comfortable as possible especially since she had inconvenienced herself by coming all the way out here."

"Wow. Well if you need rescuing at any time just call."

"Thanks. The girls have made the same offer. Hopefully it doesn't come to that."

"Okay well I have to go talk to Grandpa and rein him in."

Laughing Dixie wished him luck and turned to leave. Chase watched her swaying hips as she left and shook his head. Figure out what to do with the sexy woman later, deal with the old man now.

LATER THAT NIGHT ALL the girls were at Dixie's apartment drinking wine and eating the Italian pasta Josie had brought over.

"Did you hear that Valerie has already been skulking around Jay's shop in her low-cut tank and ripped shorts," Ariel asked as she refilled Dixie's glass with wine.

Dixie shook her head. "No. Geez, she doesn't wait long."

"Darling I haven't lived here that long, and I have heard of her swooping in on ten recently single men," Josie said.

"At least she waits until they are single. I knew women who didn't even wait until the men were single," Zoey said passing the garlic bread around.

"Honestly, if I thought she would make Jay happy I would wish them both the best. I really like Jay, and he deserves to be happy."

Ariel rolled her eyes. "Believe me, one does not find happiness with Valerie."

Dixie laughed. "No, they don't."

"Are you going to warn him?"

"Nah. Let him have his fun rebound sex. We all deserve that."

Josie swirled around her wine glass. "Ooo. So, who is going to be your rebound sex? What about that new hunk of man candy at the orchard? He would be a fun satisfaction to your sweet tooth."

Ariel perked up and said, "Oh yeah, Finn. He is yummy."

Dixie shook her head. "I love yummy men, but I don't have time for rebound fun right now. I have to get ready for the family trip. Not to mention Elena is going to stay with me instead of the B&B."

Ariel nearly choked on her pasta. "Here in your apartment?"

"Yeah, unless I could get away with making her sleep on the roof."

"Sweetie have you finished the guest room?"

Dixie winced. "No. I was going to start on it tomorrow."

"Oh. My. God. You are so screwed."

Josie looked at Ariel. "How bad could it be?"

"You know how everyone has a junk drawer?"

"Yeah."

"Well our dear Dixie has a junk room."

With an evil smile Josie rushed up and started sprinting towards the back bedroom with all the girls dashing right behind her. Josie finally made it to the door and burst it open with a rush of air blowing on the girls. Zoey let out an audible gasp and Ariel start giggling.

Dixie stood with her head hung down. "It isn't that bad."

Josie gave a loud laugh and said, "Isn't that bad? You have boxes stacked taller than us. And what is with that leaning tower of tubs over there?"

"I had to do something with all the stuff leftover from Gram and Gramps house, and some of it is my stuff."

"This is all stuff they wanted to keep?"

"No. It was stuff from the house that I wanted to keep."

Zoey held up an ugly clock with birds around for each number. "This is something you wanted to keep?"

Dixie swiped it and held to her chest. "Yes. It was Grams."

"Yes, and on each hour that dumb thing doesn't chime like a normal clock, it tweets with whatever each bird sounds like," Ariel said while peeking around some of the boxes.

Josie shook her head. "God that sounds annoying as hell."

"It is," Ariel confirmed.

Dixie glared at her friend and said, "Do you want me to even start on your yoga clock?"

"Hey yoga makes me bendy, which has come in very handy."

Josie smiled and gave Ariel a high five. "Seriously, what are you going to do with all of this stuff?"

Dixie sighed. "I have to go through some of it and donate some and move other stuff to the storage room downstairs in the studio."

"Oh, let me help you. I love throwing out other people's stuff. It makes me happy."

"You really are mostly evil," Ariel said laughingly.

"Okay girls, let's finish dinner and help Dixie with this room," Zoey said hoping to cheer up Dixie.

They all turned back down the hallway to their dinner as Josie growled in frustration. "Dixie, I am going to kill your rat!"

Dixie rounded the corner and saw Ansel standing on the coffee table eating garlic bread off Josie's plate. The other girls laughed while Dixie rescued Ansel before Josie could make hedgehog stew out of him.

After dinner was over, all the girls were in the spare bedroom going through the boxes. Ariel held up some of Dixie's old clothes from high school. "Sweetie can we please get rid of these. You are never going to fit into these again and god willing they will not come back into style."

"Well maybe I could make something out of them like a memory blanket or..." SMACK. Josie had smacked Dixie's hand as she reached out for the clothes "Ow. That hurt, you evil wench."

"I did it out of love. Now stop trying to keep all the worthless crap, and we will have you organized in no time."

"Oh my god. Dixie these are amazing," Zoey said as she held up a large print photograph of a sunflower field encased in a black wood frame. "Why aren't these in the art exhibit? The whole series is amazing." Zoey continued to look through the stacked pictures.

"Not these. These are not for anyone."

"Okay, but they would look great in your living room on that large wall behind the couch."

"No."

Ariel stepped behind Zoey and put her hand on her shoulder and whispered, "She will never put those out. Trust me. Let it go."

Frowning Zoey said okay and moved them carefully to the corner.

Dixie felt bad for snapping at Zoey, but she could never let anyone see those pictures. Especially Chase. Those were some of the best images that she had ever captured, but she couldn't bring herself to do anything more than frame them and hide them away. How could she possibly share anything from that day that killed Chase's sister and mom? Seeing the pictures just reminded her of the worst day of her life. There was one last picture of the series that she couldn't even bring herself to print on anything larger than the small proof from the originals. It was Summer, lit with a haze of orange light around her profile surrounded by sunflowers. It was the most engaging image, but also the last ever taken of her friend and seeing it just hurt her heart. She knew if it ripped her heart out, she could only imagine how Chase would feel seeing that all the time.

Dixie started absently rubbing her hip and leg up and down the length where her she knew her scar was. Ariel came beside her and wrapped her fingers around Dixie's wrist to get her to stop rubbing. Dixie stopped and looked her friend in the eyes with a silent thank you.

A couple hours later they had all the boxes ready to go and labeled to either be donated or sent to the storage room at the studio. Ariel looked down at her phone and said, "Okay the boys are on the way with Kyle's truck."

Dixie shook her head. "You didn't have to do that."

"Sweetie, did you really think we were going to walk all those boxes downstairs?" Ariel then nodded over to Zoey. "Besides little Miss Graceful over there would fall down and break an arm and then who would bake all of our goodies?"

Zoey turned over to Ariel with her mouth open and said, "Hey!"

Josie patted Zoey on the back and said, "Truth hurts darling."

Sighing, Zoey replied, "Yeah, okay."

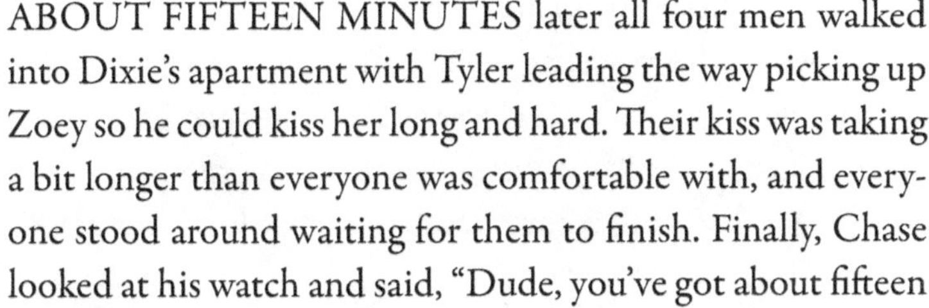

ABOUT FIFTEEN MINUTES later all four men walked into Dixie's apartment with Tyler leading the way picking up Zoey so he could kiss her long and hard. Their kiss was taking a bit longer than everyone was comfortable with, and everyone stood around waiting for them to finish. Finally, Chase looked at his watch and said, "Dude, you've got about fifteen seconds before the poor girl runs out of air. Let her go."

Slowly Tyler lowered her to the ground, smiled and said, "Guess what? Thanks to those bozos over there I am taking my girl out for a good date this week."

Giggling Zoey replied, "You took all their money?"

Nodding his head, he said, "Yup, along with some perks. Kyle over there has to wash your dishes for the bakery one day this week, Chase has to mow Mom and Dad's yard for me, and Derek has to clean our apartment."

Kyle smacked Chase in the chest. "Humiliation tasks and poker... that was the dumbest idea you've ever had, and I got the worst task in the bunch."

It only took about thirty minutes for the guys to load all the boxes in Kyle's truck for donation and take the others to Dixie's storage room in the studio. Everyone left Dixie and Chase as he walked her back up to the apartment. He guided her in with his hand on the small of her back. She felt a jolt of electricity creep down her spine.

Dixie walked over to the refrigerator and said, "You want something to drink?"

"Water will be good. I still need to drive back home. Unless you want to make room for me?"

Dixie stopped in her tracks holding the water bottle. "I, uh, have the bed cleared in the spare room now."

Lowering his voice, he replied, "That is not what I had in mind." He stepped a little closer as Dixie stepped back. Then she sidestepped him and went into the living room.

"What has gotten into you? Your flirt level has gotten out of control."

Chase shook his head. "My flirt level is still the same, maybe I just redirected it a little."

"Well stop it. You are creeping me out."

She looked as if she was fighting herself. She didn't seem to know what she wanted. He would take that. He could work with that.

"When is the last time you got laid?"

Chase shrugged. "About six months ago." It was around the holidays before Zoey had moved to town. Things were so crazy busy with work and his family and then when Dixie started dating Jay, he felt himself drawn to Dixie even more than usual. Was it fair for him to want her so much just when she looked like she was finally happy with another guy? No probably not, but he felt himself losing his friend, and at the time it felt like he was losing two of them. Tyler and Dixie. He was happy for Tyler and Zoey. They deserved each other and went through hell with Zoey's ex and almost losing her when she got shot. As time went on, he kept watching Dixie and feeling irrational jealousy. He even picked up a girl at a bar in the neighboring town trying to get Dixie out of his head. After she kissed him in the bar's parking lot, he couldn't bring himself to go any further. He said his apologies to the woman and drove back home. Then when he saw Dixie the night Jay broke things off, he felt like it was the best day he had in months. Sure, he felt bad for his friend but he knew he needed to do something soon or he would lose his chance forever.

"Six months?!? No wonder you have been so weird. Go find one of your bar flies and have some fun before you combust."

"What if I don't want a bar fly?" By now Dixie was backed up against the wall and Chase braced his arms on each side of her head. "I need more Dixie." He then lowered his head to where his lips were almost touching Dixie's ear. "I need more than just a release. I need someone who can reach—"

Just then they both turned to the sound of Dixie's front door opening and Tyler's voice, "Hey Dixie, Zoey forgot..." he paused as he saw Chase hovering over Dixie, "her um, purse."

Dixie ducked under Chase's arms and said, "Oh right, it is just in the spare room."

After Dixie walked out of the room, Chase glared at his friend. All Tyler could do was give him a wide-eyed look with a shrug of an apology. Then he mouthed, "Do you know what you're doing?"

"Yes... No."

Dixie emerged from the hallway with Zoey's purse. "Here you go. Now not to be rude but you boys need to get going so I can get some sleep. We all have early mornings tomorrow."

Tyler taking her hint, shoved Chase towards the door. "Come on Chase, let the girl get some rest."

Dixie sent a smile of thanks to Tyler and closed her door behind them.

Chapter 4

The next few days went by in a blur of work for Dixie and Chase. It was finally the day Elena was due in town and Dixie, Ariel and Josie were enjoying a destressing breakfast before she had to face her sister that afternoon. "Are you ready for the ugly stepsister?"

Dixie groaned. "She isn't ugly, just a bit removed... and sometimes condescending. Plus, she isn't a stepsister."

"Sweetie, I still say you were adopted, and I didn't specify if she was ugly on the outside or inside."

Josie sat back amused and then lifted an eyebrow. "I am mean. Do you think I am ugly?"

Ariel sat up with a smirk. "Yes, but you are not mean just to be mean. Your meanness is intended out of love and affection not snobbery and bitchery."

"Does this mean I can be let off my leash and put in my reign of terror?"

"NO," both Ariel and Dixie loudly replied.

"You guys never let me have any fun anymore."

"We let you make that tourist slut cry last week at McKenna's."

"Let me? You both egged me on."

"She deserved it," Ariel replied. "She kept on making comments about Amy being fat even though she is pregnant and not fat. Then she had the nerve to hit on Amy's husband when she had to pee for the hundredth time that night."

"I think it was the moo sounds that pushed me over the edge," said Dixie.

Josie's mouth dropped. "I didn't know about the cow noises. If you would have told me about that I would have hit her while I was at it."

Laughing, Dixie said, "Yeah, that is why we didn't tell you."

"See, you never let me have any fun."

Ariel shook her head. "No, we saved your pretty new manicure."

Josie nodded and looked down at her nails. "Well, that is appreciated. So, Dix, when are you going to spill the beans about what is up with you and Chase."

"Uh... what are you talking about?"

"Oh please, I overheard Tyler talking to Zoey about how Chase was all up in your space after we left earlier this week."

Dixie sighed. "I don't know what he is doing. For the past couple of weeks, he has been acting all weird. He has been flirting with me and has almost kissed me a few times now. Did you guys know that he hasn't been with a woman in over six months?"

"I can't believe the big bear hasn't shot anyone out of sexual frustration by now," said Josie.

"Me either. He has always been a little man whore. I just don't know what has flipped his switch. I told him that his flirt level had gotten out of control and he said that it was still the same, he was just redirecting it. He was leaning in my space and giving that low sexy whisper in my ear when Tyler came back into the apartment."

Ariel winced. "That boy sure does have god awful timing."

"Yeah, well if he didn't come back, I would have caved and kissed the big idiot. He was turning on all his sexy charm and I couldn't breathe, but I can't do it. I can't go through his rejection again."

Josie looked confused. "Again?"

"Yes again, but it was forever ago. It was after my high school graduation. Chase came back to visit for the summer. He was spending a lot of time with me since I was still trying to get full mobility of my leg and hip after the accident. He was great with the exercises and motivating me to get moving. Grams and Gramps were having a hard time paying for all the physical therapy sessions so Chase learned all the exercises that were recommended for me and worked with me whenever he was home. It was the first day that I was able to run a full mile. He was incredibly motivating. I was on such a high, and feeling good about the progress I was making. Chase had walked me home, and we were talking by the front door. He told me how much he missed me and wished he had more time to spend with me. I hugged him and said I missed him too. As we let go of the hug, we still had arms around each other. He was looking at me and I thought he wanted to kiss me. So, me being the dumb eager girl, I pulled him down to kiss him. He started to kiss back but then gently pushed me off and said he couldn't do it, that it was a mistake and he was sorry. Then left me there, standing like an id-iot."

Josie put her hand on Dixie's arm and said, "I think the important part of the story is that he started with kissing you back. There is a big difference between a man who doesn't want a kiss and a man who kisses back and then stops it. I think maybe he wasn't ready to face his feelings about you yet."

"Thank you. I said that back then," Ariel said.

Dixie sighed. "Yeah, but his rejection crushed me back then. I was such a stupid love-sick girl. It has taken years to get over him and be his friend at the same time. YEARS! And now he wants to change the rules? What happens if give in? What if I let my heart go back there and he pulls the same crap? What if he starts to go there with me and then pulls back? It would crush me... again."

After a moment Ariel said, "But what if he doesn't pull back? Can you really risk not following through on what could be the best thing in your life? You can't keep dating these safe guys who will never really capture your heart. That just leaves your heart always trying to grasp for happiness that is out of reach."

Dixie gave Ariel the side eye. "Those who live in glass houses babe."

Ariel narrowed her eyes. "My situation is different. Kyle isn't throwing any signals to me. If anything, he keeps pulling away a little more each day. If Kyle even gave a slight hint of desire my direction, all bets would be off. I would have that man naked and begging *me* for mercy."

"And Derek would kick his ass," Josie said as she emptied her coffee cup.

"I have no problem kicking big brother's ass if he gets all up in my business."

Josie smirked. "Our little princess is fierce."

Ariel nodded. "Damn straight."

"Nice to see your quality of friends is still lacking," said a feminine voice from behind Dixie.

Shit. Dixie knew that voice. She couldn't be here already, could she? Dixie turned around to see Elena standing with her Louis Vuitton suitcase and dressed in pressed black slacks with a navy button down silk shirt. She had dark hair upswept in a French twist. Her makeup was perfectly applied. The only jewelry she wore was a simple charm necklace and her wedding ring. She began drumming her fingers on the handle of the suitcase impatiently waiting for Dixie to greet her.

Dixie began looking around the bakery, for what she wasn't sure. She saw Zoey busy with customers. Mr. and Mrs. Glover eating donuts at the table next to her. A few people were in line, including Chase who was looking interestingly at Elena. Finally, Dixie resigned and stood to greet Elena. "Hi Sis, it's so nice to see you." Dixie tried to hug Elena but when Dixie wrapped her arms around her Elena's arms remained at her side.

"Dixie why aren't you at work? It is nearly 9 am and your studio was closed. Some old fat guy had to tell me that you were probably at the bakery. Really Dixie? It isn't like you need the calories, and you should be working by this time on a weekday."

Dixie ground her teeth. "The studio runs on appointments only, so it opens when I have appointments. I knew you were coming in today so I took the time off so I could spend it with you."

"That was completely unnecessary. I can entertain myself without you hovering over me."

Dixie frowned. "I just thought since we don't spend much time together it would be nice if—"

"Why? We talk to each other on the phone. You need to work. Surely you can't afford all this time off being a silly photographer."

Finally, having heard enough, Ariel stood and held out her hand to Elena. "Hello Driz. Nice to see you again."

Elena looked down at Ariel's hand that had some powdered sugar covering her fingers. "Really? I am not going to shake your hand when it is covered in... whatever that is."

Ariel shrugged and proceeded to lick her fingers slowly and with a loud pop.

Elena grunted in disgust and said, "And Ariel... I know why you call me Driz. You can stop it any time now."

Ariel giggled. "Took you long enough." Ariel started calling her Driz to irritate her years ago. Drizella was the name of one of Cinderella's ugly stepsisters and she had shortened it to Driz. Then she started calling her that to her face after hearing her chip away at Dixie's self-confidence one too many times.

Elena turned away to ignore Ariel and focused her gaze back to Dixie. "Anyway, give me a key to your apartment and I will let myself in. Then I am going to see Grandmother and Grandfather for lunch."

Josie snorted a laugh. "Grandmother and Grandfather?"

Elena turned and glared at Josie. "You clearly were not part of this conversation so it would be only polite of you to remain so."

Josie's bitch face came in full force. "Actually DRIZ, you interrupted our conversation, so it would only be polite of you to no longer be a part of ours."

Oh boy, this was spiraling fast. Dixie couldn't believe how quickly this escalated. She stepped in between the line of sight between Josie and Elena before Josie hauled off and hit her. Elena's small petite face would not fare well against an angry Josie. "Okay, Sis. Let me give you the key and I won't be far behind you." She dug around her purse and handed the key over to Elena. "I am making dinner tonight. Do you think you will be back by seven?"

"Of course. Just how long do you think lunch with our grandparents would take?"

"Well not that long, I just..."

"Just what? You really need to learn how to speak in complete sentences."

"Sorry."

"Don't apologize; simply learn how to change your bad habits." Elena put Dixie's keys in her purse and raised an eyebrow. "Is your boyfriend joining us for dinner?"

"No. He is uh..."

"Please don't tell me that you are going to have him try to stay overnight while I am there? That is so inappropriate Dixie."

"No, he won't be spending the night." Dixie shifted uncomfortably. Telling her sister that she just got dumped was going to be mortifying. She cleared her throat and started to spill her confession, but just as she started to speak, she was lifted off the ground and turned around. She only had a second to see Chase grinning at her and then he tilted her whole body back and his mouth was on her. At first, she was frozen, but then her back softened and her hands wrapped around the back of his neck. Her heart was pounding out of her chest. Chase's warm lips were enveloping hers. His tongue traced the seam of her mouth until her lips parted. Then it began a deep exploration of her mouth, and she felt her whole body awaken with arousal. Oh god. He was kissing her, and not just any kiss. This was passionate. This was a kiss that she never wanted to end.

Dixie was getting lost on Chase's scent of cedar and soap. Her lips and tongue were exploring him with just as much intensity as he was with her. Could this be real? God, she hoped so. She hoped this wasn't a pity kiss because Elena was attacking her. He just lifted her like this was how they always were. There was certainty and purpose with every movement. Dixie's hands were digging into his head as he wrapped her closer. Then breaking the spell that they were under she heard a throat clearing and a loud shrill voice. "That is enough, don't you think?"

A faint "Not even close," could be heard coming from Josie.

Chase released his hold from Dixie and parted from her lips. He looked directly into her eyes and said, "Hey sweetheart, sorry I was so late this morning. I just had a few things to clear up so I could make it to dinner tonight."

Dixie was just staring back at Chase in confusion. "Dinner?"

"Yes, dinner," Chase said with a smile on his face. "I was able to get coverage so I could have dinner with you and your sister tonight." He then turned to Elena with a giant smile and held out his hand to Elena. "Pleasure to see you again, Elena."

Elena narrowed her eyes at Chase and replied, "You are Dixie's boyfriend? She didn't mention that her new boyfriend was you."

Chase just gave his easy grin that Dixie knew all too well, and said, "We thought it would be best to explain in person. I know that I have never been your favorite person, but I wanted you to see how much I care for your sister and that we make each other happy."

"Sometimes happiness isn't enough."

Chase took down his hand that Elena never accepted and wrapped his arms around Dixie who was still standing there dumbfounded. "Well you will have plenty of time to see just how much it really is on the trip. I know I have never been happier."

Soft laughter was heard coming from both Ariel and Josie. Then softly Josie said, "Classic."

Obviously having had enough Elena cleared her throat and said her goodbyes to Dixie and reminded her to keep her dietary needs in mind when cooking dinner.

After Elena left, Dixie grabbed Chase's hand and started dragging him to the back of the bakery. She quickly looked at Zoey as she walked by and said, "We need to use your office really quick."

Zoey laughed and replied, "Okay, but keep in mind it isn't too sound proof."

Phil, Zoey's part time help, shuddered as he gave Zoey the side eye. "She's got that right."

DIXIE SLAMMED THE DOOR behind her and Chase and started to open her mouth to speak but nothing was coming out. She closed it and then started to open it again. This went on a few more times before Chase finally decided to start the conversation.

"Don't be mad Dixie. I just kept on watching her talk to you like you meant nothing to her and I couldn't take it anymore."

"So you decided to kiss me to make me feel better?"

"Yes... No." Chase sighed. "Yes, I wanted to make you feel better, but no it wasn't the only reason."

"And now we are supposed to pretend to be boyfriend and girlfriend? I am going to have to lie to my entire family?"

"You don't have to lie. We can be boyfriend and girlfriend. That way you won't be lying to your sister or the rest of your family."

Dixie's forehead creased as she studied his face. "You want to be with me, as your girlfriend, through this entire trip?"

"Yes," he replied, but he wanted so much more. He wanted to finally give in to his desire for his friend.

"This isn't going to work. We can't fake a relationship. Everyone will see right through me."

Chase leaned in and braced his arms on the desk to each side of Dixie. Her ass was leaning on the desk and he could feel the front of his body press against hers. He was sure she couldn't miss the show of interest coming from the front of his pants. "Then we won't fake it. This will be me and you together. No lies. No deceit." He bent his head to lightly kiss her neck and he continued to speak in between his kisses lining his way down her neck to her shoulder. "Let me show you how good we could be. How good we can be together." His arms then wrapped around her waist.

Dixie closed her eyes and sighed as Chase's lips traced a line to the other side of her neck. He was getting lost in the sensations of her warm skin meeting his wet lips and caressing her neck. Dixie's hands made their way up to his head and scratched his scalp trying to grab onto his short hair. "What are you doing?"

Chase's hands moved from the table to her hips and then traced up her spine. "Dixie, If I have to tell you what I am doing then I am not doing this right." He then moved his head up to take her ear lobe into his mouth and gave a gentle suck and then a small bite.

"Oh God."

His hands slowly inched up to the back of her head and he whispered in her ear, "Let me in Dix."

"I don't... I mean... I..."

Suddenly the swift movement of air blew across their faces and the door to Zoey's office opened to find a surprised Tyler on the other side.

Chase growled and said, "Seriously, don't you ever knock?"

Tyler, looking really amused, replied, "No, especially when it is my fiancée's office."

"Are you going to close the door?"

"Nah, I think I will sit back and watch the show. I might even get some popcorn and come back."

Chase slowly left Dixie's space and glowered at Tyler. "I don't know why you are my best friend. You are a complete asshole."

Tyler shrugged. "I am the only one who can put up with your grumpy ass, besides her," he said while nodding to Dixie.

"I am not grumpy."

Dixie gave a slight smile. "You are when you're hungry. That is why I am constantly shoving food in your mouth."

Chase sent a slow wry smile towards Dixie. "I am happy to taste a lot of different things, not just food."

Dixie rolled her eyes and shoved at Chase's chest to walk by. "You are such an idiot."

"Don't forget starting today I am your idiot," Chase bellowed as she walked away. Chase turned to Tyler and said, "Are you done mucking things up? I didn't get in your way this much when you landed Zoey."

"Is that what you are trying to do? Land Dixie?"

Chase scrubbed the back of his head and sighed. "Yeah, and she doesn't have a choice now."

"What do you mean she doesn't have a choice?"

"She never told her family that she and Jay broke up, so they were all expecting her to bring a boyfriend on the trip."

"And now you are that guy?"

"Yes. This will give me a chance to show her that we are supposed to be together. I am done with keeping my distance. If I don't do something now, I am going to lose her to someone else."

"Not that I am disagreeing with you, but why now? What makes now different from when you pushed her away before?"

Chase sat in Zoey's office chair and looked up at his friend. "I need her in my life. I thought keeping her as a friend would be good enough. You know how much I blamed myself for not picking up the girls the night of the accident. I hated myself. I wasn't in any shape to open up to anyone. I know I always gave those speeches about how it wasn't her fault, or my fault, but shit my heart couldn't let it go. I felt like I didn't deserve anything real."

"And you deserve it now?"

"Probably not, but I want to be selfish now. If she truly lets go and falls in love with someone else, I will lose my friend and it will kill me."

"Being afraid to lose your friend is not a good reason to turn a friendship into something more."

"I know that. I have always wanted something more than that with her, but everything was so messed up. Then she started dating Jay, and I just lost it. Man, did I lose it. Every time I saw him kiss her or wrap his arm around her, I wanted to rip his body parts off. I mean Jay is a nice guy, he didn't deserve my anger or frustration. I know that he would make a decent enough husband for someone, but I was going out of my mind thinking it would be Dixie."

"Yeah, I know."

"You knew, and you didn't think to mention it to me?"

"Well keep in mind that is when I was first together with Zoey and we were dealing with her ex and her new bakery. I was a little preoccupied."

"So was I. Watching you and Zoey was like a kick in the ass. I wanted to have what you both have. Did you know I went to Greko's bar and picked up this gorgeous blonde who wanted to go home with me and all I kept thinking about was Dixie? We were even in the parking lot and she had her tongue down my throat and all I could do was imagine that it was Dixie."

"Nice."

"Not really. I stopped it and told her that I couldn't go home with her. When she asked why I said because I would be thinking about somebody else while fucking her."

"God Chase. There are times when it is appropriate to lie to people."

Chase shrugged. "I wasn't going to see her again, so I figured why bother."

"Dixie is right. You are an idiot."

DIXIE MADE HER WAY back to the girls table in the front of the bakery and sat down. Josie and Ariel found this whole thing amusing and sat with their elbows on the table and chins in their hands looking expectantly at Dixie. Dixie decided to ignore them both and take a bite of the last muffin.

Josie quickly snatched the muffin out of Dixie's hands and glared at her friend. "Spill it shortbread."

"Hey! I am not short. I am taller than Ariel."

"Yeah and she is a pip squeak when she is annoying me, so dish."

Dixie looked at Ariel who nodded. "Yup it's true. She called me that just this morning before you got here."

Dixie looked at Josie and then to Zoey. "So what do you call Zoey?"

Josie quirked an eyebrow and said, "If I tell you, are you finally going to spill?"

"Yeah sure."

"Okay." Josie got one of her trademark grins and looked over at Zoey who was behind the counter. "Hey cream puff!"

Zoey glared and put her hands on her hips and replied, "Yes, Viper?"

Josie laughed and replied, "Nothing, just making a point."

"Viper?"

"Yes. Viper. Don't feel bad, I had to look that one up too. She has been with Tyler too long. Viper is a female Marvel supervillain who is known for extra abilities and likes to use artificial fangs filled with poison on her victims. Don't tell her but that is a kick ass nickname."

"Yeah and I get stuck with shortbread."

Josie shrugged. "Yup. Now spill."

"Well apparently while I am on this family trip, Chase is going to be my boyfriend."

"Your real boyfriend?"

"See that is where I am a little confused. I mean you don't just walk up to someone, kiss them and then declare that you are an item. I mean who does that?"

Ariel jumped up and said, "Oh I know! Alpha males."

Dixie looked questioningly at her. "What?"

"You know an alpha male. They walk around with charm and ownership of the room. They take what they want. They are aggressive and sexy as hell."

"And you think this is sexy?"

Ariel and Josie both replied enthusiastically, "Yes!"

"Where do you get this crap?"

"My romance books."

"I thought you gave that dribble up?"

"I never said I would give it up. I simply cut down to two a week."

"Don't you think these books give you an unrealistic expectation of love and romance?"

Ariel shook her head. "No more unrealistic than watching how things happened with Zoey and Tyler. Besides, I need these books to keep me optimistic for something more to happen in my life. This floating stagnant love life is getting old."

Josie drummed her fingers. "Do you think if I hit Kyle over his head with a bat it would knock some sense into him?"

"No. If I thought that would have worked, I would have bought a Louisville Slugger years ago."

Just then the girls all turned to see Chase walking out the door with a bear claw in his hand. He stopped at the door, turned and winked at Dixie and said, "See you tonight babe."

Josie belted out a loud laugh. "You are so screwed."

Chapter 5

Dixie was busy in the kitchen making the carbonara sauce and prepping the bread for the oven when Chase came through the front door with a bottle of wine in hand. He peered into the living room to find Elena busy tapping away on her laptop. He walked into the kitchen and placed the wine on the counter and wrapped his arms around Dixie from behind as she was stirring the sauce. He bent his head to kiss Dixie on her neck and felt her give a slight tense of her body before relaxing to his second kiss. "Hello girlfriend," he said with a smile.

Dixie rolled her eyes. "You are terrible, do you know that?"

"Yes, but you love me that way."

She turned around and was still being held in his arms as she narrowed her eyes. "Do I now?"

"Yes. You do. You can't resist my charms."

Dixie reached behind her back and grabbed the sauce spoon and quickly bopped him on his nose. "Obviously I can resist some of your charm."

With a shit-eating grin Chase released Dixie from his arms, wiped the sauce off his nose and proceeded to lick his finger clean. He bent over to Dixie's ear and whispered,

"That was only half power babe. I will have you melting to my touch in no time."

Suddenly, like a booming clap disturbing the quiet, Elena's loud voice could be heard from the next room. "Dixie, are you almost done? It is 7:05, and you said dinner would be done at 7:00."

Chase growled under his breath, "God forbid." Did everything have to be an exact science with this woman? A normal person knows that when preparing a dinner, it is an estimated time not like a train schedule.

Dixie plastered on her fake smile that Chase hated, and replied, "Just a few more minutes." Sighing she placed a lidded pot on the counter next to the sink and went for the potholders. Turning to Chase she said, "Can you please drain that pot and place it into the large serving bowl?"

"Of course." Chase got the strainer from the bottom cabinet and carefully placed it on the sink. He lifted the lid and peered inside. He instantly slammed the lid back down with a face of horror. "Uh Dix. There is something wrong with..."

Panicked Dixie ran over to the pot and pulled the lid off again. She peered in and looked at Chase with a face full of confusion. "It is fine. What's wrong with you?"

"Uh your pasta is green."

"My pasta..." Then Dixie burst into a fit of giggles. "That is spiral zucchini."

"Okay... so where is the pasta?"

Sighing she replied, "That is what we are eating in place of the pasta."

"No really. That isn't funny. Where is the real food?"

"This is real food. I had to substitute the pasta for the zucchini for my sister's dietary restrictions."

Growling Chase said, "She could use a few more carbs in her life." He wasn't even kidding in the slightest. She had Dixie's petite stature, but looked like she had been starved of food for months.

Dixie patted Chase's cheek and finished draining the zucchini. "Don't panic. I made some manly garlic bread for you, so you don't starve."

"I could think of other things I could feast on to satiate my appetite."

Bumping Chase with her hip she walked past him with the carbonara dish to set the table. "I am going to tell Tyler to stop buying you the word a day calendar."

Smirking Chase replied, "What do you mean? This year was the best one yet."

"Yeah, the sexual word a day calendar. *That* was such a good idea."

Laughing he said, "Don't forget it came with pictures."

"Don't brag about that sweetie. That just means he thought you needed help in that department."

Stunned Chase stood quietly for a second and blinked slowly. Finally, Dixie put him out of his misery as she walked by him for the second time with the salad and bread. "Calm down you big bear, I do still find you charming."

Grinning, he sat down to the table with Dixie and Elena. Elena opened the conversation with her visit to Grams and Gramps. She listed all the things that she felt were lacking in the facility at Whispering Oaks and then started grilling

Dixie about why she wasn't making sure that they were better taken care of.

"I don't understand. Did Grams and Gramps complain about this stuff to you?" Dixie looked lost.

Chase knew that her grandparents had always told her how happy they were there, and how much they loved being close to their friends.

"Of course not. They see the best in everyone and everything. They wouldn't want to burden anyone, but we trusted you to make sure they are in a safe and clean environment."

Chase began to take offense since his Grandpa also was living in the same community and the facility has always been run with the utmost care for its residents. "Just what exactly do you feel isn't safe for the residents?"

"There isn't enough staff. There should be more staff to care for the residents. Plus, they have to do their own housekeeping duties. That is absurd. They are too old for that."

"Actually, the ratio of staff to residents is higher than the amount required by North Carolina state law."

Dixie nodded. "They always have any help needed, and they refused the housekeeping service that was offered by the facility."

"You should have stepped in and put it in place for them anyway, and I can't believe they still cook for themselves. That is dangerous and unnecessary. For all the faults of the facility they do have a decent staff cook working for all three meals per day."

"I can't force them to take help, or make them eat their meals in the dining room. They are competent adults and thankfully do not have any illnesses that compromise their daily functioning."

"They are old, Dixie. Grandmother even said she barely recognized me, so obviously there are some memory issues going on that you are ignoring."

"God Elena, she said she barely recognized you because you never come to visit them. You haven't seen them since your wedding."

"Some people have important jobs Dixie. We can't all float around life doing jobs for fun and live in poverty."

"I don't live in poverty."

Chase could see she was getting upset, and she was right, she was nowhere near poverty. Actually, Dixie made a good living between the studio and selling her art. He knew that she had enough money to put over half down on a house if she so desired. But she always told him that she wanted to wait to make such a purchase until she met the person with whom she could spend the rest of her life. She wanted to make those big decisions together.

Chase grabbed Dixie's hand under the table and hoped he could pour his strength into her with his caring touch. He cleared his throat and looked directly at Elena. "That is enough. Dixie has been looking forward to seeing her family for this trip for a long time now and this includes you. But, if you can't start acting like a caring sister, hell a caring person, I will have no problem grabbing your things and dropping you off at the B&B for the remainder of your time here. I care about your sister and seeing you hurt her consistently with your words is pissing me off and I won't put up with it."

Elena clanked her fork on her plate and stared at Chase. She sighed. "Fine, but Dixie just know that I will be speaking with Mother and Father about the care at that place and we will make the hard decisions that you obviously can't do on your own."

A FEW MINUTES HAD PASSED since Elena's declaration, and Dixie began shaking in her seat. Panic was paralyzing her. She couldn't lose her grandparents to Atlanta or some other facility away from Blossom Hills. This has been their home... her home. She looked at Chase with tear filled panicked eyes. He placed a reassuring arm around her shoulders and kissed her temple. He then whispered in her ear, "Don't worry babe, they aren't going anywhere."

Dixie had lost her appetite and could not stomach the rest of her meal. She also had to agree with Chase. She desperately missed the carb filled pasta. The quiet table finished their meal. Elena ate all of her dish while Chase picked around the zucchini and ate almost half of the garlic bread. Dixie had brought a pie from Zoey's bakery but couldn't bring herself to force the three of them to any additional time at the table.

Elena rose and said, "I have work to do for the rest of the night so I will be going to my room. Try not to disturb me tonight."

Dixie just sat quietly and nodded.

Chase's gaze followed her down the hall to the second bedroom. "Disturb her? Shit, I would have slipped a roofie in her drink if I thought it would knock her out for the rest of her time here."

Dixie just shook her head. "Not helping."

Chase rose and began to clear the dishes. "I am helping. See?" He extended his arms with plates and glasses. "This is me helping."

They began washing the dishes in a quiet calm until only a couple items remained before Dixie finally spoke up. "She wasn't always like this you know?"

"Really? I just thought she was born like a robot. You know, smart and thoughtless in assessments."

"No. When we were little, before I moved out here, she was fun and kind. We used to play hopscotch out in the front driveway or even dress up our dolls in frilly outfits for pageant shows. She was always willing to share any new doll clothes with me, or would even try to style my hair to match the doll. Then mom and dad had her IQ tested, and it was through the roof. All of a sudden, she was going to some weird elite school where they discouraged play and fun and only allowed time for studies. Between that school and mom and dad, they trained her to believe that only scholarly things mattered and relationships with people were an afterthought. I watched the sister I loved turn into the person I didn't know. Then when it came time for me to take that same IQ test, I missed several questions on purpose. Oh, I still answered enough right so that I wasn't labeled an idiot, and I didn't want to fake it so much that my parents worried about me. They just assumed I was an average kid and enrolled me in public school. As time went on Elena and I grew further and further apart and my parents concentrated all of their time on her, having her excel in her studies. It didn't take long for my grandparents to get frustrated and suggest to them that I live with them in Blossom Hills. They explained in a very logical list to my parents the benefits of having me out here so they could concentrate on me while mom and dad could focus even more time on culturing Elena's mind to make a difference in the world."

Chase looked stunned. Dixie wasn't surprised. After all the years they had been friends Dixie had never told him about this. Chase wrapped her in a hug and caressed her with his hands gliding up and down her back. "Did your grandparents know about the faked test?"

Laughing, Dixie said, "You know Grams knew right away. She said she always thought I was smarter than Elena and there was no way my points were that much lower than hers."

"Good for her."

"Yeah. After she and Gramps had legal custody of me, they had me retested and threatened me with no chocolate for a year if I faked it again."

"Oh thems is fightin words."

"Right? So, I retook the test as they asked."

"And..."

"I scored one point higher than Elena."

Laughing, Chase picked up Dixie by wrapping his arms under her ass and said, "That has got to be the best thing I have heard all night. Please let me be the one to tell her one day. I want to see her head explode."

Dixie laughed and shook her head. "No, sorry. I am keeping that little nugget to myself. I only bring it out in my mind when I am picturing throwing something at her head. Honestly, I am just grateful that I had the opportunity to live here and get some normalcy. I'm just sad that we are not closer and I don't have the relationship that I see with the others like Derek and Ariel, or Tyler and Kyle."

Chase sighed, looked over at the picture of Summer, and wistfully said, "I know. Believe me, I know."

Dixie turned to see the point of his focus and took in a deep breath. "God, I'm sorry Chase, I wasn't thinking."

He quickly put his fingers to her lips and said, "Shhh... It's okay. We both lost her. She thought of you as the sister she always wished I was."

Dixie smiled. "No. She loved you to pieces. She just wished she had a sister and a brother. You and your dad were a very powerful force of testosterone in one house."

"Still are."

THEY FINISHED PUTTING away the dishes in silence and then went to the couch to watch a movie. Dixie laid in the crook or Chase's arm wrapped up in her favorite furry blanket. Chase was kicked back with his feet on the coffee table. As the movie ended, he kissed Dixie on the top of her head to wake her up.

"Dix. Come on, babe. Time to get up and go to bed."

She slightly stirred and shook her head. "No, I am so comfy here. Can't move or the world will end."

Chuckling he replied, "It won't end I promise, but you can't sleep like this. Believe me you will regret it in the morning."

She snuggled deeper into his body and said, "I promise I won't regret any of this."

"God Dix. You are killing me."

"That's okay as long as I can keep you as my pillow."

Chase growled lowly and then pulled himself up and scooped Dixie in his arms and walked down to her bedroom. He opened her door and placed her on the bed. "Dix don't you wanna get into something a little more comfortable?"

With a slight groan she sat up, pulled her shirt over her head to reveal a tank, did that pull your bra off from under your shirt thing and took off her pants to reveal lacy "boy shorts" underwear.

"Christ woman. Warn a guy next time."

Dixie cocked her head. "Why? You told me to get more comfortable."

"Yeah, I thought after I left." He walked closer to her and leaned down to kiss her head again. He knew she was tired and needed to get her rest. As he leaned in closer Dixie grabbed his hand and pulled him down even lower.

"Don't leave." She looked down to avoid his eyes. "Please. I just feel... I don't know how to explain it, but I know I would feel better knowing you are still here."

Chase kneeled beside her bed to look in her eyes. They were filled with tears and uncertainty. He lifted her chin to look directly at him. "I will always be here if you need me... or want me."

She nodded and pulled the blanket down on the other side of the bed.

"You know having me spend the night is going to piss your sister off."

"Don't care. I am half tempted to fake a loud orgasm just to shove her over the edge."

Pulling his pants off to his boxer briefs Chase shook his hips and replied, "Who said it had to be fake?" Then suddenly he was met with a pillow to the stomach. "Oooofff."

"You are such a great big man-child."

"Yes, but I am the best man around," he said pulling his shirt over his head.

"Oh, I don't know Derek is pretty studly."

Chase narrowed his eyes and jumped on the bed trapping Dixie underneath him. Dixie laughed as he maneuvered to trap her two hands into his one above her head. "You did not just say that to me. I am way better looking and more charming than Derek."

Dixie wiggled underneath him and Chase groaned with their hip to hip contact. "He does have that flowing brown hair and chocolate eyes."

"Sounds like you are describing a chocolate lab and not a man."

Giggling Dixie shook her head. "Although your emerald eyes do speak to me."

Chase leaned in closer and asked, "And what are they saying to you now?"

"That I am in big trouble for something that I might not be quite ready for."

Chase held his breath and let go of her wrists to stroke her cheek. "Just let me know when you are ready."

Dixie stared into his eyes and leaned into his touch on her cheek. Chase could see that she was conflicted and was struggling with what to do. He could feel every piece of his body humming energy into hers, but with the look in her eyes he may need to slow this down. He had to be sure that this was done right so that neither of them would end up broken at the end of all this. As he waited for her response, she took a deep breath. In the end all she did was nod her reply and close her eyes.

Chase knew he couldn't push her. He had to let her come to him in her time and to have faith in the two of them. He rolled to his side as she did as well. She curled her back into his front and fell asleep with Chase stroking her scar in rhythmic circles.

Chapter 6

The next morning Dixie woke up feeling coldness on her back. She felt behind her to feel an empty side of the bed where Chase had held her all night. She grabbed her phone to look at the time and found a missed text message from Chase.

Chase: Good morning babe. Sorry I had to leave to deal with something from work and figured it would be better if I was gone before Elena woke up to find me there anyway. I will call you later.

Dixie: Thanks for staying. I was a mess last night. Stay safe.

Chase: Always.

Dixie sat up and shook her head. What was she going to do about Chase? Should she let her guard down and let him in completely? But what if things go horribly wrong and she loses one of her closest friends? And what about the group? She is close with Zoey, whose fiancé is best friends with Chase. But can she afford to not take this chance? Finally, she decided she needed more help. She brought up her text messages again and started a chat with the girls.

Dixie: I need help guys. I am so messed up.

Josie: We are here to help. Or make fun of you whichever seems right.

Ariel: Josie don't be mean. What are you messed up about?

Zoey: She is probably messed up about Chase spending the night at her apartment last night.

Dixie: How did you know about that?!?!?!

Zoey: He left your place while I was opening up the shop this morning.

Josie: Are you messed up because the sex was bad or good?

Dixie: God Josie. Neither. We didn't have sex.

Josie: What? Grumpy bear couldn't rise to the occasion?

Zoey: Viper... tone it down a little.

Dixie: Do you guys want the real scoop or not?

Ariel: We are all behaving and listening now. *smacks Josie

Dixie: I had a bad dinner with my sister and Chase stayed to watch a movie with me. I fell asleep, and he brought me to bed. After ditching my pants and bra I asked him to stay because I felt like shit.

Josie: You little slut. I am so proud of you.

Ariel: Hush woman. Go on Dixie.

Dixie: He decided to stay, and we joked around for a few minutes, but then things got serious and he said he would always be there if I need or want him. And yes, it was very clear about the wanting him part.

Zoey: And you didn't have sex?

Dixie: No. I told him I wasn't ready. He told me to let him know when I am and then he wrapped me up in his arms and we fell asleep.

Ariel: So, the guy you have wanted since we were kids finally gives you a green light and you threw it in reverse?

Dixie: Not reverse. More like neutral.

Zoey: I am confused. What is the problem?

Dixie: I don't want to lose the friendship if things go bad. Or lose the friendship of our little group if it goes all wrong. What if he slams it in reverse again? I couldn't survive it.

Ariel: Okay, first you won't lose our group of friends no matter what. I mean, unless you turn into one of those crazy chicks we see on TRU TV.

Josie: I hate to say this but your relationship with Chase is going to change whether you go in drive or reverse. He is putting himself out there and do you think he will want to spend time with a woman who doesn't embrace that? If you don't take the chance you both can get hurt by doing nothing, so why not take the chance that it won't fall apart?

Ariel: Awww. Look at our little Josie turning romantic.

Josie: You guys have made me weak. I need to go make someone cry to balance me out now.

Zoey: I am sure I am breaking some relationship rule here by telling you this, but Tyler said that Chase is going all in and he is done standing by. So, if you are afraid that he is going to pull back, I think you are in the clear. Seeing you with Jay scared the shit out him.

Dixie: Thanks guys. I feel better.

Ariel: What are you going to do?

Dixie: I think I know but whatever it is Chase deserves to know first.

Ariel: I hate it when you try to be all mature.

Dixie put down her phone and walked out to the hallway to go into the kitchen. She found Elena already sitting on a stool reading her phone while sipping her coffee. Even Ansel was awake running on his little wheel.

"Morning," Dixie said in a strained voice.

"Good morning Dixie. I see your boyfriend snuck out of the house this morning."

"Chase didn't sneak. He walked out like a normal person to go to work."

"Do you think it is wise to attach yourself to a cop?"

Dixie slammed her mug on the counter. "You think that a cop is beneath you too?"

Elena put down her mug and looked at her sister. "No. I believe that police provide a critical role in developed society. There must be laws to keep order and people who enforce these laws."

"Then what is your problem with me dating him?"

"Don't you worry about him being harmed in the line of duty? What if you have a family with him and then he is killed answering a call?"

"This is Blossom Hills not Atlanta. And before you start yes, I know that violence happens anywhere. It wasn't so long ago that Chase had to shoot someone to defend another victim, but he is highly trained and smart. He doesn't make reckless decisions. Besides, both Chase and I know all too well that life can be taken even without a dangerous job. I won't limit my heart because of what he does for a living."

"Yes, I remember your little accident. I know you have seen life taken too early."

"Little accident?" Dixie's voice was getting higher pitched as she continued. "You want to call losing my best friend and her mother and me nearly dying, a little accident?"

"Perhaps that wasn't the best choice of words."

"You think?" Dixie turned to go to her bedroom. "Elena, I love you, but right now I don't like you very much and I need just a little space. I'll call you later. Come and go as you please, you have the spare key."

Dixie dressed quickly in her bedroom and stormed back out of the apartment slamming the door behind her as she left.

CHASE WAS DRIVING TO his dad's house after his long shift. He saw that the yard needed some tidying up before he left with Dixie. He went over to the shed in the back and brought out the trimmers and the large garbage can. As he was dragging the can to the front Jeff Montgomery came out onto the porch. "I was going to get that, son."

"I know Dad. You have plenty to do, and I could use it to burn off energy."

"Don't you have a house of your own to worry about?"

"Yeah, but I already took care of all the yard stuff. Cranky Ted Kransky never fails to nag me when one blade of grass goes astray."

"I still can't believe you moved next door to him. I told you not to."

"Hey, I had the inside scoop that he was getting a divorce and I thought Mrs. Kransky was going to win the house. Who knew he would hire that shark lawyer to keep everything for himself?"

"Seriously, how could you not know he would hire the shark? The man is a cranky old bastard."

Chase shook his head and started clipping the hedge by the porch while his Dad took the chair closest to him.

"Anyway, I just wanted to come by and help out before I leave town for a week."

"A week? When is the last time you took off that long?"

"Dunno, a couple of years ago."

"Try more like five. Where are you going for this special occasion?"

"We are going to the beach."

Jeff quickly stood up and leaned over the railing to look closer at his son. "We? Who is we?"

"Me and Dixie." Chase snipped the next branch a little harder than needed. He knew this was going to be a surprise for his dad and didn't want to upset him.

Silence. Jeff studied his son in silence for a minute and finally said, "Dixie."

"Yes, Dixie."

"I feel like I just got dropped into a movie halfway through the plot. How long have you and Dixie been a thing, and why didn't you tell me?"

Chase sighed and set down the clippers and leaned on the flooring of the porch below his dad. "We aren't really a thing, at least not yet."

"And you are going to the beach with your close friend who isn't really a thing... yet?" His dad looked confused.

Well... he could join the club.

"I am working on convincing her to let us be a real thing."

"Since when did you want it to be a real thing?"

Chase looked down at the ground and started kicking around the mulch chips. "I don't know exactly. A long time." Actually, it was much longer than he wanted to admit.

Jeff then flicked his son on his head and said, "Get your ass in the house. This is obviously going to be a longer conversation that needs some privacy."

Chase continued to look at the ground and nodded, but still wasn't moving. He was trying to delay the conversation, but moved quicker when his dad growled, "Move your butt Chase."

Jeff grabbed some drinks from the fridge and ordered his son to sit at the breakfast table. This table had served for so many discussions growing up. Whether it was good or bad, serious conversations were handled here. Chase began tracing the design of the flowers of the tablecloth that his mom had bought just before she died, while Jeff sat waiting patiently for him to start. Jeff finally had enough of the silence and repeated his earlier question. "How long have you wanted this to be a real thing?"

Chase dragged his hand down his face and groaned. "Since she was in high school. She just turned into the amazing beautiful girl with an incredible heart and she just fit with us."

"She always did. She was like family." Chase knew that. His parents were always so open and warm with Dixie when she was around. They even bought her presents at birthdays and Christmas as if she was their own child. It wasn't until after the accident that his dad took a step back from Dixie.

"Yeah, but I was too old for her then. I was going away for college and then there was Summer to think about. Dixie was her best friend, and I didn't want her to feel like I was stealing her away from her. I always saw my friends with their siblings who weren't close with their sisters, and were actually quite mean to them, but it was never like that with us. Summer was great. She just knew when I needed her and when I wanted my space. She always seemed to be intuitive like that with a lot of things. We could talk about anything and I never worried about her blackmailing me or saying anything to anyone else inappropriately. I was afraid if I attempted to date Dixie and it went well, she would be frustrated that I was taking her best friend away from her. Then if I did date Dixie and it went bad, then it would put a strain on their friendship and Dixie wouldn't feel comfortable here. So, I waited. I figured the feelings would go away, and then the accident happened." Chase's eyes became unfocused and tears gathered just waiting to overflow. "I felt responsible. I was supposed to pick them up. Mom and Summer were gone and Dixie would never be the same."

Jeff placed a hand on his son's forearm. "We have been over this. It wasn't your fault. They would—"

"I know Dad, but you have to understand that the guilt just stayed there pounding me into the ground for years. I had decided that I wasn't good for Dixie, and I knew she was starting to have feelings for me so I put up this giant wall of friendship and kept her there. I didn't want to hurt her, but I couldn't stay away either. Jesus, I even only dated girls from other towns so it wouldn't be flaunted in her face."

"So, what changed?"

"Time, mostly. Dixie and I have this amazing compatibility as friends and the more I spent time with her the more I just wanted... more. The guilt lessened, but I know it won't ever completely go away. I have watched her date other people here and there and then she started dating Jay and it was killing me. Jay is a good guy, and I knew he would treat her well." Chase started tapping his fingers on the table and continued. "It almost killed me. I wasn't spending as much time with her and I was watching Tyler fall in love with Zoey, and there I was just losing my mind."

"Why isn't she going on this vacation with Jay?"

Chase looked up at his dad with a self-deprecating smile. "Well, it isn't because I got up off my ass like I should have. This vacation is the anniversary party for her grandparents. It's a big deal. Her entire family is going to be there and Dixie had said that she would be bringing her new boyfriend, but then her and Jay broke up."

"She broke up with him?"

"No. He broke up with her. He felt like she wasn't as into him as he was to her, and he didn't think it was going to change so he ended it."

"Oh. I didn't see that coming."

"None of us did. I thought he was willing to do anything to be with her. He has had a thing for her for a long time now."

"Do you think that, like you said, he saw how happy Zoey and Tyler are and he realized he wasn't getting what he needed or wanted from Dixie?"

"I don't know. Maybe. I kept my distance from him when we would all go out. I wasn't exactly up to bonding with the guy."

"I get that. So how did you slide into his spot?"

Chase's face eased into that grin he always used when he had gotten away with something he wasn't supposed to. "Dixie had confessed to me that with the exception of her grandparents, her family didn't know who she was dating because they never took the time to listen to her. Then I saw her sister berate her about her date at the bakery and I couldn't take it. I just jumped in and basically took over as her role of the boyfriend."

Jeff raised his eyebrow. "So you lied to her family? That isn't a good idea."

"Yeah I know. Dixie pulled me aside after the whole thing with Elena and said basically the same thing."

"That it wasn't a good idea to lie?"

"Yup, so I told her that we could not lie and be together for real."

Jeff pulled his hand down his face and groaned. "Christ son. If I would have known your moves were so bad, I would have given you pointers years ago."

Chase bristled. "My moves are not bad. I have awesome moves. This was the best I could think of to have Dixie save face with her god-awful family. I had dinner with her and her sister last night, and Dad, it was just horrid. Elena is so condescending to Dixie. I was just so damn happy I could be there to support her."

"I don't disagree that someone should be helping her with her family, but don't you think they will see right through this fake relationship?"

"It isn't fake for me."

"Okay, but what about her?"

"I think she is getting on the same page. She let me stay with her last night."

"You stay with her all the time. That is nothing new."

"Yeah but this time I was upgraded from the couch to her bed."

Jeff stayed quiet for a minute and looked at his son. Chase started fidgeting in his chair. Jeff finally cleared his throat and said, "I am trying to decide if I want to be the cool dad and ask about the sex part, or if I want to stay with my instinct of not wanting to hear about my son and sex."

Chase quirked up a smile and said, "Don't worry, there is no sex stuff to hear about. Just flirting and kissing. No sex. Last night her sister had her off balance, and she just wanted me to stay with her."

"And you just jumped at the chance."

Laughing Chase replied, "I may have even jumped into the bed." After enjoying a couple minutes of silence, he looked at his dad and continued. "In all seriousness Dad, I want to be with Dixie. I want this chance with her. I know you were uncomfortable around her for a while. Is this going to be a problem for you?"

Jeff sighed and cleared his throat. "I know that right after the accident I was silent and awkward around her, but that was never because I didn't like her. Mostly I felt guilty that she was always in so much pain because of us. I know she still has problems with her hip and leg sometimes. Then there was the whole thing that she saw..." Jeff had to cough back his emotions before continuing. "She saw them die. Chase, she was so young and never should have been subjected to that kind of horror. I just never knew what to say to her, or how to make her feel better."

"You know that she felt responsible for the wreck. She also thought that you didn't like her anymore because of it."

"God no. Jesus, that poor sweet girl. I had no idea she thought that. I should have been clear with her back then and that is my fault."

Chase put his hand on his dad's arm. "Not your fault really. None of us communicated very well back then. We were all working through our own issues about this."

Jeff smiled and said, "Well, after this trip and the two of you get settled, bring her over for dinner. I want to make it clear to her that she is always welcome in this family."

"Thanks, Dad. That means a lot."

DIXIE WALKED INTO ENCHANTED Gifts and saw that Ariel was busy with a customer at the counter. Dixie nodded to Ariel and headed over to the cards to pick an anniversary card for her grandparents. After looking at several options she found an acceptable card and headed to the checkout where Ariel was still talking to her customer. After a few minutes, and some skillful deflecting of terrible flirting from her customer Ariel smiled at Dixie. "Hey, sweetie. You here to pick up the topper?"

"Yes. I can't wait to see it." Dixie had special ordered a glass blown topper made of hibiscus flowers and a picture frame to hold their original wedding picture.

Ariel pulled out a pink box from below the counter and gently opened the lid. Dixie pulled the topper out and gasped. "Oh, Ariel it is perfect."

"It is, isn't it? Jerry did a great job with it. And he said send his best to your grandparents."

"How is Jerry doing?"

Sadness crept into Ariel's face. "Not much is changing. His cancer is still getting a bit worse. His son is hoping to move back to town and help take care of him."

"How is Bax doing?"

"He is still good. He is still teaching in Charlotte and trying to mend his broken heart."

"Oh. I heard about that. She left him for another woman, right?"

Ariel's lips turned down at the corner. "Yeah, I thought that was just a rumor at first but his dad told me all about it. Bax walked in on the two of them when he came home early to surprise her one day."

"Guess he is the one who got surprised then. Wasn't he with her for years?"

"Yeah since their second year of college. He didn't understand why she kept dragging her feet about the wedding and well... now he knows."

"Yup. Poor guy. I just don't get it. Why do people cheat? It isn't like anyone ever really gets away with it. Want someone else, then just break it off and move on."

Ariel finished repacking Dixie's gift and rang up her purchases.

Dixie knew not to interrupt her friend when she got on one of these rants about cheating. Her dad cheated on her mom, who was one of the most amazing and beautiful women. Seeing that Ariel was calming down, she gave Ariel her credit card to pay. Once Ariel went to hand it back, she held it just out of Dixie's reach.

Dixie gave Ariel a puzzled look. "Are you planning on giving my card back?"

"Not until I get some answers."

Sighing, Dixie waved her hand in a bring-it-on motion.

"First, have you talked to Chase today?"

"No." Dixie held out her hand.

Ariel shook her head. "Second, are you going to jump in with both feet with Chase."

"No."

"You better give me more details or I will mug you for your whole wallet and hold it hostage."

"Geez, you have been hanging out with Josie too much."

"Josie wanted to tie you down and torture more information out of you."

"So, avoid Josie. Got it."

"Details."

"Fine. I am not going to jump in, but I tested the waters with my toes and I think I am going to use the stairs to get into the pool rather than just jumping from the high dive."

"But you are getting in the water, right?"

"Yes, I am slowing wading in."

"Well don't take too long or the sun will leave and the water will get too cold."

"Fine. And when are you going to fix your love life?"

"There is nothing to fix, and I have a date Friday."

"Really? With who? Please tell me not another blind date from some dumb app."

"Not a blind date. I met him in person and then he asked me out."

Dixie quirked a smile. "Details."

"I went to Kyle's office to drop off the details for the coupon in the next circular and there was this tall guy standing in the front waiting on Kyle. Kyle was still in the back and so we started talking. His name is Cord, and he just moved into town and is working out of his house as an accountant. He was at Kyle's office to put in a new ad. He seems like a nice guy and he does have a very nice body, or at least it looks like it under his khakis, polo shirt and black-rimmed glasses."

"I am trying to figure out if you are serious about the nice body or not."

"Oh, I am serious. I watched him bend over to pick up a stack of papers he knocked down and he has a very firm ass under those pants."

"You have to appreciate the fine asses of the world. Did Kyle hear him ask you out?"

Ariel straightened her spine. "Yes, and it was the same as always. He just gave me a blank stare and doesn't seem to care."

"I don't get him."

"Me either, and I am not going to waste my life trying to figure him out."

"Good." Dixie gathered her purchases and started to leave, but Ariel stopped her at the door.

"When are you leaving for the beach?"

"Tomorrow morning."

Ariel hugged her friend and whispered in her ear. "Please have fun and just let things happen with Chase."

Dixie just nodded and turned to leave.

Chapter 7

Dixie made it home that evening after running errands to gather last-minute things for the trip. As she picked up the many bags and draped them over her arms, she heard a noise come from behind her in the alley. She turned quickly and dropped half of her bags. Dixie growled in frustration and bent over to start picking up the items that scattered on the ground.

"Jumpy much?"

Startled, Dixie looked back up to find Chase leaning against her car.

"Jesus Chase, you scared me to death."

Chase bent down to help Dixie pick up the rest of her things. "I wasn't trying to scare you... at least not this time." He leaned over and picked up the sun screen and travel sized toiletries and then stopped when he found a small black box that landed by her tires. He picked it up and turned it over and suddenly had the brightest grin on his face. He held up the box of Magnum condoms and smiled at Dixie. "I am so glad you at least got me the right size."

Dixie's face went pale, and she gaped her mouth open. She took a deep breath and closed her eyes for a second.

Finally, she cleared her throat and said, "What makes you think those are for you?"

He took a step closer to her and started walking her back to the wall. "A few things. First, you do not get along with your sister enough to buy those for her. Second, I doubt you bought those for your grandparents, and if you did, let me just say... eewww. And finally, no girl would buy these for their parents."

Dixie snatched up the box and stared him directly in the eyes. "Fine. I bought them for me, just in case something does happen. But keep this in mind Montgomery, this in no way is a green light for you." Dixie started poking him in the chest. "You got me?"

Chase didn't answer. The big lug just kept grinning from ear to ear.

Dixie growled. "Chase."

Laughing, Chase replied, "Yeah, geez I get it. I still have to earn it." Chase heaved a big sigh and cupped Dixie's face in his hands. "But listen to me now. I am going to earn it, and we both will reap the benefits of my hard work."

Dazed Dixie was frozen in her spot. It was several breaths in and out before she remembered this was the same guy who backed off in the past and nearly broke her heart. She raised her hand up to Chase's face and squished his cheeks together. "Well you haven't earned it yet, so help me bring all this stuff upstairs and I will feed you."

"Real food?"

Shaking her head Dixie replied, "Yes. Real food."

"Promise."

"Yes, I promise. I never lie to you about food."

"Thank god."

They finished gathering all of the purchases and walked up to Dixie's apartment. Upon entering they found Elena sitting at the dining table with her laptop furiously typing away. She cleared her throat and started to speak without looking away from her computer screen. "I went to the market and made us a salad with baked tofu."

Dixie stared wide eyed while Chase made a gagging noise and mumbled something about not real food. "Sis, I was going to make dinner for all of us again."

Elena looked at Chase with a frown and continued, "Well, I only made enough for the two of us. I didn't think you would be bringing him back for dinner again."

Dixie looked down and played with the hem of her t-shirt. "It's okay. I will make something else for me and Chase and you can package up the leftover salad for you to snack on during our trip."

"If you insist. I was trying to be a good sister and show appreciation for your hospitality."

Dixie winced. "I can eat it and just make something else for Chase."

Chase shook his head. "Babe, I will make my own dinner. I know my way around your kitchen. Then I will help you pack up the rest of the supplies."

Elena walked past Chase and opened the refrigerator. She grabbed a small sealed bowl and placed it in front of Dixie. "Here, I already ate and I have some things to work on so I will be in my room."

Dixie watched her sister walk down the hallway with her laptop cradled under her arm and then looked down at the offending bowl of salad. After grabbing a fork, she moved the greenery around to inspect the ingredients. Then Chase's voice boomed from the inside of the refrigerator. "Oooh, you have fried chicken. And look at this you were hiding mashed potatoes and biscuits too."

Dixie bed a green leaf and inspected it. "What do you think this is? And where the heck is the lettuce in this salad?"

Chase inspected her fork and frowned. "I swear that looks like a dandelion leaf."

"What? No way."

Chase picked up his phone and typed something and smiled as he looked at his screen. "Yup. Dandelion leaf. I hope she didn't pay a lot for that. I just pulled a bunch from mine and dad's yard this week."

"Let me see that." Dixie grabbed Chase's phone from his hand and gasped. "Oh my god it is. Do you think there is an app to identify the rest of this crap? I just want to know what I am eating so I can tell the hospital what she poisoned me with."

Chase took the bowl from under her and threw the contents in the trash. "You are not eating that crap. One of those things looked like it had thorns on the leaf."

Dixie peered into the trash can disbelievingly and then shook her head. "No thorns, just jagged little edges."

Chase slammed the garbage lid down and growled. "No. Friends don't let friends eat garbage. Now... hot or cold."

"Huh?"

"Hot or cold?"

Dixie still looked at Chase with a glazed look. Laughing he said, "Hot or cold chicken?"

"Oh, cold is fine, but please heat the potatoes and biscuits."

"Yup."

The two worked quietly together to prepare dinner. Chase used the microwave while Dixie got the plates and drinks. She was sitting at the table waiting on Chase when it hit her. They were so comfortable with each other. They knew how to read each other and adapt to everyday tasks. When she was dating Jay, they always kind of stumbled over each other in the kitchen or even trying to get ready at the same time. They were awkward, while her and Chase had this perfectly choreographed way with each other in everything they did. But does this mean they just have a friendship or something more that they just haven't allowed to breathe?

CHASE LOOKED AT DIXIE, who was staring at him, but it wasn't as if she was seeing him—it was almost as if she was staring through him while deep in thought. He carefully approached the table and set the chicken down. "What? Is there something on my face?"

Dixie gave a very slight shake of her head. "No. I was just thinking."

Chase grinned. "About my sexy body?"

Dixie laughed. "No, you little perv."

"Then what?"

Dixie grabbed a biscuit and stared intently at it, not responding.

"Dix? What were you thinking about?"

"Just drop it please. A girl has to keep some secrets."

Chase grabbed the biscuit and put it on his plate and then took her chin to turn and look at him. "Know this Babe, there are no secrets between us. Not us. Never us."

Dixie gave a slow blink and sighed. "Okay maybe not a secret as it was so much as a thought. I can keep my thoughts to myself."

Chase grinned. "Okay but it will cost you."

"Cost me?"

"Yes," he said lowering his voice he continued. "Cost you." Then he leaned in and touched his lips to hers. He lingered there before touching his forehead to hers and then moved his hands into her hair. They kissed again only this time Dixie completely melted into Chase. His hands tightened their grip in her hair as she parted her lips to allow him entrance and dance his tongue along hers. He heard a soft needy moan release from her throat and then Chase grabbed her by her hips and pulled her into his lap.

His lips glided down her jaw and stopped by her ear as he groaned. "Do you know what you do to me?"

Dixie wiggled her hips, and he knew that she had to feel his erection on her thigh. Then she gave a loud sigh as Chase bit and sucked on her earlobe.

"No, but I am getting a pretty good idea." Dixie took her hands and started playing with Chase's hair as their foreheads touched and they stared into each other's eyes.

"What?"

Chase cleared his throat, unable to hide his grimace and looked down. "I think Ansel is trying to dig his way down my pants."

Alarmed Dixie jumped up and looked down as she saw Ansel with his head half way down the back of Chase's jeans and his little legs sticking up in the air as he was trying to wiggle his way down. She gently grabbed Ansel by the midsection and pulled him away from Chase. She smiled and rubbed under Ansel's chin. "Bad little hedgehog. You are not allowed to bury yourself in his clothes."

Chase shook his head. "It is your fault. You let that little pain in the ass crawl down your shirt all the time."

"It is just my sweatshirt; I still have another shirt on underneath it. If he was digging his way down your pants, you still had your underwear between you and him."

Chase shook his head. "Uh, no Dix. I don't."

Dixie looked at him a minute and then gaped her mouth open. "Oh you... uh... don't have any... I mean you went..."

"Commando?"

"Uh. Yeah."

"Yup. All the quicker to please you with..."

Dixie tilted her head and rolled her eyes. "Yeah. Now the moment is gone. Come on, let's eat."

They finished their dinner and Chase helped Dixie load the car with all the supplies for the trip. Chase stood by the door and shook his head. "You don't pack light, do you?" Sarcasm dripped with every word.

Dixie shook her head. "Only the one suitcase and that case over there is mine. The rest is all supplies for the party and beach. The other two suitcases are Grams and Gramps.

Since they were riding with Elena, she wanted the extra space in her car. That little open spot over there is for your stuff."

"So, what is Elena taking in her car?"

"Nothing besides people."

Chase wanted to say something about how she could have helped more, but Dixie put her hand over his mouth and shook her head.

"Nope. Don't even think about saying a word. I know how you feel about her and I am super tired. You can complain about my loving sister tomorrow on the drive down."

Chase mumbled a response that resembled an okay so Dixie released her hand from his mouth. He ran his hand down the side of Dixie's face and gave her a small kiss. "I will meet you here in the morning. What time did you want me to get here?"

Dixie shook her head. "I can pick you up."

"No. You will have enough to worry about and at least if I leave my truck here it will look like someone's home."

"And if you don't have your truck at your home, it will look like no one is home."

"Nah. I am leaving one of the cruisers there. Who will try to rob a house with a cop car in the driveway?"

"I don't know, there are some incredibly stupid people out there in the world."

"I know. I have arrested most of them in town."

"True. Okay Montgomery, meet me here at 7:00. We will stop at Zoey's for breakfast before we leave."

Chase groaned in approval. "You know me so well."

"Yes. Feed the bear and keep him happy."

Chase wrapped his arms around Dixie and drew her in close. "There are other things that keep the bear happy."

Dixie wiggled in his arm and smiled. "Yes, I know that too, but if I don't get some sleep soon you won't like the kind of bear I will be tomorrow."

Sighing, Chase gave Dixie a kiss that felt rushed and left both of them wanting more. "I will see you in the morning and try not to kill your sister before I get here."

"So, it is okay if I kill her after you get here?"

"Stop it."

"Fine. I will behave."

Chase began to pull away and watched Dixie in the rearview mirror. She was standing next to her car, watching him, and then seemed to bump her head a few times on the car door. He knew that she was struggling with moving them forward but he was positive that she was going to let him in and everything would be good. He just had to help her get through this trip without having a breakdown.

Chapter 8

Dixie woke up with her head pounding. *Thump. Thump. Thump.* She moaned and pulled the covers over her head and instantly regretted her late-night wine and cleaning spree after Chase left. *Thump. Thump. Thump.* Finally, she sat up and looked at the clock. It was only 4:30. Then the thumping came back again. Blinking to clear the fog she realized that the thumping was coming from her door and not her head.

"I am going to kill her." She threw off her covers and rubbed her eyes and began walking to her bedroom door. "Elena, I don't know who you..." Dixie stopped suddenly coming face to face with a metal walker making contact with her forehead. She stumbled back and fell to the floor. "Owwww," she cried rubbing the spot where she knew it was going to bruise.

"Oh God sweetie. I am so sorry. I didn't mean to whack you in the head." Dixie's grandpa put the walker down and started to walk into the room.

Dixie was still blinking hard and rubbing her head as she gazed up into her grandfather's kind eyes. "Gramps, what are you doing here so early? And why did you hit me with your walker?"

Sheepishly grinning he replied, "Well I tried to knock with my hand but it wasn't very loud and you weren't waking up. So, I decided to use my walker to jolt you out of bed." His chest puffed up. "And look it worked."

Dixie sighed and rolled over to pull herself off the floor. "Okay that answers one question but for the love of god why are you here at 4:30 in the morning?"

"Your grandmother was acting like a kid at Christmas. She woke up at 3 am and just stared at me with a stupid grin on her face. I woke up, and she scared the crap out of me. I thought she was finally going to kill me in my sleep or some-thing."

"I see you are still alive."

"Yup. Turns out she still likes and loves me. Go figure. Anyway, she told me that she was so excited about our trip that she couldn't sleep and wanted to get started right away. She made me get ready and bring her here so we could leave early."

"Do you remember that Elena is the one driving you there?"

"Of course I do. Your grandmother wanted the joy of waking her up and left you to me."

Dixie laughed. She always loved how her grandmother had a slightly evil streak. "She does love to torture her."

"Yes, she does. Do you know that she is planning to have a come to Jesus talk with your sister almost the whole way?"

Dixie grimaced. "Grams' 'you need to go to church' speech?"

"Yup."

"But she doesn't even go to church anymore. And she hasn't given me that speech since I was a teenager."

"She just wants to get a rise out of Little Miss Scientific."

"I am so glad I am going to be in a separate car."

"I wanted to talk to you about that." He walked over to her bed and sat down and patted the bed beside him for Dixie to sit next to him.

"About what?"

"You are coming with Chase now?"

"Yes."

"As your boyfriend?"

Dixie took a minute to think about how to respond and after deciding that everything sounded ridiculous, she simply nodded.

"When did you and Chase become more?"

"Not long ago."

"Not long. You mean about when Elena came into town and ran into you at the bakery?"

"How did you know about that?"

"Is that really a question? I live in a high school for old people. All they do is gossip all day. At least four people from the community told me about Chase kissing you at the bakery."

"Oh."

"What's going on? Are the two of you finally together?"

Dixie began picking lint off her blanket and couldn't look at him while answering. "I don't know. He is acting as if we are, but he only started it because Elena was being mean to me. And now he is treating me as if this is real, as if he is really interested in me."

"What makes you think this isn't real?"

"It took him pitying me to start this, and when I tried to show him how I felt years ago, he rejected me."

He put his arm around Dixie and started squeezing her closer. She rested her head on his shoulder and let a tear fall. Gramps always made her feel safe and like she could be that vulnerable little girl in his arms.

"Can I tell you what I know and a little about what I think?"

Dixie silently nodded on his chest.

"Okay. You and Chase have always been close and I know he cares about you and loves you. When you tried to show him how you felt before things were still a mess with all of you. You were still recovering from the accident and losing your best friend. Chase was recovering from losing his sister and mother in one day; not to mention how much his dad had changed after their deaths. The two of you have been close all these years and neither of you found someone you loved enough to claim as your own. That poor mechanic of yours adored you, but you never looked at him the way your grandmother looks at me. You both have the same hearts and you show all your emotions in your eyes. Your eyes have only ever looked at one person that way. Chase wasn't ready, but I think he is now and he finally saw an opening and took it. Should he have handled it differently? Sure, but he is a man and sweetie we never do things the way we are supposed to."

"That is not very reassuring Gramps."

"There isn't much about relationships with men that are reassuring. We are morons. We screw things up a lot and just hope we find the love of a woman who will always forgive us and find some of our faults endearing."

"You have faults?"

Dixie could feel the rise and fall of his chest while he laughed. "Oh, so many my dear. From the very first moment I met your grandmother I showed her my faults. I thought I was hot stuff as you say. I started walking over to your grandmother to ask her out and I tripped over my own feet. I was so sure of myself and my charms that I brushed it off and kept walking over to her to ask her out, and do you know what I said once I got to her?"

Dixie shook her head and replied, "No, what?"

"I looked her in the eyes and said, 'You pretty. You want to uh... um... go to... uh... dinner with me?'"

"Smooth Gramps."

"Turns out it actually was. Your grandma once told me that she was tired of the men who were full of themselves and thought the world should fall at their feet. When she first saw me coming over with a cocky grin on my face, she was going to turn me down, but then she saw me stumble and stutter like a fool and decided to take a chance on me."

"She went on a pity date?"

"Nah. It wasn't pity. She still thought I was the most handsome man in the world."

Dixie let out a sharp laugh. "Oh, really?"

"This is my story, sweetie. Let me tell it. Anyway, she thought I was the most handsome man in the world and not a cocky jerk. We went on our date and I wouldn't let her get rid of me after that. Just keep in mind I had a ton of screw ups here and there. I am constantly asking your grandmother to forgive me for something stupid I did or said. Chase is going to screw up but I have faith that he will always make a fool out of himself for you."

"I hope you're right."

"If I am wrong, I know how to make a person disappear."

Dixie looked at her grandpa and saw a serious light in his eyes. "You scare me sometimes."

"I have scared a lot of people over the years sweetie, but they were all for good reasons." He gave a mischievous smile and grabbed his walker to leave the room. "Now get ready so we can all have a nice morning before we leave."

Dixie got up and looked at the clock. It was just a little after 5 am and Chase would be there in a couple of hours. After her conversation with her Grandpa she was feeling a little better about the direction things were going with Chase. Bringing down her walls with him would be hard. She hadn't truly ever let any man fully into her heart, but if she let anyone in it should be Chase, shouldn't it? He had consistently been by her side for whatever she needed. She wanted a kind of love that she had seen with Tyler and Zoey and others like Ariel's parents and Chase's parents before his mom died. She didn't want to see an empty side of the bed or only see it filled with a spoiled hedgehog. Dixie sighed as she thought about waking up wrapped up in Chase's warm arms and felt flutters deep in her stomach. As she finished packing her makeup into her travel bag, she gave a short silent nod and decided to give this a real chance. No holding back. No hedging. And if this didn't work out, she would live. She had gone through so much in her life and loving and losing Chase sounded much better than never knowing how it would feel to truly love him with her whole heart.

After getting her shower and packing some last minute necessities, Dixie jumped when her phone suddenly went off with her text message alert. She picked up her phone and gave a bright smile.

Zoey: Did someone die or is the world ending? I saw that your light was on before 5 this morning.

Dixie: Nobody died. And you are just now texting me? It is almost six now.

Zoey: I was busy mixing icing for the donuts.

Dixie: Priorities, of course. Pastries, then your friend.

Zoey: Didn't want to interrupt sexy time.

Dixie: Ugh. Grandpa was in my room talking to me. No sexy time.

Zoey: Oh. I thought Chase was doodle-bopping you.

Dixie: What? How old are you?

Zoey: Hush. Sounded better than batter dipping his corndog.

Dixie: Ew

Zoey: Stuffing the muffin?

Dixie: You have been around Josie too much. Just stop.

Zoey: Wait one more. Glazing your donut.

Dixie: Remind me to never ever eat your glazed donuts again.

*Zoey: *Gasp. And to think I made you road treats for this morning.*

Dixie: Chase and I will be stopping by on our way out of town. I have to see my girls before we leave.

Zoey: What about the boys?

Dixie: Meh. I am taking the good one with me.

Zoey: Don't know about that. You may go broke feeding him.

Dixie: Tell me about it. Gotta go. See you soon.

Dixie gathered her bags and walked into the kitchen to see Grams and Elena talking about the drive down. Elena was gritting her teeth while Grams was listing all the places she wanted to stop on the way to the resort.

"We can't stop at all these places or we will never get there," Elena said clenching her hands into tight fists.

"Sure we can. Some of those trips will be necessary for potty stops anyway. We have plenty of time."

"We have a schedule to keep."

Grams shook her head. "This is a vacation, sweetheart. There shouldn't be any schedules involved except the events that start much later tonight."

"There is no need to stop at Ted's Curiosities or the Old Town General Store."

"There is a need for us. I want to see what kind of new things they have. If you are a good girl, maybe I will buy you a present while we are there."

"Grandmother, I don't need a present from these places."

"Are you trying to tell me that you are too good for these kinds of stores?"

Sighing, Elena replied, "No, of course not, but I don't need anything from there."

Grams' face lit with a bright smile and said, "That is the idea of a gift. It's something nice I can buy that you may not need but will always bring a smile to your face."

Dixie was desperately trying to hold in a smile as she thought about her grandmother's last gift of a bowl made out of glass eyeballs. "Hey sis, if you don't like your gift you can trade what she got me last time."

Grams shot her a warning look and replied, "You will do no such thing. You needed a good-sized bowl for snacks for your little get togethers with your friends."

"Ariel said the blue eye in the middle freaks her out because it follows her around."

"Pish posh. Nonsense. Now Elena dear, gather your things so we can get breakfast before we all hit the road."

Dixie looked at the clock and saw that she had about twenty more minutes before Chase would arrive. "Grams, Chase and I are picking up some food from Zoey's that she made for us this morning before we go. He should be here soon."

"No worries, my dear. We will just spend some more bonding time with your sister."

Dixie grinned as she saw a small grimace on Elena's face. "Sounds perfect."

A short time later Dixie put her last bag by the front door and then promptly got hit on the head again when the door swiftly opened. "Ow. God bless it. That is twice now." She began to hold her head where the collision happened when strong hands cupped her face and made her look up.

"God Dixie. Are you okay? I didn't know you were right there. God, I am so sorry."

Dixie looked up into Chase's remorseful eyes and blinked a few times to clear her head. "It's okay, it is just that

Gramps already wacked me in the head this morning with his walker."

Chase looked over at her Gramps in confusion as she continued, "Don't ask."

"Do you need me to get you some ice?"

"No. I just need a minute."

"Here. Just sit on the couch for a few and I will take your stuff down to your car."

After Chase bounded down the stairs, Dixie shakily stood up, eased over to Ansel and picked him up along with his travel bag of supplies. She took one more look around the apartment to make sure she had everything and went down the stairs to join Chase.

She found him leaning into the car trying to reorganize the back seat and watched his ass as it swayed back and forth. She stood silently for a moment and then heard his voice break though the silence. "Do you need me to wiggle it some more or are you done gawking?"

Dixie gasped. "I was not gawking. I was just waiting for you to get done doing... whatever it is that you are doing."

"Uh-huh."

Chase turned around and watched as Dixie felt the heat creeping up from her neck to her cheeks. She hated that blush. Chase just grinned. She knew that he could always read her emotions since she could never control her reactions.

"Anyway, Tyler said we have to stop at the bakery before we leave."

"Yeah, Zoey said the same thing. We have treats waiting on us."

"Thank God."

Chapter 9

Chase and Dixie walked in the bakery to find everyone waiting for them at the table with the exception of Zoey. Zoey was behind the counter helping a customer as she waved them on over to the table of their friends. Dixie sat beside Ariel who had a large basket with a bow on it sitting in front of her.

"What's this," Dixie asked while restraining herself from greedily grabbing the basket.

"We all pitched in and got you guys road trip goodies."

Chase quickly grabbed the basket off the table. "Awesome, more food."

Josie and Ariel looked at him with wide eyes as he peeled back the cellophane wrapping.

With a disappointed frown he said, "Aw. Not food."

Dixie held out her hands and stared at him. "Give it to me, you big lug, and go see Zoey for a snack."

Tyler got up to walk with Chase to the counter, as Dixie peered inside. As she pulled out each item her friends laughter kept increasing. First, she pulled a mad libs book, then a crossword book, and as she pulled out pink fuzzy socks, she looked questioningly at the girls.

Ariel smiled and explained, "For your feet. You're always complaining how Chases' house is a freezer. Just imagine how cold it will be when he has free rein of a thermostat without an electric bill."

"Good thinking," Dixie replied as she dug deeper and pulled out the Tide to Go wipes.

"That is for the big guy. He wears most of his food when he gets too hungry," Josie explained. "Keep digging, the good stuff is at the bottom."

"Wireless headphones."

Josie nodded. "Either to tune out your family or Chase. Works good both ways."

"True."

Ariel then leaned over and whispered, "Okay now for the stuff in the black wrapping, you may want to be a little discreet about opening those."

Dixie had just lifted the last items when Chase and Tyler walked back over and sat down. Dixie unwrapped the first item and as she realized that it was a blue box of condoms, she quickly put them below the table out of sight.

Chase frowned. "You guys got the wrong size. I need extra large."

Tyler shoved him in the arm and laughed. "You wish."

Dixie glared at Josie who laughed at her. "Don't look at me. I didn't buy that. That came from Tyler and Zoey."

Chase looked at his friend who laughed and said, "Be glad I didn't buy you the extra small ones."

Chase shrugged and said, "We all know they keep those in stock for you. It's okay."

Dixie cleared her throat. "Okay boys, play nice."

Ariel smiled as Dixie grabbed the next one and said, "This one is mine."

Dixie pulled out what seemed to be a knotted mess of black strings and lace. Knowing that it had to be some sort of lingerie she couldn't help but hold it out to try and detangle the mess. "How are you supposed to wear this thing?"

"Ha!" Josie shouted as she slapped a piece of paper in front of Dixie. "I told you we would have to show her the picture. That thing is a mess."

Ariel pouted. "Fine."

Dixie saw one last item wrapped in black and shook her head. "Nope. I think we can wait to unwrap it."

"Like hell we can." Chase lunged his arm into the basket and took the last item and quickly opened it. "Oh my god. Wait why does it have a face?" Held in Chase's hand was a large purple vibrator with a face where the penis head would normally be and a smiling rabbit attachment.

Then an older woman's voice came from over Chase's shoulder. "That is because of overseas shipping laws. They can't import sex toys but regular toys are okay, so they have to make a face on it to call it a doll."

They all turned to see Mrs. Glover, Zoey and Tyler's landlord, with a giant smile on her face.

"What? Do you guys think you invented the idea of sex toys, or we shouldn't know about it because we are old? Please, we were being creative about our sex lives long before you all came along." She then turned and threaded her arm through Mr. Glover's who turned around and winked at them all.

Josie smiled and said, "God, I love that woman."

Chase shook his head and gently put the toy back in the basket. "I think I have been traumatized, and I lost my appetite."

Everyone continued their breakfast and Dixie enjoyed the conversation and laughter being with her friends. She was going to miss them all week, but at least both sides of her family would be there and she should have fun. Her parents were not as outright condescending to Dixie as her sister. They were just distant and didn't show affection well. Her Gramp's side of the family were completely opposite—loud, expressive and loving. Watching the two families mix together was always interesting.

Dixie and Chase said their goodbyes and left the bakery with the gifts and baked goods to begin their journey to the beach.

AS THE DRIVE CONTINUED, Dixie began to feel a little uncomfortable. Clearly all of their friends assumed that her and Chase were going to start having sex on this little trip. Was that what she wanted? Would their friendship survive if it didn't work out? Could she afford to not take this chance? She obviously wasn't doing the whole dating others thing very well. And maybe it was because she always held out for Chase to date her, but she dismissed that because she saw how Ariel waited for Kyle and that is not what she had been doing. She just hadn't found the one person to make it all fit. With Chase everything always fit. Everything except romance. Her head was beginning to hurt, so she picked up her phone and looked through nearly every app she had before Chase finally grabbed her hand with his and brought it to the middle of the two seats.

"Dix. You are beginning to make my head hurt, your thoughts are so loud."

"What? That doesn't even make sense."

"I know you. I know when you are overthinking things. It is as if you have all these ideas and worries running around in your head and when I look at you, I can almost hear the echoes of the craziness humming in my head."

"Sorry. I will try to think less," she said as she rolled her eyes. That was just annoying. She hated that he could read her so well.

"I know you are worried about this week, but please don't be. Everything is going to be okay. This is your family and they do love you. Albeit some better than others."

Dixie sighed. "It isn't just that."

"You are worried about us?" Chase took her silence as confirmation. "Don't be. No matter what, we will always be good, but take this chance with me. Give me this week and if at the end you don't think it is worth the risk, we will go back to how it was before."

Dixie took a deep breath and looked at their joined hands and weakly replied, "I am afraid of falling."

"Don't be afraid because I will be falling by your side."

Dixie nodded, reclined the seat back and closed her eyes, then fell asleep for the remainder of the drive while Chase rubbed his thumb back and forth across her hand.

CHASE WOKE DIXIE WHEN they pulled up in front of the resort. It was much larger than it seemed in the pictures and had beautiful landscaping with flowers lining the paths to the front door. Chase rounded the car and opened the door for her as they entered the lobby.

The lobby was just as picturesque as the outside. The main area by the registration desk was gray with cool tones of blue and aqua accenting the space. The lighting was surrounded by spiraling colored glass that resembled ocean waves and the middle had a square opening that showed all the way up to the roof with some rooms lining the edges with balconies and walls made to look like the afternoon sky.

They made their way to the registration desk and were greeted by an attractive dark-haired man in his thirties. He smiled at Chase and asked how he could assist. Dixie cleared her throat and said, "Yes, I have reservations for Dixie Hewitt."

The man nodded quickly and smiled as the information flashed on his screen. "Ah yes, here you are. The starlight bungalow."

Dixie shook her head. "No. We should have just a regular room. The starlight is supposed to be for my grandparents. You know, the guests of honor."

"There is no mistake, Miss Hewitt. Your grandmother called and insisted to trade rooms with you."

Chase couldn't help but smile. He really did love Grams. That woman would meddle until her dying day.

Dixie continued to shake her head. "Well, I can't afford that room on my own, so you have to switch it back, or give me a regular room at least."

"I am sorry ma'am but as you are probably aware, we are sold out for the week, and besides, your room was paid in full."

"That can't be right. I didn't even pay for the standard room yet."

"Someone paid for it on your behalf."

Dixie turned and glared at Chase. He held up his hands in self-defense. Not that he wouldn't have done it if he would have thought about it, or at least had the time, but this time it wasn't him. "Hey don't look at me. I didn't even know they had a bungalow."

Dixie shook her head. "We will be right back. I have a phone call to make."

Dixie and Chase walked over to the couches where she opened her purse with annoyance and pulled out her phone. After a few seconds she took a deep breath and took out her sweet voice. "Hello Grams. Did you trade rooms with me?"

Chase could hear her grams on the other line since the old woman still thought she had to practically shout into cell phones to be heard. "Well of course dear. The bungalow is a nice gesture, but it is too far away from the rest of the family and main grounds of the hotel. You know Gramps and I can't take long walks like we used to and we want to be close to the family. Besides, you and Chase need the privacy."

"Can't take long walks my ass, Grams. You just walked that half marathon earlier this year, and I saw Gramps using the treadmill for a walk last week."

"Maybe so, but the boardwalk will be uneven and it would be best if we don't have to trudge through the sand. Now you be a good little girl and say thank you to your

Grams and enjoy the breathing room from your relatives. You do a lot for us and we wanted to do this for you. Now go settle in with that big handsome man of yours."

Chase was going to have to send this woman some flowers and a thank-you card for this one. He couldn't have asked for a better set up to win Dixie over for good.

Dixie looked over at Chase. "He isn't mine, Grams."

"Pish Posh. Of course, he is. Now go have fun and we will see you soon."

Dixie hung up the phone and looked at Chase. "Well, it looks like we are staying at the bungalow."

AFTER COMPLETING THE check in they walked down the boardwalk to the bungalow. Dixie gasped as she caught her first glimpse. It was beautiful. The house was colored in the same blue, aqua and gray tones from the lobby and had an extended front porch with a built-in gazebo complete with a hot tub and shades for privacy. Chase turned around with a devilish smirk when he saw the hot tub. Shaking her head, she kept walking and said, "Clean up those thoughts, Montgomery."

"Who me? Obviously, your thoughts were not much better than mine to know where I was going."

"You're a guy. Your mind only goes three directions. Food, sex and sleep."

Chase stopped in his tracks and looked down at Dixie with a frown. "Is that all you really think of me?"

Dixie stopped and looked up. Shit. She really hurt his feelings. "Aw. Come here."

Chase stubbornly stood his ground, so she walked up to him.

"Okay, I was just picking on you. I know you have more feelings than that."

He was still frowning.

"I'm sorry. You know I love you."

She wrapped her arms around him and felt his chest shake. She looked up and saw him laughing. She pushed off his chest. "You are such a jerk."

"But I am your jerk."

Chase unlocked the door and they entered the bungalow. The inside was just as beautiful as the outside. It was all one great open space with an oversized white couch with blue and gray pillows. The coffee table was a giant white coral with a free formed glass table top. A large screen TV hung on the wall with glass sculptured sea creatures surrounding it. Dixie saw that he was admiring the TV when she saw the bed. She let out a squeal of delight and jumped into the giant soft bed with low sounding flumps. Chase turned around just as Dixie was rolling on top of the bed in the middle of a giant-sized white down comforter and what looked like a hundred pillows.

"This bed is amazing. Do you think they would notice if we accidentally packed it up and took it home with us?"

"Uh, yeah."

"Come on, where is your sense of adventure?"

"I could see Kyle printing the headline now. Town sheriff gets arrested for stealing a bed."

"You would be legendary."

"This is not the type of thing I would want to be legendary for. Saving a person's life. Yes. My incredible athletic skills, of course. And I..." the rest of his words were mumbled and cut off as she held his lips together with her fingers.

"I know where the rest of that was going and you need to stop right there."

Chase smiled and threw them both back on the bed. They laid there staring at the ceiling and saw a bunch of gears towards the left side. He lifted his head in confusion then gave a slight jump when it began to slide to the side.

He felt Dixie's breath in his ear as she said, "This is why they call it the starlight bungalow. It opens for you to see the stars at night, and all at the press of a button." Dixie handed him the remote. "Here have fun. I am going to get ready for dinner."

Dixie changed into a blue dress with spaghetti straps and a lace knit sweater and strappy sandals. She felt ridiculous. She hadn't worn a dress in years but she also hadn't seen her parents in years and wanted to make a good impression. She nervously adjusted the bottom of the dress trying to lower it and beginning to regret buying one that was so short.

She walked back into the room to find Chase still pressing the ceiling button. "When I said have fun and let you have the remote, I didn't think you would still be pressing the button ten minutes later."

"Come on. It is a remote-controlled ceiling. That is worth at least fifteen minutes of entertainment."

Why are men mostly like grown children? She wondered if they were like pets too. Give them a box and they would be entertained for hours. Looking around she asked, "Where's Ansel?"

Chase nodded over to the corner. "He is in his playhouse over there. The poor little guy is tuckered out from the drive."

"Why would he be tired?"

Chase grimaced. "I may or may not have tried to reenact that scene with Bill Murray with the groundhog steering the car while you were asleep."

"And how did that go for you?"

"Good for a few minutes until he rolled off and fell on my crotch."

"Good lord. Are you ready to go?"

Chase nodded and held his hand out to Dixie. She hesitated for a moment and finally took his hand, and they walked together back to the main hotel.

THEY WALKED INTO THE banquet room and saw that much of the family had already made it to dinner. Dixie first saw her sister and grandparents speaking to her Great Uncle Kalino and his wife Mary. She saw other cousins talking on the other side, but could only recognize a few of them and what she assumed were their spouses. As she scanned the room, she suddenly felt arms wrapped around her waist and her feet lifted off the ground as a loud deep voice said, "Dixie, my little sprite, how are you?"

By now her legs were still dangling while they swung from side to side. "Bronc. It's good to hear your voice again."

"Hell girl, I have missed you. Why haven't you come to visit? I miss your cute little face."

Dixie looked at her legs still lifted off the floor. "Well you could see my face better if you put me down."

Laughing he set her down and released his hold. "Sorry about that. I just got so excited to see you." The two hugged while Chase stood back watching them with amusement. Once Bronc let her go, he turned to Chase and eyed him from head to toe. "Is this your new guy?"

Chase nodded. "That's me." He extended his hand in greeting, "Chase Montgomery, and you are Bronc?"

"Actually, my name is Bronco, but everyone calls me Bronc." The two shook hands and squeezed more than necessary. Bronc was a large man standing at 6'5" and close to three hundred pounds. "I am Rose's nephew and Dixie's favorite relative."

Dixie smiled. "He isn't wrong."

"You both need to meet my new wife, Anne."

"You got married again?"

"Yup. Fourth time is the charm. She isn't like the others. She is smart, independent and doesn't take my shit."

Dixie bounced from foot to foot. "I definitely have to meet her."

Just then a short red headed woman approached the trio. She wrapped her arm around Bronc's middle and gave a warm smile in greeting. Bronc lit up at her smile and proudly said, "This is Anne. Anne this is my little Dixie and her man, Chase."

A bright, warm and genuine smile came from Anne as she extended her hand in greeting to Dixie and Chase. "It is so nice to meet you. Bronc told me all about you and showed me your photography page. You are an amazing artist."

Dixie blushed. "Thank you. I didn't even know Bronc knew about the page."

Bronc smiled. "Of course I do. Aunt Rose won't shut up about how well you are doing. She emailed me your page a long time ago."

"I didn't even know she knew how to use a computer."

"She told me she took those classes at the retirement village so she could keep up with all the trouble we get into. She social media stalks all of us now. She sent me an IM when I got engaged to Anne and told me that she was happy that I finally got my head out of my ass."

Anne wrapped her arm around his middle and said, "Well dear you were kind of a big mess."

"And now I am your mess." He turned to Chase and asked, "Are you going to the golf outing tomorrow morning while the girls have their spa day?"

Chase grimaced. "I am going, but I have to admit the only time I have held a golf club is at mini golf."

"No worries man. Most of us don't golf. Uncle Hale just wants to show off to the rest of us his mad golfing skills."

"Is Dixie's dad going?"

"Yup. Last I heard, so don't worry there will be someone there worse than you." Bronc looked over Chase's shoulder and smiled. "Speaking of the devil, here they come."

They turned to see Elena, her husband Charles and a boy in a little suit with bowtie. Everyone gave polite greetings while the young boy stood quietly by Charles' side. Chase bent down to greet him and said, "Hello little man. I don't think I have met you yet. I'm Chase."

The little boy looked wide-eyed at Chase and then up to Charles who gave a slight nod to the boy. The boy extended his hand and looked at Chase directly as he said, "Hello Mr. Chase. I am Martin."

Chase smiled and gently and politely shook the small hand offered to him. Chase stood to his full height and extended his hand out to Charles. "Good to see you again."

Charles gave a polite smile and shook Chase's hand. "Hello, Mr. Montgomery. Elena told me that you would be Dixie's escort for the trip."

Chase shook his head. "If by escort you mean her boyfriend, then yes I suppose that I am."

Charles shook his head. "You will have to pardon my confusion. I was always under the assumption that you and Dixie were just friends."

"We were, but things changed."

"You will have to forgive my curiosity then, sir. What provoked the change?"

Dixie saw Chase's eyes narrow on Charles. She knew that he did not intend for the question to offend Chase, but like Elena, Charles had a lack of social grace for common conversations. She used to believe that Charles did not like her at all until they had a conversation one night after he found her crying after dinner. Dixie's reminiscing thoughts were interrupted by Chase's deep voice. "Is that your way of asking me why are we together now after all this time?"

Charles nodded and said, "Yes."

"Well then, I guess the best way I can explain it is that I had all the right things in my life. I love my job as sheriff. I get to provide security and help to the members of my community. My family is close and we all care for each other deeply. I have amazing friends who support one another and remind me how to have fun, but at the end of the day I would leave behind one friend who filled my heart completely, and I couldn't deny that she belonged with me anymore. She is that missing piece of everything I want, everything that I need."

Dixie felt her fingers drift to her lips as her mouth parted hearing his words. Were they true? Did he really feel this way, or was he just saying this to prove a point to her family? She felt Chase's arm wrap around her waist as she was drifting off in her thoughts and heard Anne's voice, "Well that is just about the sweetest thing I have ever heard."

Dixie tried to ground herself back into the conversation. She looked at Anne and asked, "What, doesn't Bronc talk about you like that?"

"Ha! That man was nearly all grunts and commands for the first month. The first time he told me that he loved me he said 'I love you, and you are moving in with me today.'"

Dixie looked over to the obviously unapologetic man who just shrugged. "What?" he replied. "If you ask then they can turn you down. I wasn't going to risk it."

Chase chuckled. "I like that idea."

Anne gave a light slap to his forearm. "I could have turned you down. You were just lucky I didn't want to be without you."

"Baby, I would have just made love to you until you couldn't see anything but us in our future."

"Pretty sure that was how you won me over the first time," Anne said with a sly smile.

Dixie could feel Chase's chuckles as they watched the two banter about who was really the boss in their relationship. Dixie looked up, gazing at his face, as his smile continued to widen. She rested her hand on his chest, enjoying the feel of his heartbeat as the conversation continued. It felt comfortable and even natural to embrace each other. When did that happen? She felt Chase pull her hand from his chest and bring it up to his lips where he lightly kissed her palm. The waves of her pulse raced down her neck and traveled down her spine. That simple kiss, the light touch of his lips to her palms, was more electric than nearly all the touches from her previous boyfriends. This man was potent, and he may very well be the death of her.

As the three couples continued to talk, the banquet manager announced that dinner was ready. Chase led Dixie to the beginning of the buffet line and took two plates as they reached the first station. Shaking her head Dixie asked, "Are you really that hungry?"

"Yes, but both plates are not for me. One is for you and one is for me."

"I can carry my own plate."

"Maybe, but I am trying to be a gentleman."

"Okay, how about I serve up my own food and when I am done you can carry my plate to the table?"

Chase looked at the two plates and then to the first serving dish and nodded. "Probably a good idea. I don't have any hands left to scoop the food."

As they approached the end of the line, Dixie could hear the whispers and giggles as people would eye Chase's plate. It was stacked like a mountain of food. He had ham on the bottom, with turkey directly on top, two chicken breasts and then there were side dishes of potatoes, rice, corn, and vegetables that surrounded the meat. Chase suddenly stopped at the end and looked longingly at the basket of rolls and then to his plate.

Laughing Dixie said, "Don't worry, I will get rolls for the both of us. I would never let you suffer." He continued to look with his puppy eyes at the rolls. "Geez. Okay, I will get you two rolls."

Beaming, he took the now two full plates and found his way to their table. Dixie sat next to her dad, Keith, and greeted him with a hug before they sat down. Dixie's mom, Alani, was already eating her dinner while reading what appeared to be an email. Frowning, Dixie looked at her dad. "I thought mom promised not to work this weekend." Both of her parents were workaholics but her dad would often remind her mom that there was an importance to recharging and resting your mind.

"This is her off work. I got her away from the building and to the beach. I had to allow her access to emails and phone calls or she wouldn't have come."

"She seriously wouldn't have come for Grams and Gramps anniversary?"

"You have to understand sweetheart. We are very close to making a breakthrough and it could make both of our careers if we can validate our conclusions."

Resigned, Dixie sighed. "I am happy for you both then. I hope you get everything you are looking for." Because apparently it would never be time with their family.

Dixie looked down at her plate, slowing losing her appetite when she felt Chase's hand on her knee placing a gentle squeeze. She brought her hand down below the table and laced her fingers into his. She needed this. She needed the solid support of someone who understood the dynamics of her family. She loved them all but never seemed to find that connection she needed with her parents and sister.

Elena, Charles and Martin joined the table and Dixie and Chase found the discussion steered towards science and new grant foundations that were available for funding Elena's new research. Dixie continued to feel smaller and smaller as the discussions continued. She had nothing to contribute and felt that injecting her opinion would create tension. Chase however did not feel the same way. During a brief pause he quickly said, "Did you all hear how well Dixie's last art exhibit went?"

Alani paused for a brief moment and looked at her daughter. "I thought that you owned a photography studio and did family portraits and events?"

Dixie blushed. "I do, but I—"

Keith quickly interrupted and gave a pointed look at his wife. "I told you about her little project."

Dixie bowed her head, not wanting to be the center of attention. Her family didn't understand her love of photography and capturing images of light, life and love. Chase squeezed her hand and continued. "It isn't a little project. She is amazing. Did you know that she made ten thousand dollars for her first showing?"

Alani looked at her daughter with her eyebrows drawn down. "Your father did mention that you were selling photographs, but he did not explain that it was at a gallery. I wouldn't think that a gallery in Blossom Hills would bring in that kind of money."

Feeling a little more confident Dixie replied, "It wasn't in Blossom Hills. I had the exhibition in Raleigh. I sent you and Elena the invitation for the opening."

Elena briefly looked up from her dinner and commented, "I sent you a text that I would not be able to attend."

Dixie remembered getting that text. She also remembered how she had expected Elena to not be able to attend but she thought that maybe her sister would at least call to congratulate her on such an accomplishment. Every time Elena won a research grant or was provided an award in her field, Dixie had always called to support her sister and show she cared. Dixie cleared her throat so her voice would not crack. "Yes, I got your text."

Alani showed a brief moment of contrition and then cleared it as quickly as it came. "Well dear, it is nice that you did so well. I am... proud of you."

Dixie wished that her mom's tone matched her words. She may have said that she was proud of her but her tone seemed to infer that Dixie could still do more, do better.

Chase leaned next to her and whispered, "Let it go babe. Just know that I am amazed by you, okay?"

Dixie nodded and began to shovel heaping amounts of food into her mouth. She just wanted to leave the table and get back to that amazing bungalow. Maybe she would just jump on Chase as soon as they got into the doorway. Drowning her feelings in his arms seemed like a fantastic idea. Then what Elena said next made Dixie stop her thoughts cold.

"Mom, don't forget we are supposed to pick up our dresses for the foundation's award dinner next month. We need to make sure the tailoring has been completed correctly this time."

Dixie gave a slow blink to Elena then her mom.

"Of course, dear. Your father and I are looking forward to your dinner."

Looking forward to her dinner? Better yet, another dinner for their perfect daughter, but they couldn't bother to even call Dixie when she had an exhibition at a well-respected gallery? Hurt beyond words Dixie stood up from the table and gave a small quiet, "Excuse me, I have to... have to go now."

With tears in her eyes she quickly left her table and rushed by others including her grams who had a worried look in her eyes.

CHASE COULD NOT BELIEVE the conversation Dixie's family had in front of her without a small consideration of Dixie's feelings. He watched Dixie practically run out the door trying not to make a scene. He gently placed his napkin covering the remaining items on his plate and looked at each of them at the table. "You know, for smart people, you guys really are dumb."

Elena started to open her mouth, but Chase cut her off with his hand in a stopping motion. "Not now, Elena. See if you all can figure this one out on your own, and we will see you tomorrow."

Chase walked past Grams and gave a gentle kiss on her cheek. Gramps also gave Chase a worried look as he pulled away. "Both of you enjoy the rest of your night. I am going to take care of Dixie."

Gramps frowned over at the table where Dixie's family were talking in hushed tones. "Chase, is there anything I can do to make this better?"

With a sad smile Chase replied, "Yeah, no more assigned seats this week."

"Done. Now go get our little girl."

Chase gave a slow nod and walked out the door to find Dixie. Once he made it out to the beach, he could see in the distance the little wooden bridge just before the cottage and saw that Dixie was sitting on the middle step leaning her head against the railing. Once he reached her, he sat down next to her. She took a shaky inhale and shifted her position from leaning on the railing to leaning her head on his arm.

"I thought I might have to wait for you until you got your second helpings."

Chase took her chin and turned her to look in his eyes. "Know this Dixie Hewitt, you are the most important thing in my life. No amount of food would stop me from coming to you when you are hurting."

"That might be the sweetest thing you have ever said to me."

Giving a small laugh Chase replied, "Nah. Maybe just the most shocking."

They sat quietly for a few minutes and her tears started to fall again. Chase couldn't fight it any more. He stood and picked her up, cradled her into his arms, and walked her back to the cottage. After opening the door, he laid her on the bed and kissed her on her forehead. "Stay here."

Chase opened Dixie's suitcase and grabbed her pajamas and set them on the bed. "I will be right back."

Chase was beyond frustrated with Dixie's family. They barely see her, hell they barely talk to her, and they can't even pretend to show an interest in her life. Just because she didn't follow in the same steps as her family shouldn't mean that they disregard her in so many ways. Chase winced as he realized he slammed the microwave door when he was heating water for tea. He needed to calm down. Dixie needed him to be level headed and be there for whatever she needed.

He walked over to Ansel's playpen and set down the mugs so he could feed him. Ansel came scurrying over to Chase's hand and nuzzled him. "Don't worry little guy. We can take care of Mom and show her she is loved, right?" Ansel seemed to huff in reply and then walked over to his food.

Chase brought the two mugs of tea to the bed to find Dixie already asleep, curled up around a pillow. Chase walked over to the other side, set down the two mugs and stripped to his boxer briefs. He sat and drank some tea while he watched her rhythmic breathing fall in time to the slow moving ceiling fan. If today was any sign of things to come, it was going to be a long week, and he had plans for the two of them. She was going to realize that they belonged together, and he didn't want their beginning to be tainted by the inconsiderate actions of the people who were supposed to love her.

Deciding on a plan of action for tomorrow, Chase lifted the blanket and curled around Dixie to get a good night's rest.

Chapter 10

Dixie woke up the next morning to a warm palm on her breast. She looked down to see Chase's hand firmly gripping her like she might try to escape. She loved the idea of him taking more control of their morning and seeing where it could go, but she really had to use the bathroom. She fought with herself for a moment. Let Chase take advantage of her body and start the morning off right, or let her bladder win this fight. She wiggled her butt into his groin where she found him already hard. He started to moan, and she loved the reaction she was getting from him. She wiggled again to see what would happen, but finally her bladder won the fight for control and she threw off the covers trying to quietly go to the bathroom.

When she walked back in, she found Chase sitting up in bed already on his cell phone. "No, sir. I didn't forget. Of course. I will meet you at the lobby in fifteen minutes. Yes, sir. I will bring Dixie too."

Dixie looked at Chase while he gazed up and down her body. Figuring out that he wasn't going to say anything without prompting she said, "Who was that?"

"Gramps. He was kindly reminding me to meet them for golf and that you are supposed to be there as well for the girls' spa day."

"Thank god I am not doing the same things that most of the girls are. I might be able to have some private time."

"What are you getting done?"

"That is my little surprise for later."

Growling, Chase sprang from the bed and pinned her to the wall. "And am I going to like this surprise?"

Dixie wrapped her arms around his neck and rose to her toes to whisper on his lips, "You are going to love this surprise. I promise."

Chase took her lips and dove his fingers into her curls. Dixie melted into him. She wanted to wrap her legs around him and have him take her up against this wall. Dixie's mouth parted as Chase glided his tongue over hers. Her fingers were searching for something to hold on to. His hair was cut so short she found herself searching his body for something else to grip. Chase took this as an invitation to pull her in closer and lined up his pelvis to hers, gently lifting her up from under her ass cheeks. Their bodies were heating up as Chase moved his mouth down to her neck and licked her just where her collarbone led to her shoulder. Dixie moaned and tilted her head to give him even more access.

Chase was the first to speak. "We don't have enough time. I want so much more babe. God so much more than this."

Dixie held onto him tighter. "We can make it quick."

Chase sighed and put Dixie back on her feet. He cupped her face and looked directly in her eyes as he responded,

"Dixie, the first time we make love it isn't going to be up against a wall, or a rushed event. This will be me and you finally connecting the way we have always meant to be. I will be exploring every inch of your precious body and you will know that you are the center of my world."

Well, how was she supposed to respond to that? Her stomach quivered and her heart wouldn't stop pounding against her ribs. She finally nodded her head. "Okay." She kissed him lightly. "Tonight then?"

Chase returned the kiss and nodded. "Yes, tonight." He finally turned her body back to the bathroom and swatted her ass. "Now go get ready before we're late and your Gramps hits me with a golf club."

CHASE AND DIXIE ENTERED the lobby hand in hand as they saw two distinct groups gathered by the front doors. The men were all clustered dressed in polo shirts and khaki shorts or pants, with the exception of Gramps who had his loud plaid pants that could be seen from nearly a mile away. The women were all dressed casually in pants or shorts and looked like they all just rolled out of bed with messy buns and pony tails. Dixie's shorter curly hair didn't really allow for either of those styles so she just looked like a windblown curly mess.

Chase bent down and gave her a light kiss before he joined the men and gave her a small wave of goodbye. Anne made her way over to Dixie and said, "Wow the looks that man was giving you could melt a glacier."

Dixie nodded. "He has definitely been turning up the heat."

"Where's Bronc?"

Anne pointed to a large form standing behind a potted palm tree. "There he is. He keeps trying to hide because he said he looks ridiculous."

Dixie gazed over at him and saw that he had on a bright orange polo shirt that looked like an upside-down traffic cone with his broad chest and narrower waist. His biceps were nearly splitting the sleeve apart and his brown pants looked really snug around his ass and thighs.

Laughing, Dixie said, "It doesn't look like there is much room in those clothes."

"There isn't. He didn't bring golf clothes so we had to buy from the gift shop, but apparently they don't typically carry big beefcake sizes."

"Oh. Poor guy."

"Yeah, I told him that if he manages to golf the whole day without ripping anything, I would have a good surprise for him when he gets back."

Dixie looked around to see if anyone was listening and whispered, "I told Chase I had a surprise coming for him too. I signed up for the full Brazilian."

Anne squealed in delight. "Me too. Bronc has never said he wanted it, but I know he will love it."

"I figured I might as well since we will be either beach-side or by the pool all week."

"Good thinking. What else did you sign up for?"

"The hot stone, facial scrub and hair treatment. I am not into the whole mani-pedi thing. Besides, I didn't want to get paired with Elena or mom, and I knew they were both getting nails done."

"I didn't sign up for those either. I have to use the computer too much for work and nails just get in the way. I am always amazed by women who could type with two-inch nails and not have a million errors."

The concierge approached the women and led the group up to the elevator. He pressed two different floors and called out names of which person would be getting off which floor. Many of the women got off on the first selection, and left Dixie, Anne, Grams and a couple of the cousins to ascend to the top floor. Once the concierge led them out the two sets of doors, they found themselves on a rooftop oasis. There were a couple fountains and several massage tables with dividers that overlooked the ocean view. Light music permeated through speakers and each woman was greeted by a masseuse. Dixie was greeted by a stocky woman whose brown hair was pulled in a tight bun. Anne was led away by a smaller Asian woman who pulled her along in strong strides. Anne looked back pleadingly at Dixie as if she was being led away for slaughter.

Grams was the lucky one. She was approached by a muscular attractive man in his thirties who lavished attention on her immediately. He kissed her hand in an introduction and led her arm-in-arm to the massage table. Dixie could hear Anne grumble, "Lucky bitch," as Grams giggled at something the young man said.

Dixie walked to her table and found a robe neatly folded on top. The masseuse advised that she could change behind the small curtain across the roof or there by the table separated from the others by a divider. Dixie chose to simply change there. She was not modest or ashamed of her body and most of the other women were already preoccupied anyway. The woman explained that she would be getting her massage and facial scrub here and then be sent to the other services.

She heard Anne call from the other side, "Are you ready to have your troubles rubbed away?"

Dixie laughed. "God yes."

Anne's attendant suddenly spoke up, "Do you want me to remove the divider so you both don't have to scream at each other?"

Both women giggled as she replied, "Yes, please."

Dixie laid on her back as the woman began giving her a facial. She felt her face relax as the music lulled her almost to sleep. The quiet was broken by a shrill scream in pain. Dixie turned to see Anne wincing as her small masseuse dug her elbow into the small of Anne's back. Dixie gasped as Anne's legs bolted up in reaction to another movement up her back. Dixie's masseuse finally smiled and said, "Don't worry about your friend. Soon she will be good as new, she just has a few kinks to get worked out."

"Are you going to be nicer to my kinks? Wait that sounded wrong."

"You will be fine. The stones are more relaxing than the method your friend chose."

"If I refer a friend, can I request that massage and that woman to give it to her."

Laughing she replied, "Doesn't sound like much of a friend to me."

"Eh. She's my sister."

"Say no more. I completely understand. My sister just upgraded the broom she rides on."

After about five more minutes Dixie was able to turn over and prepare for her massage. Anne looked like she was much more comfortable with her rub down of torture. "Feeling better now?" Dixie asked.

"Yes. Apparently, you have to get completely broken before it feels better."

The girls sunk into a deep state of relaxation for the rest of their massages and were in a quiet reflective mood. Dixie appreciated the view watching the wave roll in and out of the ocean. It was absolutely beautiful. She was also enjoying Anne's company and loved hearing the occasional laugh coming from Grams on the far side of the rooftop.

All too soon she heard the concierge return and tell everyone that it was time to go to their next appointments. Dixie gathered her clothes and walked beside Anne to return to the elevator. Grams joined and linked her arms with the two women. "How was your massage my dears?"

Dixie leaned her head towards Grams and smiled. "It was lovely Grams. I really enjoyed it."

"Where are you girls off to now?"

"We are getting waxed."

Grams winced. "Ouch. One of the only good things about getting older girls is that a lot of hair stops growing in inconvenient places. I hope you both enjoy the appreciation your men will give for your efforts."

"Grams!"

"What? I am not dead or stupid. I know why you are doing it." She gave a small wink at them as they stepped off the elevator for their next appointment.

Dixie sat on a table waiting for her waxing specialist to show up. She had never been waxed before, except for her eyebrows. She figured she could do this without any problems, but the longer she sat there on the table, the more nervous she got.

Just before she chickened out a tall man in his twenties with impeccable blonde hair and crazy long lashes walked into the room. "Hi, I'm Aaron and I will be your waxing specialist."

Dixie looked at the attractive man and began to stutter. "I...uh... well... I kind of thought..."

"That you would be getting a woman named Helga."

Dixie winced. "Well not that exactly."

"Let me guess you have some burly alpha male waiting for you and he wouldn't like another man to see your girly areas?"

Dixie looked at him for a minute. There was no menacing or rude tone, in fact he seemed amused and as if this happened all the time. "Well you do have the burly alpha part right."

"Sweetie, if he asks about who did this, just put his mind at ease that you have no parts that I am interested in being intimate with. I would be more inclined to enjoy his burly man bits."

Dixie couldn't help it. She laughed. "Oh god. He would not take that well either."

Aaron sat down on the stool and looked at her. "Sweetie, trust me when I say you want me. I will try to make this as painless as possible. You won the coin flip honey. Trust me." He suddenly put his fingers to his lips in a shushing motion and about fifteen seconds later a scream in agony could be heard in the next room.

"Oh god, maybe I don't need this."

"Trust me sweetie. You want this. That alpha you have waiting on you will make it all worth it."

"Painless, huh?"

"No sweetie. As painless as possible. It's still going to hurt like a bitch."

After taking a deep breath Dixie nodded. "I like you Aaron."

"I think I like you too sweetie," he replied with a wink.

"Are you sure you are gay?"

"If not, I pissed off my parents for no reason."

Before too long, Dixie found herself on the table with her feet clasped together and legs wide open in a clamshell position with the first coat of wax ready to be ripped off. "You know Aaron, maybe this wasn't such a good idea. Maybe we should just wash this all off."

"Too late now. Besides nobody wants to have a one-sided mohawk on their va-jay-jay. Ready..." Aaron was pausing for dramatic effect then quickly said, "One, two, three."

"Ahhh... That fucking hurt." The sudden burst of pain ripped through Dixie's body. Why do people do this? This had to be the dumbest idea she ever had.

"Don't be a baby. We all suffer for beauty."

"I don't see you suffering over there you little monster."

Aaron gave her a smile that almost showed a little sympathy. Almost. "Sweetie this chest isn't bare on its own. I get this baby waxed for my man's pleasure. If you keep this up, you just kind of grow numb to it and it won't be so bad."

"You will forgive me if I don't want to be numb down there. I like feeling the good stuff."

"Oh believe me... you will feel the good stuff." Then quickly as he did before, to where it was almost no warning he said, "One, two, three." *RIP*.

"Holy crap! Oh my god... what is wrong with you?"

"I take pleasure in the simple things in life. Like knowing someone is hurting more than me. One, two, three." *RIP*. That excruciating sound came from down below again.

"I am going to take your manhood from you, if you say 'one, two, three' one more time," Dixie said gritting her teeth together.

Aaron just shrugged. Shrugged... like the man got his life threatened all the time and it wasn't a big deal. "Okay," then just as quickly as his previous phrase he said, "ready, set, go." *RIP*.

Dixie must have reached the beginning stages of numbness because she laid her head back and said, "That was *not* any better."

"Hmmm... okay... Beyoncé, Cher, Madonna." *RIP*.

Dixie sucked in a harsh breath. "How many of those do you have?"

Aaron shrugged again. "Ten or so. Unless I get sasquatch in here for a wax, I haven't needed any more than that."

Dixie suffered through the remaining soul deep tears from her personal areas and listened to Aaron talk about his boyfriend and how his parents had originally disowned him after coming out, but that they were working towards re-building a relationship after a health scare for his mom.

"Do you find it hard to be close to your family now, after so many years apart?"

"Actually, I found it much harder to be apart. It isn't natural for people to sever family ties."

"What if you never really connected to your family to start with?" Dixie looked into Aaron's face and she saw a small sadness take over his eyes.

"Those can be hard, but it's up to you to make sure the effort is worth the reward."

CHASE WAS QUICKLY LEARNING that he hated golf. It took a certain finesse and control of strength that he did not have. The green looked so far away so he just tried to smash the ball as hard as he could in that direction. So, what happened? He hit a tree, and it bounced back and hit Dixie's dad in the head. Of course, it couldn't have hit one of Dixie's obnoxious cousins who bragged about their conquests from the night before. Chase had his fair share of casual sex, but he never had to lie to a woman to get her in bed.

One of the cousin's nudged Chase in the arm after his third time landing in a sand trap and said, "I hope for Dixie's sake you have better aim in bed."

Chase snapped his head to the side and gave the man a glance up and down sizing him up. He really wanted to tell the guy off, but he didn't want to cause any issues with Dixie's family. "You're hilarious," he grumbled as he started walking down the hill for his ball.

Chase looked at the green and then back to the man still chuckling to himself at Chase's lack of golf skills. Maybe he could just shoot him in the kneecap. A small bullet, like a .22. He could recover from that quick enough. The laugh grew louder and he said, "Come on little piggy."

Chase's head snapped up and watched the man still laughing and now making little snorting noises. Just as Chase was about to throw down his golf club and throttle the guy, Gramps put a hand on the man's shoulder and said, "Stop pissing off the cop, Wee Willie. I won't stop him from giving you a lesson in manners."

"Grandpa!"

"Hush. Now go catch up to your dad and brothers. I am going to hang back here with Chase and Bronc. We'll catch up." Willie wasn't moving. Gramps raised his eyebrow and cleared his throat. "Now go on. Scoot!"

Chase held his breath to keep from laughing too loudly. He could hear him grumbling as he passed and said something about the guy not even really being family. Chase looked up at Gramps who had walked back to the golf cart. He finally had to ask. "Willie?"

A twinkle came to Hale's eyes as he said, "His name is actually Wilbert, but he used to run around naked everywhere not afraid of his teeny weenie hanging out, so I used to call him Wee Willie Winkle. He hates that now, so I only bring it out when I am pissed."

Bronc put a hand on Hale's shoulder. "I love your mean streak Uncle Hale. I want to be just like you when I grow up."

Hale eyed him from head to toe. "Son, if you grow up anymore there won't be a stitch of clothes around that will fit you."

Chase watched Hale walk and hop in the golf cart with a little too much ease. "Hey Gramps, what happened with your walker? You are moving around pretty good here."

Hale turned with almost lightning speed. "This is just between us men. If Rose thought I could walk around this well she would have me running all around town and doing damn chores all day. If I look like I am struggling just a little, I finally get to enjoy my retirement. Plus, I told Rose I might putt a couple times but would mostly ride around in the cart and enjoy some quality time."

Bronc threw back his head in laughter. "You conniving old man. Aunt Rose is going to hang you out to dry by your balls when she finds out."

"Nah, beside she won't find out."

"Famous last words old man. Chase, don't pull the same crap with Dixie. She'll knock you on your ass."

After the last hole the men all gathered back at the bar to enjoy some beer before meeting the women back at the hotel. Bronc and Chase had been joined by one of Dixie's cousin's Scott. Scott's father, Maleko was the oldest child of Rose and Hale. Maleko worked in personal security after serving as a Navy Seal, before being injured in a recovery mission. Maleko had three sons—Scott, Erik and Wilbert—that he raised on his own after their mother left them for another man and dreams of becoming a movie star.

During the second round Scott gave his money to the bartender first. "Let me pay for this round. I heard my brother was kind of a dick to you earlier."

Chase shook his head. "You don't have to pay for your brother's actions.... literally pay."

"I know, but I feel a little responsible for him. He is the youngest and neither dad nor I can seem to get him to act like a real man. He seems to think acting like an asshole is going to earn him respect by fear."

"It's all good. Hale just embarrassed him to get him to shut up. It was completely worth it."

"Good. Now I am going to sound like a big brother for just a minute."

Chase eyed the man while he took a long slow pull of his beer waiting for him to continue. When Scott didn't continue, Chase made the circular "come on" motion to have him spit it out.

"What are your intentions with my cousin?"

Chase was expecting this. To be honest, he thought he would get the threatening big brother speech from Bronc not Scott. He knew of Scott and his brothers vaguely. Dixie rarely talked about them and the only time she saw them was when she would visit them with her grandparents. Sighing, Chase put down his beer and looked at Scott and then Bronc who was waiting patiently beside him. "Dixie is one of the most important people in my life. I care about her very much and forgive me Scott if I have a hard time defending my relationship with a man who never visits and I know rarely ever calls. Do you know how I know this?"

Scott looked a bit chastised but shook his head to answer Chase's question.

"I am there just about every damn day. I am the person who watches crappy romance movies with her while we eat pizza. I am the person lifting the damn couch to find that pain in the ass hedgehog. I am the person she talks to when her parents or Elena does something to hurt her again. Do you know how many times I have heard her phone ring from her family besides Grams and Gramps, or because someone wants something from her?"

Scott and Bronc looked a little ashamed now and Scott finally said, "No."

"None. Not once have I seen that phone ring from an Aunt, Uncle or cousin, until they wanted something. Until they wanted her to organize this party for Grams and Gramps. And you know what? She was happy to do it. She loves her family. I just wish her family loved her as much as she does them."

The two other men looked down at their drinks. Bronc was the first one to speak. "Does she think that we don't love her?"

Shit, he may have gone a little overboard with his speech, but he had been frustrated with her family for so many years now it just all blurted out. "No. Not at all. I just see everything first hand. We may have recently gotten together romantically, but I have always been there with her. I just wish that her family would make more of an effort with her. I am sorry if I stepped over a bit, but she is my first priority."

Bronc clasped a hand on Chase's shoulder. "And that is how it should be, and what we want for her."

Chapter 11

Chase made his way back to the bungalow and found Dixie laying on the beach in her shorts and tank top. Her face was covered by a towel but he would recognize that hyacinth tattoo on her ankle anywhere. He stopped next to her, casting a shadow over her body and cleared his throat. Her face moved and only to have the towel go with her as she was trying to look at him.

"How can you breathe through the towel?"

"This towel is horrid and is practically thread bare. It isn't blocking anything."

Chase shook his head and sat beside her. "Can I at least see your beautiful face?"

Dixie sighed and pulled the towel away. "Hi."

"Hi sweetheart. How was spa day?"

"The usual. It had its good moments and bad moments. How was golf?"

"Same. Good moments and bad moments."

"Bad how?"

"Some of your cousins are assholes. Nothing major."

"Ah. Wilbert."

"Yeah, he definitely led the pack. So, what is on for tonight?"

"The luau dinner is tonight. Roasted pig, limbo, the anniversary hula and fire dancing."

"Fire dancing?"

"Yeah. Akoni and Lonan will be doing the fire dancing." Akoni and Lonan were cousins from Hale's side and his great nephews. They were pretty well known on the islands for their performances and trainings.

"Well that is awesome. The only talent I have is shooting someone between the eyes."

Dixie gave a shrug. "That could come in handy too."

He loved her sense of humor. She always knew never to take him too seriously or lectured him about his bad and sometimes inappropriate jokes. "How much time do we have before you have to go and help with the set up?"

Dixie pulled out her cell phone to read the time and gave a slight groan. "Almost two hours, but I have to get ready too."

Chase stood and extended his hand to hers to help her up. "Come on, let's go. I will help you too, but I need a shower to get all this sand out of all the weird places."

A FEW HOURS LATER CHASE and Dixie were putting the final touches on the place settings and appetizers in the outdoor tent while the catering staff was rushing to finish the food preparations. Dixie had traditional Hawaiian music playing in the background and Chase watched her move slightly to the music as she walked from place to place. As she started to pick up a stack of chairs, she winced and dropped them quickly. Chase rushed to her side knowing that he was showing a little too much panic on his face.

"I am fine. Don't hover."

"Was it your hip?"

"Yes, but it isn't a big deal. I just lifted too many chairs. I forgot I'm not He-Man like you."

"If I was He-Man, I would have a cool pet tiger."

"Just what you need. Instead of a police dog you would have a police tiger."

"That would be awesome. Imagine the drop in crime. Nobody wants to mess with a tiger and I could become king in the zombie apocalypse too."

Dixie pinched his ribs and replied, "You watch way too much TV."

Chase dropped his jaw in mock horror. "Blasphemy woman!"

"What's blasphemy?" Dixie and Chase turned to see Bronc and Anne approaching with handfuls of leis.

Dixie approached and took some leis from their arms. "Chase is complaining that I said he watches too much TV."

Bronc opened his mouth and widened his eyes. "There can never be too much TV woman."

"Exactly," Chase said puffing out his chest.

Dixie was looking at each lei examining for flaws and as she came to the last lei she frowned. "Is this all the leis from the florist?"

Bronc nodded. "Yeah, the delivery guy just left and we grabbed all of them."

"We are missing one. I ordered one lei to be open ended. These are all closed."

Chase gazed upon the flowers, frowning. He knew there were many traditions that he didn't understand, but Dixie was looking frantically at the pile for something that wasn't there. He placed his hand on her back and began to rub in small circles. "Okay, calm down. What exactly are we looking for?"

Dixie sat in the chair beside the pile of flowers and sighed. "All of these are complete closed circles. I ordered one that would not be closed for Linda."

Chase knew that Linda was new to the family and married Dixie's cousin Jeremy. "Why would she get a different lei?"

"For a pregnant woman a lei can represent the umbilical cord, the cord of life. It is considered bad luck to have a closed lei. It would represent the cord wrapping about the baby's neck."

Chase cleared his throat. "Okay, we don't want that. We can just fix one of the leis we already have."

Then in a small voice Anne said, "Actually, you better make that two."

Everyone snapped their heads up to look at Anne whose eyes were watering and a small smile across her lips. Dixie finally spoke up first, "You're pregnant?"

Anne nodded her head.

Dixie and Chase looked at Bronc who was blinking wide eyed at Anne. Finally, he cleared his throat. "Baby? You have a baby? We have a baby? I mean... We are going to have a baby?"

Anne kept nodding her head with happy tears now falling down. "Yes. We are going to have a baby."

Bronc picked up his wife and squeezed her to his chest. "Hot damn! I'm gonna be a dad!"

Chase watched as the couple celebrated with kisses and intimate words to each other. He looked over at Dixie and felt a warmth heat up his chest. He could see her holding their child. A little girl with Dixie's love and determination. This was it. Dixie was his, and he just had to convince her that they are meant to be and always were. She was now standing, hugging Bronc and Anne to give her congratulations. He was still planted to his spot watching her. Dixie finally looked at Chase with her brow raised in question. Chase cleared his head and walked towards the happy couple. He extended his hand in congratulations towards Bronc. "Congratulations."

Bronc took Chase's hand and then jerked him in for a big hug. Chase stumbled in not expecting the big man to pull him in. "Oh, okay we're hugging now."

Chase was finally released and he couldn't help but see the giant smile Bronc had expanding on his face. He looked over to Dixie who was leaning into Anne and smiling at the two men. Bronc turned to his wife and didn't break her gaze as he said, "We'll be back. I have to make love to my wife now." He grabbed Anne's hand and nearly pulled her up off the floor as he led the way back out of the tent.

Sighing Dixie picked two leis from the table and began to inspect them. "I think we can make these open, we just need some wire, vine or rope."

"I think I saw something on the concierge desk earlier that could help." He made quick strides to the lobby and spoke to the concierge about the floral wire he saw on the desk earlier. The man agreed to give him the wire and disappeared to retrieve it. As he stood by the desk, he felt a graze on his ass and a hand firmly cup him.

"Have you missed me?" came a soft voice from behind him.

Wait... that was not Dixie's sweet tone. It was practiced and overly husky. Chase froze.

"If you missed me, you could have just called."

Chase turned around holding his hands up and came face to face with a tall blonde wearing too much makeup. It took a moment, but he finally recognized her. Lucy. He hadn't seen her in almost a year. He had spent a few nights with her but he was very clear he didn't want more from her. "Lucy. You need to stop touching me." He was gently pushing her back away from him by her shoulders.

"You always enjoyed my touches before," she cooed as she pressed her body closer to his.

Chase gently pushed her away from him and looked around. Thankfully he didn't see anyone to witness this disaster. "Well I don't want them now. I am here with Dixie."

Lucy tilted her head. "So, you are not here to see me?"

"Why would I come here to see you?"

Now she looked completely offended. This was probably something he shouldn't have needed to ask. "This is my father's resort; our family owns Lenoir Properties. I am the Creative Director for the company. I told you about this before and that I rotate visiting the properties."

Chase could see how annoyed she looked now. She did tell him that, but he never paid much attention to which hotels and resorts they owned. There were so many and they always found other ways to fill their time together. "Sorry. Honestly, I didn't know this was one of your family's properties, and like I said I am here with Dixie."

"Your little photographer friend?" Lucy clicked her tongue in disgust. "Just tell the little girl you need to spend some time with a real woman and you will be back later."

Chase was reeling. Was she always this rude? Maybe she was, but they didn't spend much time getting to know each other. Lucy's hand was grazing up his chest again, and he softly wrapped his hand around her wrist and put it down. "I don't think you understand. Dixie and I are in a relationship now and you and I won't be doing anything."

Lucy gave a little shrug. "If you change your mind, you have my number, and I will be here all week."

"I won't but thanks." Chase turned back to the desk to see the concierge had returned and was studying Chase with a curious gaze. "What?" He growled.

The short man jumped back a bit at Chase's tone. Shakily he held out his hand with the floral wire. "Your wire, sir."

Chase sighed. It wasn't this guy's fault he had a run in with Lucy. He tried to paste on a grateful smile and said, "Thanks." Seeing the scissors on the desk he picked them up and lifted an eyebrow in question.

"Yes, of course. Just bring them back to my desk when you are done, sir."

Dixie was sitting at the table with the leis and gently fingering a petal as Chase walked back in holding up the wire and scissors in the air like a conquering hero. She stood up shaking her head. "You act like you went away to slay a dragon."

Thinking about Lucy he responded, "Maybe I did."

"Well then where is my dragon head trophy?"

"Uh... I left it in the car?"

"Do you think the carwash knows how to get out dragon's blood?"

There was that sense of humor again. His hands itched to grab and pull her into his arms.

"Well, what kind of place can't even get out dragon blood?"

Dixie handed over a lei and said, "Okay goof. Help me fix these leis."

They both worked in a comfortable quiet silence while they arranged the flowers and wire to complete the open leis. Dinner would be served soon. The strong aroma of the pig roasting was wafting over to the tent. This was the first time Chase had seen a whole pig roasted over a fire, and while the smell was amazing, the actual animal being cooked still looking like the animal was a bit disturbing.

Dixie looked at the time and made her way up front to greet everyone as they came in. She handed out the floral leis to the women while Chase greeted the men and gave the other tea leaf leis that were primarily made of nuts and leaves.

Dixie and Chase finally joined Anne, Bronc and her two cousins Scott and Erik. Chase watched as Dixie breathed a sigh of relief as the dinner started. With the exception of the confusion of the leis everything had fallen into place. It was only a couple minutes before the entertainment portion of the dinner was to begin. She leaned over and kissed Chase on the cheek promising to return soon. Chase nodded and watched her as she left the tent.

DIXIE ENTERED THE TENT that was behind the wooden platform that they were going to use as a stage. She found her garment bag hanging up by the edge next to the extra chairs. She gently unzipped the bag and had to sit down as she gazed upon the garments. Her top was a strapless blue and white wrap that would cover her breasts and then crisscross her midriff. The skirt was a traditional white flowing material accented with blue tassels around the waist. She took a deep breath. She could do this. She learned the wedding hula that her grandmother had performed for her grandfather at their wedding through several Skype sessions with her great Aunt Naia.

Dixie gazed upon her reflection in the mirror after putting on the finishing touches with the hair and wrist garlands. Realizing that it must be close to time she checked her phone. They only had five minutes before the performance. She looked around the tent trying to find her sister. Elena had also learned the dance and was supposed to perform it with Dixie. Then a voice came from behind her, "Calm down Dixie, I am here and ready to go."

Dixie turned to see Elena wearing a white bodice trimmed with lace and pearls, then the matching flowing skirt without a midsection. Studying it closer, Dixie gasped. "Is that Grams wedding dress?"

"Yes. She gave it to me when I got married."

"Yeah, but you didn't use it." Dixie could feel pains in her chest. She had planned on borrowing the dress for when she got married someday.

"I thought it would be fitting to wear it for the anniversary hula. Grandmother would be happy that I put it to use to celebrate her anniversary."

"But you sliced it all up." Dixie wanted to break down into tears and maybe yell at her sister. She couldn't believe that she destroyed the antique wedding dress, Gram's dress.

"Yes, of course I did. We had to modify it to fit my slimmer frame and to be a more appropriate dress for the dance."

Dixie couldn't breathe. Her heart was breaking, but she knew that Elena didn't do this maliciously. Elena wasn't sentimental, and by wearing the dress for the dance she was making an effort to be sentimental. This was progress... sort of. Dixie just had to suck it up. It couldn't be changed now. "Okay. Here are your wristlets and floral crown."

Elena took the flowers, placed them accordingly and Dixie had to admit she looked stunning. "Let's hurry up and get this over with. I have some things I need to work on tonight."

Ah there she was. The sister she knew and.... loved? "Aren't you going to stay for Akoni and Lonan's fire dance?"

"No, but Charles is staying so Martin can experience it."

"Good. Martin will have so much fun with it. They have been performing at some of the exclusive resorts and are making quite a good living from it now."

"I am surprised the family is okay with them exploiting our culture at these resorts."

"It isn't the only thing they do. They have been able to open a school for the locals and even provide scholarships for those with economic need. They want to keep the traditions alive and the only way to do that is to teach the young and perform for others. By engaging with the tourists, it also brings in much needed money to the economy. Without the tourists' financial support, the island would be in a lot of trouble. Tourism is critical for our family there."

"That is understandable. It is good that they are helping the community. Grandfather has expressed his concerns about the family at the island before, and how he feels guilty that he isn't more involved there anymore."

"He is old. He can't keep traveling there as much as he used to." Dixie thought she saw concern and sadness as she looked at her sister. Maybe she had more of a heart than she thought. Just as the sisters were beginning to have a moment to bond, a tall blonde woman entered the tent.

"Hello, ladies. My name is Lucy Lenoir. I am the Creative Director for Lenoir properties. My manager told me about the activities that you had planned this week and wanted to know if it would be acceptable to take some pictures for our social media page. We would like to show how our event spaces could be used for future customers."

Dixie studied the woman. She looked familiar, but she couldn't quite place her. She had done so many wedding photography jobs that she may have seen her at one of the resorts where a wedding was held so she didn't think about it much more. "I don't see any problem with it, but I would ask that you get permission from each individual before you post any pictures with them on your site or publications."

Dixie dealt with releases often with her business. Often, she would use examples from events that she would photograph, but would always get a release from the client and any people in the images used.

"Of course. I have waivers my staff can provide for permission. Is it okay if I attend your performances tonight with the photographer?"

Dixie looked at Elena, who was studying Lucy with narrowed eyes. Dixie could tell that her sister didn't trust Lucy, but figured there was no harm in helping the resort with promotions. Dixie tried to search Lucy's face for any trace of deception, but finally agreed.

Dixie watched Lucy leave and she could feel Elena stepping up beside her. "I don't trust that woman. Keep a close eye on her. Something just feels off."

"That isn't very scientific of you sister dear."

"There is a bit of instinct that goes into science too. I get some kind of feeling that prickles just before an experiment fails, and she gives me those same prickles."

CHASE WAS ENJOYING his conversation when he saw Lucy walk into the tent with a photographer close behind. He thought about getting up to see what was going on, but then music started to play and lights brightened the stage. Then a vision of beauty walked into the spotlight. Dixie walked in wearing the traditional hula dress and bodice wrap. She looked amazing. There was a back light that glowed from behind giving her an ethereal glow as she walked up to the front of the stage. She was stunning. He was staring trying to soak it all in. Dixie looked around the room a bit uncomfortably until her eyes locked with Chase's. He could see her shoulders relax and her smile brightened the room.

A moment later, she turned to her side where Elena joined her. She nodded as the DJ stopped the current song and gave the microphone to Dixie's great Aunt Naia. She tapped the microphone a few times until the loud screech of feedback came through the speakers. "Oh, good. You are all awake now. To start tonight's performances Dixie and Elena will be recreating the hula dance I taught Rose all those years ago to perform at her wedding. I couldn't be happier to celebrate this great milestone with my brother and his wife. All those years ago my husband was the best man and said at his toast that Hale once told him that life without Rose would never be an option, and he would spend the rest of his life making sure that her light would always shine bright. Rose would never know anything but love and acceptance. Before the wedding Rose told me that she would move heaven and earth to make sure he never doubted her devotion to him. They have definitely given all of us inspiration for how a marriage should be, and with that I present to you the wedding hula."

The light dimmed and the sound of the guitar floated through the air as Dixie began swaying her hips. Chase watched as she rhythmically floated back and forth. Her arms gracefully glided in a side to side waving motion. As the music continued Dixie and Elena moved in synchronized motions. Chase could hardly believe it when he saw a smile form on Elena's face. He thought the woman didn't know how to upturn her lips. Suddenly, he heard a small commotion coming from the side of the stage. It took a moment to focus but soon he realized he was seeing Rose make her way up the stage and began dancing beside her granddaughters in perfect steps.

It wasn't long before scraping sounds were made as Hale tried to move his chair up front and center to the stage. Chase immediately stood and helped him get his front-row seat, so he could watch the women he loved. As Hale sat, he kept wiping at his eyes. His smile was bigger than Chase had ever seen before. Chase continued to watch Dixie gracefully move her hips. His heart constricted in his chest and he knew that tonight would be the night he showed her just how much he loved her.

AFTER THE DANCE WAS finished, Grams wrapped her arms around the two sisters and whispered, "Thank you. That was the most beautiful present we could have ever gotten. I love both you girls so much."

Dixie thought for a moment she saw Elena's eyes grow soft and a smile start to form on her thin lips. Then as quickly as it was there, it was gone and Elena's posture stiffened and she gave a polite response, "Glad you liked it Grandmother." And with that she left Grams embrace and walked back to the staging tent to change.

Grams gave a small sigh and looked again at Dixie. "Okay, now go change so you can get back for the fire dancing."

Dixie held her hands with Grams and gave a small nod. "Okay. Make sure Chase stays out of trouble."

"Oh, I think he would get into more trouble with you if you stayed out here in that outfit. I know your Gramps always loved it."

"Ewww... Don't do that again. You know I can't stand to hear about you and Gramps and your escapades. No... just no."

"I know. That's why I do it. Gotta have a little fun. Now scoot!"

As Dixie approached the staging tent, she saw her nephew standing by the front opening playing with a cell phone. "Hey sweetie, where is your dad?"

Martin pointed at the opening indicating he was inside the tent. "Dad said to wait out here and he would be right back."

"Okay. I will go inside and see if he is ready to come back out. I'll be right back." Martin didn't even look up from his phone as he gave a small shrug.

Dixie walked in and saw the small curtain divider drawn shut and then heard soft moaning. Is that... no it couldn't be. More moaning and then a masculine grunt. Dixie stopped in her tracks. Her sister was having sex. Oh... my... god. She was having sex, and from the sound of it good sex. *This would be a good time to move*, she thought. As she tried to move her feet Charles' deep voice boomed through the tent. "Damn baby you looked to fucking hot up there. I almost carried you off that stage to remind you that is my body you were showing everyone."

Wow. Charles is an alpha in bed. That was a shock. She figured Elena would run their sex life the way she ran her professional life, cold and with a step-by-step plan. Then she could hear the slapping of skin on skin and knew she had to get out of there.

She grabbed her clothes that were on the chair and scurried out of the opening. Martin was still standing there playing with the phone. Dixie stopped beside him and tried to figure out what to do. Should she leave him there or take him with her? He tapped the phone to push pause and looked up at Dixie. "Are they done wrestling?"

Dixie drew her brows together. "Huh?"

"Mom and Dad wrestle all the time and say that I can't play and it is an adult game."

Dixie nearly choked. Well that was a true statement. "They should be done soon. How about you and I go over to those chairs and wait for them to finish with their game?"

Martin closed his hand around Dixie's fingers and nodded. "I wonder if Dad will win this time. He says Mom always wins. I don't get it. He is bigger than her, so he should always win."

Dixie stopped walking and desperately tried to find an answer that would be appropriate for a child. "Um. Well part of being a man is letting the woman you love win at games sometimes."

"That is dumb. I want to win all the time."

Believe me kid, I think your dad is winning more than you think. "Well, you will find someone someday who you won't mind losing to."

They both reached the chairs. Dixie sat down and felt Martin's arms struggling to crawl up onto her lap. She helped him up and settled him sideways across her legs. His huge eyes looked at her appearing to be trying to figure something out. "Does Mr. Chase let you win all the time?"

Dixie smiled. "No, not all the time but he does a lot, and it isn't just about games. He lets me pick the movie, or decide what we are going to do for the day or even what we have for dinner."

"Mom never lets me pick what we have for dinner," said with a cute pout to his lower lip.

"That is because your mom is smart and knows what a growing boy like you needs to be healthy and happy. What would you pick for dinner if it was up to you?"

Grinning, he smacked his lips together and slapped his hands onto Dixie's arms. "Chocolate cake with chocolate sprinkles."

"There you see. It is a good thing your mom decides, because while that sounds like an amazing dessert, it wouldn't make for a very good dinner." She wasn't going to mention that she'd had that for her own dinner a number of times when she was upset.

"Did someone say something about dessert?" asked Chase in a laughing voice from behind.

Dixie rolled her eyes. "Of course, you walk in on the food portion of our conversation."

Martin tilted his head back to Chase and said, "Aunt Dixie said chocolate cake with sprinkles isn't a good dinner and it is only good for a dessert."

Chase frowned. "As much as I hate to say it buddy, she's right, but there are so many things that are really awesome for dinner food. You got chicken, steak, hamburgers and pork chops."

Martin screwed up his little face. "You eat a lot of animals."

Laughing, Chase replied, "Yeah I guess I do, but they taste delicious."

Bringing a finger to his lips Martin whispered, "Don't tell Mom, but Dad sneaks me chicken nuggets and French fries. He says it is our little secret."

Dixie wanted to laugh at Charles' blatant rebellion over Elena's strict menu. "I bet he gets a big cheeseburger when he gets those for you."

Martin nodded. "Uh huh, and fries as big as my head."

After looking around Chase asked, "Where is your dad?"

Martin pointed to the tent. "He is wrestling with mom again."

Mouth agape Chase looked at Dixie for confirmation. "Does that mean?"

"Yes, and let's not talk about this again." She did not want to think about Elena and Charles' sex life. That was almost as bad as when Grams would try to overshare with her all the time.

Chase sat next to Dixie and the two of them helped Martin with his game until they saw Charles walk out of the tent with a satisfied look on his face. There was a momentary panic when he didn't see Martin by the front entrance, but then he visibly eased when he saw his son on Dixie's lap. He walked over to them with an awkward smile. "Martin, I thought I told you to wait by the front."

"I did, but Aunt Dixie and I decided to sit down while you and mom finished your wrestling game."

Charles' eyes glanced from Dixie to Chase who both were giving amused smiles back to him. "Well, say thank you to Aunt Dixie for sitting with you."

Martin tilted his head and kissed her cheek. "Thanks, Aunt Dixie."

Dixie's heart warmed up in her chest. "Anytime, little man. And Charles, I would love to spend some time with him again if you and my sister decide you need a rematch."

Dixie could hear Chase's snort, trying to cover up his mouth as Charles gave a short awkward word of thanks.

The four of them began walking back to the main area and Dixie watched Elena walk out of the tent with a small smile and nod to her husband as she walked back to her room. Chase held Dixie's hand as she felt another small hand grab her other one. She looked down at Martin who was grinning and humming a song. He stopped suddenly and looked at his dad. "Can we sit with Aunt Dixie and Mr. Chase?"

Charles looked down at his son and nodded. "Sure, I don't see why not."

"Yeah!" Martin's little smile was huge as he celebrated by swinging his and Dixie's hand back and forth.

This was how Dixie sat through the fire dancing with Martin on her lap clapping and cheering with each woosh and swirl of the poi. Once Akoni and Lonan finished the first portion with the fire sticks and chains they gave a wink and smile to Martin who had been their biggest and loudest fan.

The music changed to a louder deeper bass beat and the two men brought out the Samoan Ailaos, which were traditional war knives. Dixie watched as Martin's mouth dropped and it stayed open from the sight of the long intricate blades. Martin leaned back on her chest and whispered, "You're not supposed to play with knives. Mom said they can hurt you."

Dixie couldn't help the giggle that came out. "Don't worry. They are professionals, and they know what they are doing. You know how policemen carry guns, right?"

"Yeah?" he said as a question not understanding why she was asking that.

"And you know how they are dangerous, right?"

"Uh-huh."

"Well, policeman are specially trained to carry and use the guns so they don't get hurt or hurt others, just like they are trained with the fire and knives."

"Oh. I get it." Martin's body relaxed again in Dixie's arms, and she felt Chase's hand circling between her shoulders. She eased back into his touch and felt a comforting deep feeling in her chest.

Leaning over, Chase whispered in her ear, "Using my gun isn't the only thing I am an expert at."

Dixie sucked in a breath, trying not to react to the bear of a man. "You are evil. Behave, Montgomery."

She could feel his smile against her ear as he whispered, "Okay... for now."

DIXIE WALKED INTO THE bungalow and heard little bells and a high-pitched squeaking noise. She walked over to Ansel's pen and found six new balls with bells inside and a very happy Ansel running to each of them and ringing them as he ran by. Chase's shadow loomed over her as she bent down to give some affection to the hedgehog. "You got him the balls?"

"Yeah. The poor guy was going to be bored with us out most of the day. He has been behaving so well I figured he deserved a present. We just need to remember to take them out before we go to sleep or he'll drive us crazy with them all night."

"I brought him back some fruit. He is going to be a spoiled little guy at this rate."

"Not nearly as spoiled as you made him after he ate that cricket that was torturing you."

"The dumb thing wouldn't shut up at night. I couldn't sleep for two days. I let Ansel free roam and he tracked the little asshole down in no time. I think he was mad about losing his beauty sleep too."

Dixie stood and gave a kiss to Chase's cheek. "Thanks for thinking about him. I am going to get a shower. All I can smell is the smoke from the fires tonight. Give Ansel some attention while I am gone."

Chase leaned in closer. "I would rather give you attention in the shower."

She put a hand on his chest. "Not yet. My shower first and then yours, and for now go bond with Ansel."

Pouting, Chase replied, "I've bonded. He loves me."

"Yes, for him to keep loving you, you need to continue to bond." She gave a wink as she grabbed her clothes and a towel only to disappear in the bathroom.

After enjoying the shower that had five pulsating heads that surrounded her, she walked back by the bed to find

Chase curled up on his side with Ansel snuggled up against his neck. Shaking her head, she picked up Ansel who gave a slight huff in protest at being moved and placed him back in his pen.

Dixie slid into bed, curled up next to Chase, and found herself drifting off to sleep enjoying the warmth of Chase's body next to hers. It felt as if she was only asleep for an hour or so before she felt the bed springs jerk under her. She heard Chase muttering whispered curse words and moving the blankets around. "Shit. She's gonna kill me."

Waking up a little more she was about to roll over when she felt a hand on her shoulder. "Don't move."

"What? Why?"

"Don't be mad, but I lost Ansel." Chase was a bit more frantic now lifting up pillows and throwing the blanket and sheets off the bed. Dixie thought about letting him panic for a little bit longer, but that was just too mean. Well, maybe just another minute or two. Dixie sat up in bed as Chase nearly fell to the ground, looking under the bed, then behind it. He stopped and then looked at her. "Why are you not panicking with me?"

With a sly smile she answered, "Because I put him away when the two of you fell asleep cuddled up with each other."

Chase pounced on the bed and pinned her underneath of him. "You little vixen. You let me freak out looking for your damned rodent knowing he was safe in his pen?"

"Yes. But to be fair, I was asleep most of the time you were looking for him."

"I thought I squished his prickly little butt."

"I think you would have noticed if you rolled over on a hedgehog. He isn't exactly a fluffy kitten."

"That's for damn sure."

Dixie looked at Chase, still leaning over her. In a flash his gaze intensified and his breathing grew deeper. She could feel him growing harder against her thigh. Her hands were itching to graze downward and dive under his boxer briefs for skin to skin contact. "Are you going to do something with that or do you need a little more encouragement?"

"Babe, I could always use some encouragement. That is half of the fun."

Before she could respond his lips were on hers in a desperate intensity as if he needed her to breathe. She brought her arms around his back and dug her nails in as he lowered his body further onto her so there was now no part of her body that wasn't touching his. Her lips parted to allow entrance of his greedy tongue and she heard a soft moan that she realized came from her. She needed this man, all of him. There were no more games, no more questions or concerning, or thoughts if this was right. It was the two of them in this magical bungalow under the canopy of the stars. She was grateful that Chase had opened the ceiling. She wanted their moans and passion to reach beyond the bungalow up to the night sky.

Chase's hand grazed down the bottom of her top and he lifted it slowly to feel his way up to her breasts. He lovingly focused his eyes on her chest and smiled as he finished working her shirt off her body. He took a shaky breath and said, "I need to see all of you. I don't want anything between us tonight. This is us. This is us forever."

How could she say no to that? She quickly discarded her bottoms and watched as Chase did the same. God, he was magnificent. His chest was perfectly sculpted, which she already knew from him playing sports back home, but wow he had that magical V from his hips that lead to his enormous cock. She held her breath as she looked at the pale pink skin of his shaft with a slightly darker mushroomed head. It was beautiful and big. Nobody she had ever been with was quite as large as Chase.

Dixie finally brought her eyes to his where he was smiling back at her. She could tell he knew what she was staring at. Her skin grew red hot as she could feel herself start to blush.

He brought his hand up to her cheek as he gently moved his thumb back and forth. "You don't have to be embarrassed. I want you to look, because believe me baby, I am definitely enjoying my view too, and this blushing thing... that is sexy as hell."

Dixie brought her hand to his wrist and nodded. Chase moved his hand away from her face and put his hand into hers interlacing their fingers. Dixie could feel their connection growing stronger. They weren't discarding their friendship, but instead building this new amazing connection and using it as a foundation. Chills ran through her body as she felt Chase's tongue make a line down her neck and to her chest. He lavished attention onto her nipple making it hard and rounded from his touch. He wasn't someone who would neglect the other one; she felt him move his mouth over to her other nipple to suck and nibble on it until it was a matching set. He pulled away looking satisfied with his work and began kissing his way downward.

Chase stopped once he was in full view of her pussy and then looked up to her. "You're bare. Was this my surprise?"

All Dixie could seem to do was nod.

"This is the best surprise I have had all day. Well, that and your awesome body performing that dance. It was amazing. You have no idea. It took everything in me not to drag you off that stage to have my way with you." Dixie felt warm huffs of air as he drew in closer. He dragged his tongue from the bottom up to the top of her clit and then back down to dive in deep.

"Oh god."

Her words only encouraged him further. He grabbed her by her hips and drove in deeper. Jesus, any deeper and he would reach her g-spot with his tongue. When he finally removed his tongue from inside her, she was a panting and writhing mess. He grinned wickedly as he placed two fingers inside of her and then sucked her clit in a matching rhythm. Her body was moving with him involuntarily—their pace matched perfectly. Then he moved his fingers and crooked them in a come here motion and it pressed that magical button sending her screaming in delight. Tingles started from her toes and moved all the way up her body.

Once the orgasm slowed, she opened her eyes to see Chase over her again and moving in to kiss her. The leftover sensations from her orgasm made her lips electrify to his touch. She felt the head of his cock playing back and forth with her opening nudging only about half an inch each time.

"Chase, I need you inside me now. Please don't make me wait anymore."

Chase looked at her and paused. "I'm clean, I promise. I would never do anything to put you at risk. I know you have the IUD." He stopped and waited still with his head only slightly inside.

"I'm clean too. I just got tested before we came down. Give me all of it." She saw Chase's relief as he slowly moved his hips down, but slow wasn't going to do it. She needed it all now. She slammed her feet onto the bed and quickly thrust her hips up to immediately take in his full length.

"Holy shit, Dix. Slow down or this will be over in two minutes. You feel so good I won't last." He reached out and pinched her nipple. That got her attention, and she slowed her hips down. As she gasped from the bite of pain, he brought his mouth down to suck and soothe it away. In the meantime, his hips moved in a slow melodic rhythm that she could have sworn matched the beat of the wedding hula from earlier. She could hear in her mind the guitar and drums as his body moved in time.

Her orgasm was building again as she looked past his shoulders to the stars and watched as a few twinkled when Chase and Dixie finally crested over together.

Chapter 12

Chase felt a satisfaction that he had never felt before with Dixie in his arms. He moved his arm up and down her side and only stopped for a second when he felt the scar from the accident. His heart registered a sharp pang as he remembered his role in what happened that day. He knew that she didn't blame him, nor did his dad. The guilt would always be there, but he would no longer let it stop him from being with this incredible woman. For too long he thought she would be better off with someone else. He waited for that to happen, but now he knew no one would be better for her than him. He would be devoted to her. He would always be her friend, but he was going to make sure she knew that she was his everything.

Dixie's light snores gave Chase a small sense of peace. He brought his nose up to her head and breathed her in. Looking up, he saw the morning sky fading the dark blue into orange to greet the day. He always thought of his sister when he would see the sunrise. From the time she was about five she would crawl out her bedroom window onto the porch roof to watch the sunrise. Chase was always worried she would fall off so he would join her on the roof to watch the start of the day. The first time he caught her he asked her what she was doing, and all she did was point at the rising sun and say, "Pretty." Soon that was their ritual. He started setting the alarm to join her on the roof to make sure she was safe and they could enjoy the morning together. Before long she stopped going out her window and just came in to wake him up and go out of his together.

"I promise I know what I am doing now," he said to the morning sky. After his mom and Summer died, he talked to them at sunrise. He felt the strongest connection to them both as the sun broke the night's darkness and thought this would be the best time for them to hear him.

A few minutes later he heard a soft knock at the door. Chase gently eased Dixie off his chest and slid a pillow under her to curl up with and replace his body. He quickly put on pants and opened the door to find the hotel attendant with the cart for breakfast. He had almost forgotten he set up room service for breakfast last night. He directed the man where to leave the cart and got his wallet and tipped him.

Chase gently got back on the bed and began kissing Dixie's shoulder and worked his way up to her cheek and whispered in her ear, "Wake up sleepyhead."

Dixie gave a slight moan and dug her head further into the pillow. It sounded like she said don't wanna, but it was so muffled, he couldn't be sure. To give her a little more encouragement he continued to kiss her shoulder and rub small circles on her back. His body was curled into her, and he was trying to restrain himself from taking her again already. But he knew she was not a morning person and didn't want to push his luck. "Come on... I have a surprise for you."

Dixie groaned as she turned to face him. "I hate to tell you this Montgomery, but your morning hard on is not a surprise."

Chase barked out a laugh. "No, it isn't, but that's not the surprise you dirty girl."

"Oh? What is my surprise?"

"I got us room service for breakfast. Now come on before the eggs get cold."

Dixie sighed but didn't move.

"Pancakes too, and bacon." She moved but only slightly. "You going to get up?"

"Breakfast does sound amazing but I am too lazy."

Chase got up from the bed and stood to the side. "Okay, I gave you a chance to get up nicely."

"What? Oomph." Chase had grabbed her and put her over his shoulder in a fireman's carry and walked her over to the dinette and dropped her in the chair.

"I tried to do it the nice way, but it didn't work. Besides nobody likes cold eggs."

Chase lifted the covers to reveal eggs with hollandaise sauce, bacon, sausage, seasoned potatoes and pancakes all decorated beautifully with berries around the sides of the plates.

"I don't know. Do you think you ordered enough food?" Dixie said sarcastically.

"This is enough to start my day. Don't worry I will probably get a snack later."

Dixie shook her head as she took her first bite of the eggs. Chase joined in with her and groaned at the taste.

"These eggs are incredible. That fancy sauce stuff is mmm... and the bacon. God, I love bacon."

Dixie pointed her fork at his plate. "That fancy sauce stuff as you call it, is hollandaise sauce. It is a combination of egg yolk, butter, lemon, Dijon, salt and sometimes cayenne pepper."

Chase stopped eating for a minute and stared at her.

"What?"

"Why do you know that?"

"Don't you remember after I watched *Julie and Julia,* I went on this cooking spree and tried to learn how to cook some of Julia Child's recipes?"

"Oh yeah. Was that when you made me help you kill a lobster?"

"Uh-huh. I figured if you could shoot a person, you could help me kill a cockroach of the sea."

"Nice. I think you just ruined lobster forever."

Dixie shrugged. "You didn't complain while you were eating it."

"You didn't call it a cockroach back then."

"Can I ask you something?"

"Mm-hmm. What's up?"

Chase looked over at the unpacked camera bag and then back to Dixie. "This is the first time I have seen you go more than a day without a camera strapped around your neck. What gives?"

Dixie put down her fork and met his eyes. "Grams."

"I kind of need a little more explanation than that."

"Grams had a talk with me before we left for the trip. She said that she didn't want to see me at any of the events with my face behind a camera. She wants me to be a part of the festivities. She thinks that if I break out my camera that I will treat it like a work function and won't have any actual fun. So... since this is their party, I am honoring her wishes. She did say that I could at least use my camera on my phone."

"Good for her. You need time off. I know you love photography but connecting with your family is important too."

"Yeah. It didn't take long being here to make me realize that she was right."

Chase quickly finished the rest of his meal and watched as Dixie finished hers. She was eating one of the last of the strawberries wrapping her lips around each one before biting down and sipping the juices. It was torture. He wanted her lips wrapped around him and sucking his juices off. Suddenly she smiled almost knowing what she was doing to him.

With a quirk of her lips she asked, "What? Something wrong?"

Chase shifted uncomfortably in his seat. "No, by all means continue torturing me with your mouth and the fruit sucking."

Dixie smiled and picked up another strawberry, leaned over the chair and put it to his lips. "Open up and take a bite."

He did and as she pulled it away, she wrapped her lips around his and kissed his breath away. The taste of Dixie and strawberries was intense. Suddenly he felt a firm hand grab his cock and rub it up and down. She was trying to kill him. His hips thrust up into her hand and she smiled against his lips.

"You know... I am still hungry. I think I will see what I can find down here."

She dropped to her knees and grabbed the sides of his waistband and pulled down his pants. That was all he had on. He never had a chance to put his underwear on so his cock sprang free straightening for her attention. She gave a small laugh. "Well good morning to you too."

Chase grabbed the base and gently stroked up waiting for her to lavish attention on him. "Don't tease him babe. He is a sensitive soul."

"Aw. Well let's see just how sensitive he is." She brought her head down to his groin and gently touched her tongue to his base and licked it lightly up to his head. Once there she twirled her tongue around the head as he sucked in his breath.

Chase was gripping the side of the chair desperately trying not to grab her head and take over control. She was running this seduction, and he was going to enjoy it. He felt her hands grip his hips as she completely devoured his cock, and she took all of him. He could feel himself hitting the back of her throat as she bobbed up and down. It felt so god damned perfect, and then she started this pulsing sucking thing that was driving him out of his mind.

With a loud pop she let go with her mouth and began stroking him with one of her hands from base to tip. Before he could look down at her, she had one of his balls in her mouth and sucking while rolling her tongue around in a circle. This was amazing. Her warm mouth on his balls and her small but firm hand stroking with just enough pressure, he wasn't going to last long. He was just about to tell her when she surprised him again with her other hand replacing her mouth on his balls and then she went lower still to suck on that tender spot between his balls and anus.

"Holy shit, Dixie." He groaned as his release pulsated and fell across his chest. With each pulsating spurt she squeezed a little harder each time almost as if she was trying to make sure every drop was spent from him body.

She finally released him and leaned back over to kiss him. As he was kissing back and gripping her hair, he heard her phone ring. "Don't answer that."

"Mmm... I don't want to but I have to."

Chase kissed her again. "They can wait. It won't kill them."

"Maybe... I..." Their mouths continued to explore each other as the ringing stopped, but then after only about fifteen seconds it started again. "They will just keep doing that until we answer."

Grumbling, Chase replied, "Fine. Go. I'm going to get cleaned up."

DIXIE GOT OFF THE PHONE with the concierge who confirmed the reservations for today for the dolphin cruises and boating adventures. She was thankful that for the most part today everyone was just going to enjoy the beach. She had divided up the family into two groups for the dolphin cruise and let everyone else choose their other adventures individually. Her and Chase were in the first group for the tour, and she was thankful they wouldn't be in the more powerful afternoon sun.

Looking again at the phone she saw that she had four missed text messages. Opening the texts, she rolled her eyes. Of course, it was a group text from the girls.

Ariel: How is it going? Make love yet?

Josie: Screw that. Are you using the toys and having good monkey sex?

Zoey: When did you do it? Tyler and I have a bet... and I reaaalllyyy want to win this one.

Ariel: Ewwww. I don't even want to know what the bet was for.

Dixie gave a little smirk. She missed her friends. They could be nosy little deviants, but they were all hers.

Dixie: We had sex for the first time last night.

Dixie's phone immediately began a rapid fire of pings.

Josie: What took you so long?

Ariel: Oh... I am so happy for you.

Zoey: Ha! I win... oh yeah and that is awesome sweetie.

Josie: Is he big? I bet he is big.

Ariel: Who cares about size? That doesn't mean anything if he can't use it.

Josie: Yeah. Nothing sadder than finding Godzilla who can't destroy his way to an orgasm.

Dixie: OMG guys. Yes he is big, and wow... his Godzilla demolished through to orgasm in one amazing stroke.

Zoey: I am not sure if I should be proud or horrified at our conversation.

Josie: Proud. Always proud.

Dixie heard the water to the shower shut off and Chase's voice boomed through the door. "Why is Tyler texting me calling me a disappointing asshole? Are you talking to the girls?"

Blushing at being caught she loudly replied, "Yeah. Apparently, Zoey and Tyler had a bet on when we would have sex and he lost."

Chase came out with a towel wrapped around his waist and his hand scrubbing through his hair. "Oh. Serves him right then, betting on a friend's misery."

Dixie crossed her arms and frowned. "You and me having sex was misery."

"What!? No. Betting to see how long I would be miserable until I claimed you as mine."

"I am yours, huh?" Dixie asked as she wrapped her arms around his neck.

"Damned right you are. We already established that. Do I need to remind you again?" He was practically growling now, vocalizing his possession of her.

"No, and we don't have time for that. We are going on the dolphin cruise in a couple hours. I need to get a shower ready and get our bag together."

"Fine. Go," Chase said as he smacked her ass as she walked by. "I will call Tyler and tell him to be a man and suffer the consequences of his bet to Zoey."

Chapter 13

Dixie smiled, feeling the warm breeze across her face as the boat left the dock. She sat on a bench with Chase and watched the others get settled on the remaining benches. Grams and Gramps were up by the front. Grams was talking to the first mate who looked completely charmed by the elderly woman. Her cousins Scott, Erik and Wilbert each took a bench each of their own while their dad, Maleko sat with Dixie's parents.

Bronc's loud laugh could be heard on the other side as he talked to his parents and grandparents. Chase leaned over into her ear and said, "You can't miss him if he is nearby," referring to Bronc's loud voice.

Dixie giggled and shook her head. "Nope." She glanced over to a bench that was kind of secluded from the others where her sister, Charles and Martin were sitting. Martin was on his dad's lap and using his hands to squish Charles' cheeks together. "We are going to see fish, and they look like this."

He squished even harder and then started laughing even harder. It was the most adorable thing Dixie had ever seen. She looked at her sister, who while she was not participating in the conversation, still looked relaxed and dare she say it? Almost happy.

"Your sister seems to be turning into a normal person on this trip."

"Funny. I was just thinking the same thing. You have no idea how happy it would make my heart that I could see even a glimpse of that. I really want to be closer to her, but we never seem to be on the same page." Dixie looked up at the sky to stop the tears she knew were about to fall. Getting that relationship she wanted wasn't going to happen by itself. She needed to make more of an effort too. "Come on, they are over there by themselves. Let's sit by them and talk."

Chase kissed her temple. "I am proud of you."

"Yeah well, remind me of that later when I want to kill her." At least they were only on this cruise for a few hours, so if Elena pissed her off, she could talk to someone else until they got off the boat. Or if she was really desperate fake motion sickness and hide in the bathroom.

"Maybe you will be pleasantly surprised," Chase said in an unusually upbeat tone.

They rose from their seats and made their way to the empty bench beside her sister. Elena gave what seemed to be an appreciative smile and nod to Dixie, and it almost felt like a small bridge had been built between them. As she looked around, she realized that during the week she never saw the family interact with Elena, Charles or even Martin. Did her sister feel like an outsider to her own family? Dixie's heart was breaking a little. She decided to make more of an effort, both on this trip and when they got back home.

As they continued out further into the ocean Martin proved to be the best icebreaker that was ever created. He spewed one fact after another about dolphins from the fact that dolphins only take naps with their brains for fifteen to twenty minutes and don't actually sleep, to the fact that a super pod can be as big as a thousand dolphins. During all the fact spewing, Martin would look at his mom to make sure he said each one correctly and she would give a nod and a small smile with each correct answer.

Once Martin was done, Elena explained, "It is important for him to see nature and experience the world around him. Charles and I always make sure that he understands what he is going to see before we go, and just how amazing it all truly is."

"I think *he* is just amazing. He is an incredible kid." She looked over at Martin who was now by the railing with his dad pointing out something at the shore. Chase stood up and squeezed her shoulder as he joined the two at the railing. She was thankful he was giving them space to try and bond a little better.

Elena was also looking at them as she continued. "Charles is good with him. He is more socially adjusted, and I want that for our son. I want him to have everything... education and to know how to interact with people. Charles was patient with me. Is patient with me. Did you know that he was my first?"

Dixie didn't quite know what to say. "Your first person you had sex with?"

Elena gave one short laugh. "My first everything. First time I had sex, first boyfriend and really my first friend."

"What?"

"Well I guess that's not true. You really were my first friend."

Dixie was confused. She never thought Elena thought of her as her friend. "I was your friend?"

Elena looked at her sister with her eyebrows crinkled and a bit of hurt in her eyes. "Yes, of course you were my first friend. Did you think that I forgot about all the time we used to play together before you were gone?"

"Well, kind of... yeah."

"Well you were... and my only friend at the time. But then I was sent to school and when I came back you were gone. Did you know that Mom and Dad forgot to tell me that you moved in with our grandparents?"

Dixie only shook her head and Elena continued.

"I came home for break from school and you weren't there. Your room was cleaned out. It was like you never existed. Just a few weeks earlier we had a girl die at school from a heart condition. The school cleared out her room like she never existed, just like mom and dad did. I sat in the middle of your empty room crying, because I thought you died and Mom and Dad were too busy to tell me."

"Oh god, Elena."

"Mom found me in the room and didn't understand why I was crying. When she finally explained that you moved to Blossom Hills I ran into my room and started packing my bag. I wanted to go with you. I thought that we would finally be together again. Mom stopped me and sat down with me to explain that I was too smart to waste my life there, and that I had more important things to do. I was supposed to change the world with my brilliant mind, and I needed to get my emotions under control. She said that our grandparents were the right choice for you, but not for me. I know it wasn't your fault, but I resented you for having opportunities I never would have. Eventually I met Charles, who is unbelievably brilliant but also has a drive and passion for people. No matter how cold or indifferent I was he never gave up on me. He still teaches me every day how to be a woman with desires and how to be compassionate."

"Elena, I am so sorry. I had no idea. I knew how miserable you were at that school and I knew that wasn't a life that I wanted." Dixie took a deep sigh and continued. "I have a confession to make."

Elena arched an eyebrow and waited.

"I missed answers on purpose for that IQ test. At least just enough to be regular smart and not an obvious idiot." Dixie waited for a reaction from Elena. At first nothing. Just a blank stare. Then Elena just started laughing. An uncontrollable laugh to the point she was wiping tears from her eyes. Dixie didn't quite know what to do or say. "Are you okay Elena?"

"Well shit. You may be the smarter one out of the two of us after all. You little shit. All I probably had to do was fail miserably at the school and they would have shipped me off with you to live with our grandparents. For all of my stupid big brain I couldn't figure that out on my own?" And then she just kept laughing.

Charles came back looking at his wife with concern. "Did you break my wife?"

Dixie just shrugged. "Honestly, I don't know."

Elena finally stopped laughing and Martin crawled on her lap, and wiping one of her tears away and then kissing her in the same place. "All better now Mom?"

Elena smiled, looked at her sister and said, "Yes. All better now. Thank you baby."

Dixie joined Chase at the railing to look out onto the ocean. He wrapped his arm around her and in a low voice said, "We heard everything. I don't think I am allowed to hate her anymore."

"You didn't hate her," Dixie said as she leaned onto his chest.

"No, but I hated the way she made you feel all the time, but this was good. I think we can understand her better, and I think Charles and Martin are good for her."

"I can definitely agree with that."

The cruise continued with Martin switching his time between his parents and Dixie and Chase. They were able to see two large pods of dolphins and a couple sea turtles. Everyone seemed to enjoy it as the first mate pointed out the wildlife and provided a humorous narrative about the history of the area.

After leaving the boat, Dixie and Chase went back to the room and made a lunch to take to the beach. Dixie had made some of Gramp's favorite chicken salad sandwiches and heaven in a cup which consisted of whipped cream, cherry Jell-O, cherries, strawberries and raspberries. He always loved to use the excuse that you have to eat dessert first since it ruins in the hot sun.

Dixie carried the towels and food while Chase grabbed the chairs, umbrellas, a bag with sunscreen and other necessities and also wheeled a cooler behind him. Dixie shook her head. "You know I could carry a little more.

Grunting and readjusting the chairs Chase narrowed his eyes. "I got it woman. Keep walking your fine little ass to the beach. I need motivation to keep going."

"You're terrible."

"Yeah but you like me that way."

Arriving at the beachfront Dixie found that Elena had rented a cabana for her family and was diligently working on her laptop. Anne and Bronc were already in the ocean with his brother and parents. Chase began setting up the chairs and umbrellas as Dixie set down all the food. She was scanning the beach for her grandparents and wasn't able to find them. She heard Scott's voice over her shoulder. "Who you looking for?"

Turning, Dixie responded, "Oh hey Scott. I was looking for Grams and Gramps."

"Oh. Grams said that they were going to cuddle and take a nap."

Dixie screwed her face with a horrified look. "Ugh. Thanks for that."

"Thanks for what?"

"That is their version of Netflix and chill."

Dixie heard Chase let out a loud laugh that he tried to cover up with a cough, while Scott grew a few shades paler.

Scott finally cleared his throat and changed the subject. "Hey Chase, me and my brothers are going to play some football. Want to pair up with me and kick their ass?"

Chase looked at Dixie with questions in his eyes. She sat in her chair in the shade of the umbrella. "Go. Have fun. I will just probably read my book."

Chase lifted one side of his mouth. "A porn book."

"Not a porn book, but I do expect the couple to have sex at some point."

"You're reading porn."

"You know that thing I did for you earlier?"

"Uh, yeah."

"Where do you think I got the idea from?"

"Keep reading good woman."

Scott slapped his hand on Chase's back and cleared his throat. "Now that I have had to clear my head of grandparent sex and how you are defiling my cousin, can we go kick some ass?"

Chase nodded and Dixie watched as the two men walked away to go play a sport to beat the crap out of each other. At least she could busy herself with her new book boyfriend.

CHASE WAS ENJOYING the game. Scott had a decent arm and Erik and Wilbert were athletic enough to make it a small challenge. Playing in the sand also added a level to the intensity. Chase managed to catch another perfect spiral and dodge his way past Wilbert. He could tell that Wilbert was getting frustrated because he was starting to try to play dirty. After the latest touchdown Wilbert had tried to trip Chase by extending his leg out as they were walking back. Chase easily caught his balance and looked back at the man with a glare.

"Watch where you are walking old man," Wilbert shouted as he walked back to Scott. Seriously? Old man? Chase was thirty-five, and how old was Wilbert? Maybe three years younger at best.

Chase tried to shrug it off. He really did. Besides if calling him an old man was the best that he could do, Chase could let that go. He continued to walk towards Scott ignoring the unending comments. This time Chase was defending Wilbert as Wilbert attempted his pass to Erik. He easily took him down to the sand with a resounding thud. Chase rose up first and extended his hand to assist Wilbert back on his feet. Wilbert grabbed a handful of sand and threw it at Chase's face.

Chase's eyes stung as he tried to wipe away some of the sand that was lodged in. He had endured worse. Hell, at the academy they made you suffer through pepper spray and tasing in preparation for being a police officer, so it really was like a minor annoyance. He could hear the brothers arguing with Wilbert while he tried to regain his focus. It seemed that having Erik and Scott yell at him for being an ass only provoked him further.

"Tell me Pig, how much did she have to pay you to pose as her date? Everyone knows that she is all messed up in her head from that accident and her mangled up leg."

Chase had reached his limit. He could take any insult about him, but shit, this was her family and they were treating her like an enemy. He started walking to the still blurry forms clenching his fists ready to take out some frustration of his own on the asshole's nose but then he heard two thumps. After refocusing, he found Wilbert lying on the ground with both Erik and Scott looming over him.

"That's enough. Get your shit together and stop making everyone else suffer for your bullshit," Erik growled.

Scott then loomed over Wilbert and dealt a final blow. "I'm done. Get your shit out of my room and find someone else willing to put up with your sorry ass. Go to Dad's room if you have to, but stay away from me. I am going to enjoy the rest of my vacation without trying to coddle your spoiled ass."

Chase watched as Erik and Scott left their brother on the ground. He didn't quite know what to say and obviously there was a lot more going on underneath this trip between the brothers than he or Dixie knew about.

"Are you happy now? This is your fault, you know. We were getting along fine before you came along."

Chase just let the comment roll off his back. The guy had already been put in his place by his brothers. There was no need to pay attention to a man who was acting like a child throwing a temper tantrum.

As he returned to Dixie, he found her grandparents enjoying some food with her. He sat down in the chair next to her and started to dig into the cooler. She tilted her head in question. "Do I want to know what started all that?"

Chase shrugged. "Wish I knew really. He hasn't liked me from the start and isn't hiding it from anyone."

"It's because you are a cop, and you are with Dixie," Grams said in a calm tone.

"Why me? What did I do?" Dixie asked.

"He has been arrested four times in the past year, the damned little fool. And one of those times was at your exhibit at the gallery."

"What? Why didn't I know about this?"

"Your uncle asked me not to tell you. He didn't want to upset you. Wilbert showed up with some floosy on his arm trying to impress her by taking her to your opening night gala. His name wasn't on the approval list, so he was denied entry."

"He never said he wanted to go. I invited everyone and only reserved spots for those who said they were coming."

"I know dear and so does your Uncle Maleko. Anyway, he threw a big fuss at the door and security noticed he was drunk. The girl he was with didn't help either, she was just as rude making a scene. A police officer was coming out of the deli across the street when he saw Wilbert assault the security officer. He got arrested again and when he didn't make it into work the next day, he also lost his job."

"Well I guess that is a double whammy for me and Chase then. You said he was arrested four times. Was that the first?"

Rose's face fell. "No that was his fourth. The other charges were related to drinking and driving, possession, and breaking and entering."

Chase frowned. He remembered her cousins from years ago when they would visit Dixie's grandparents and they even played with Summer when they were young. "What happened? I don't remember him being this messed up."

"Oh, he got kicked out of college for being lazy."

"Lazy?"

"Yup. He cheated on an exam and got caught. It also didn't help that he tried to reach out to his mother and she treated him like a stranger. She actually told her new husband she didn't know who he was."

Chase couldn't imagine any mother not acknowledging their own child. He knew that Tabby had left the family to start a life as an actress in California and hadn't been in touch, but it never occurred to him that she cut ties so drastically. "Well it makes me hate the guy a little less."

Rose sighed as Hale put his hand into hers. "I love him. He is my grandson, a bit of a screwup right now but I have to have faith that he will figure it all out. Out of all the boys he took his mother leaving the hardest. The other two realized she was distant as a parent before she left, but he was so young he idealizes how she was."

"How has he managed to avoid prison?"

"Maleko is a well-respected man in the community and has enough money to hire an excellent lawyer. I know the last arrest was tossed out on a technicality of some sort. But Maleko put his foot down and told Wilbert he isn't going to bail him out anymore, and he has to make a better effort with the family. I know that is the only reason he showed up here this week. He is my grandson and I love him very much. I just wish he wasn't so much of a dumb ass."

The afternoon drifted away, and the sun was starting to set leaving the sky in bursts of orange, pink contrasting the approaching blues of the night sky. Most of the beach was empty now with only a couple family members and other hotel guests quietly lingering in the sand. Thinking it was time for a romantic swim Chase stood and extended his hand to Dixie. Smiling she put her book down and took his hand and they waded into the water. The waves were calmer than they were earlier in the day and they were far enough out to only feel a gentle push moving them up and down with each passing wave.

Dixie kissed Chase's ear and whispered, "You looked incredibly sexy playing football with your bare chest all sweaty in the sun."

"I knew you liked me for my body."

"It does have its charm."

Their lips glided across each other's in a soft lingering exploration. Dixie wrapped her legs around Chase and rubbed her lower body against his hardening length. Chase groaned. His body was lighting up with each kiss and movement of her body against his. If she kept this up, he was going to take her right there in the ocean. His hands grabbed her ass, and she squeezed him harder around the waist.

"Dixie, if you don't slow down, I am going to take you right here. In the ocean. In front of everyone."

Dixie gave a long exhale. "God please do. I want you right now, they can speculate all they want. They can't see what we are doing out here."

Chase didn't need any more words. Holding Dixie with one arm he pulled his pants down far enough to release his erection and then moved her bikini bottoms off to one side so he could find his way home. Home. That's right... Dixie was his home. Her heart, body and soul was all he needed to be home. No more empty feeling inside his chest. She would always be there to warm him up. He locked his eyes to hers and whispered, "Ready?"

"For you, always."

Chase moved her hips slightly and lined himself up to her entrance, slowly thrusting his hips forward. Dixie threw her head back once she fully took him in. He kissed her exposed neck and licked her collarbone tasting the sweetness of her skin and the salt from the ocean. It was an intoxicating combination. She began to move up and down on his cock nearly making him lose his mind. Every so often the wave of the ocean would lift them up off the ground only to have him land back down and thrust further in with more force. He felt her walls clenching around him and he knew that she was close.

Moving his hips faster he slid his hand between them and pinched her clit. She gasped and came pulsating around his dick, which caused his own release to join hers. She started to pull away and release her hold around him, but he held her in place. "Wait, please. I want to stay connected like this for just a bit longer. Me inside of you. Me a part of you."

Dixie nodded, and they continued to give gentle kisses. Chase felt himself hardening again and Dixie gave a quirk of an eyebrow. "You can't be ready to go again?"

Repeating Dixie's words back to her, he said, "For you, always."

After their second round Dixie and Chase made their way back to the beach and started to pack up their gear to head back to the cabin. As Chase was bent over picking up some loose items, he felt sand being tossed across his back. Annoyed he turned around to see Wilbert walking with his arm around a woman who looked like one of the catering waitresses he had seen yesterday. Figures. He was probably going through a different woman each night.

He looked over to Dixie who had been stopped by Akoni and Lonan. She was talking animatedly and looked so happy. He was glad she was getting some time to spend with her grandfather's side of the family. Since most of them lived in Hawaii, the contact was usually through Skype or Facetime. Chase couldn't stand video chat but Dixie loved it for people that she didn't see very often.

A loud high-pitched scream broke through the night as Chase was folding the last chair. Instinctively Chase turned to see where the scream was coming from. He thought a woman was in distress but when he found the source it was coming from Wilbert, who was standing in the ocean bent over while the woman he was with was running back to the shore and just left him behind. Before Chase could put any thought into it, he was sprinting back into the ocean to help. Once he started to touch water, he checked the surroundings. What if he had been bit by a shark? Not seeing any immediate predators, he waded further in. He was able to make it to Wilbert, and the man was still screaming like as if someone was slicing him open.

"What happened? Where are you hurt?"

Wailing, Wilbert replied, "Jellyfish."

Chase had been stung by jellyfish before and he knew while it was painful it didn't deserve the screaming banshee death yell. He heard splashing behind him and turned to see Lonan running to join them and Akoni remaining with Dixie on the shore. "Watch for jellyfish."

Lonan stopped immediately and looked around before continuing.

"Okay where did you get stung?"

"Holy fuck this hurts," Wilbert moaned in desperation.

"I know, but where?"

"My fucking balls!!"

For all Chase's professional training and the odd situations, he had seen as a cop he really should have been prepared for this, really, he should have been. He should have been able to keep his cool and not want to die from laughter, but this was his vacation, so screw it. Laughing he said, "I'm sorry, your what?"

He heard Lonan's snort behind him. Everybody heard what he said, but Chase wanted him to repeat it. Just for fun.

"My fucking balls man!! Help me get out of here. I can't walk."

Chase took one side and wrapped his arm around his neck while Lonan did the same with his other side. The two men took most of Wilbert's weight as they waddled back to shore. Dixie and Akoni walked up looking like children who just heard the funniest joke ever and were trying not to laugh.

"We need to sit him down and pour some vinegar over his... uh... the infected area," Akoni said trying not to look at the man's crotch.

Wilbert looked up and screamed, "Get me out of here!"

Chase looked back at the hotel and then over to the bungalow. Their bungalow was a lot closer than the hotel and they needed to get him relief quick. Nodding to Lonan he said, "Help me get him to our bungalow and we will get him some vinegar."

The two men began to pick him up as Akoni said he would help Dixie carry the beach supplies back to the bungalow.

Chase was trying to be sympathetic; he really was, but the man was a bit overdramatic. He was moaning and carrying on like this was his last day on earth. Dixie and Akoni ended up making it back first since Wilbert made them stop every so often saying that his balls were sticking to his legs.

Dixie rushed out saying that she was running to the front desk to get the vinegar. A plea from Wilbert came asking her to hurry. Once they reached the front door Akoni was waiting to help them ease him into the bathroom.

"I put the cooler in the bathtub for him to sit on so when he pours the vinegar on it can just go down the drain."

Chase nodded. "Good thinking."

Once the three men got into the bathroom with Wilbert, it was a tight fit. Lonan looked at each of them and asked, "Okay who is taking off his shorts?"

Chase almost vomited a little. "What? Why do we have to take them off?"

"The man can't stand on his own to use his hands to pull down his pants."

Akoni groaned. "We carried the asshole. You can de-pants the man."

"I don't want to see his nasty balls."

Wilbert finally perked his head up and said, "Hey."

Lonan shrugged. "Nothing personal dude. All other guys' balls are nasty."

Chase was getting tired of holding the man up. "So, close your eyes and drop the pants. Then we will move him into the tub and leave him there until Dixie gets back."

Lonan must have realized he wasn't going to win this battle because he squinted his eyes shut and dropped the swim trunks to the floor, easing each foot out one at a time. The other two men were able to move him onto the cooler and sat him down. Wilbert grabbed the support bar on the wall and hung his head. Chase threw a hand towel at him to cover his junk and then walked out of the bathroom.

Akoni was leaning on the kitchen counter and grinned. "A hand towel?"

"What? that was all he needed to cover up. Not going to waste a perfectly good bath towel to hide his small dick."

The two other men laughed and continued to banter until Dixie walked in with what looked like a to-go cup with a lid.

Akoni grinned. "Oh please tell me you switched it out with lemonade. Because I would pay good money to see that go down."

"No, you big jerk. It's vinegar."

Chase extended his hand out. "Here let me. You don't need to see that mess."

Wilbert looked up at Chase as he entered the bathroom. "You are going to have to pour it on me."

"Have you lost your god damned mind? Why would I pour it on you?"

Hanging his head, Wilbert replied, "Because I am going to have to hold my dick off to the side while you pour across my balls and move my balls to the side where he got in between my thigh. I can't do that and pour."

"Jesus Christ. Fine, but we are never to talk about this again. Ever... and you need to stop being an asshole to me and Dixie."

Wilbert just nodded.

Chase took off the lid and waited patiently as Wilbert took off the towel and cleared the area. Wow, that jellyfish got him good. There were a few large angry red stripes horizontally across his balls. Tilting the cup Chase poured the first portion across the affected area. "Okay... Next."

Wilbert moved everything aside, and sure enough more lashes on his thigh and the side of his balls. He almost felt sorry for the guy. "I am going to turn on the water so it chases the vinegar down the drain."

Wilbert's face eased a bit as he relaxed against the wall. "Thank god that is helping. It is starting to feel a little numb." Then he started scratching his hands. Chase watched curiously as he continued to scratch.

After a few minutes Chase asked, "Do you need me to pour another round or are we good now?"

"Pour another round?"

Chase swirled the to-go cup. "Of the vinegar, dumbass."

"No. I don't think so. Burns a little more but its s-okay."

Wilbert was slurring his words now and Chase was actually getting concerned. He didn't see him drink today, and he was coherent earlier. Wilbert's head perked up, and he groaned. "Maybe I do. Starting to hurts again." He lifted the towel and holy shit his balls were swelling. Like not normal swelling. It was more like someone took an air pump and started to blow up a balloon. That can't be good.

Chase snapped his fingers to get Wilbert's attention. "Hey look at me. Are you allergic to vinegar?"

He shook his head. "No, but I am allergic to apples."

Chase looked at the slightly brown liquid and opened the door. "Hey babe, what kind of vinegar is this?"

"Apple. It was all they had, but should still work the same."

Chase looked at the cup and back at Wilbert who was looking more intoxicated. "Shit! Get the EpiPen out of my suitcase. Now!"

Dixie sprinted across the room, got the vial and handed it to Chase. He opened the tube with determination and jammed the needle into Wilbert's thigh. The man screamed again as if Chase was killing him. He helped him stand up and he couldn't help but to stare at the ever-swelling balls. Wilbert followed his gaze to his balls and gasped in horror. "What the fuck man?"

"I know. We're taking you to the hospital."

Dixie and Chase started walking him out of the bathroom when she looked at Chase and said, "We can't take him to the hospital naked."

"Well I can't put his trunks back on him. They will be too tight and restrict the blood flow from the netting."

"Oh. Let me get your sweats." She heaved his arm over to Chase and rummaged through his luggage. Dropping to the floor she fished each leg into the pants and rushed to pull them up. She apparently did that too quickly and rubbed the band across the infected area. Wilbert screamed and dropped to his knees. "Oh... Sorry."

Chase looked at the man writhing in pain and did have a bit of sympathy for the guy. How could you not see the man's balls grow into practically cantaloupes and not feel sorry for him? They finally had him dressed and ready to go. Chase nodded to the car and said, "I am going to take this guy to the hospital. See if you can find his dad or at least his brothers to meet us there. There is no sense in ruining both of our nights."

Dixie nodded and started to buckle him in, but Wilbert shook his head vehemently and said, "God no. Please it will squish them."

Dixie let go of the belt and put both hands in the air as the universal sign of backing off. Chase kissed her and said he would see her later and not to wait up for him. Chase started the car as it flickered a bit and then came to life. As he left the resort, he had to suffer with groans and whimpers coming from the back seat as he watched Dixie wave in the rear-view mirror.

Chapter 14

Once they arrived at the hospital, all eyes were on them as he wheeled the moaning man in on a wheel chair he found at the entrance. As Chase was telling the nurse Wilbert's information, Wilbert burst up from the chair and exclaimed, "They need to breathe!" With lightning quick movement, he dropped his pants in the middle of the waiting room and waved his hips in a circle attempting to create a cooling breeze. Chase thought security was going to kick them out until the staff saw why he ditched the sweatpants. One of the guards had grabbed a nearby blanket and just said, "Dude, cover that up. Nobody needs to see that."

Maleko showed up about forty minutes after they arrived with a couple of coffee cups in his hands. At this point they had sedated Wilbert, who was now peacefully resting in the bed. The two men talked while they waited for the doctor to return. Maleko was gracious to Chase and apologized for his son's behavior.

"You don't need to apologize. He does. He needs to learn to man up and accept responsibility for his actions. Until then he is going to continue to hurt everyone around him. I can take it, but if he attacks Dixie again, we are going to have a problem."

"I wouldn't expect anything less from you. You are a good match for her, and I know how much Mom and Dad adore you. They have been telling me for years that you are really the only choice for her, and you both just needed time to figure stuff out."

Chase sat quietly in the chair looking down at the ground and gave a small nod of understanding. When he didn't say anything Maleko asked, "So, have you figured your shit out?"

Chase looked over at Maleko's defined muscles, inked arms and broad frame that came from years of being a Navy Seal and now a specialist in personal security. Even if he didn't have his stuff figured out would he really say something that would upset the man? Laughing with a small smile he spoke what he knew to be true. "Yes. It took some time, but she is my everything."

"Good," he exclaimed with a harder than necessary slap to Chase's back.

Chase tried to recover with some grace and said, "Thanks."

Time flew by quickly as they watched Wilbert get treated and float in and out of consciousness. Chase really enjoyed talking to Maleko, learning about his time with the Seals and what it was like growing up with his parents and Dixie's mom. He never spent much time with Dixie's uncle and he found that he had a lot in common with the man. It was just baffling how Wilbert could be so different from his father.

IT WAS A LITTLE MORE than four hours after seeing Dixie's small wave in the rearview mirror before he was pulling back into the resort's parking lot. He was still trying to forget the image of the super-sized swollen balls he had seen when Wilbert dropped his pants for all the world to see.

As he walked into the bungalow, he heard soft music and noticed the dimmed lighting. He walked to the bed and found a note on his pillow.

I made you a sandwich and put it in the fridge. I also snagged you a piece of apple pie in honor of our victim. Enjoy and then come and warm me up in bed.

Chase devoured the food with a ferocity he wasn't expecting. He must have been hungrier than he thought, but when it came time for the dessert, he couldn't help but laugh with each bite of the apples.

After finishing his meal, he went to the bed to find that Dixie had not moved an inch the whole time he was eating. Peeling back the covers he found her in his sheriff's t-shirt and it gave him a fierce sense of caveman ownership. She was his. She would definitely object if he hauled her off over his shoulder and never let her out of his sight, but this woman would be by his side and he would protect and support her with his life.

He eased his way onto the bed and curled his body next to hers. He placed a gentle kiss on the back of her neck and she snuggled back into him. She gave a slight moan and entwined her fingers into his. "Welcome back."

"Thanks." He kissed her again this time on her shoulders.

"Did his balls explode?"

Chase gave a huff of a laugh. "No. Thank god. That would have been a terrible mess in your car."

"Mmm... yeah. We would have had to lie to the detailers and said it was taco meat or something."

Chase winced. "And now you have ruined tacos for life."

"It's okay. They're not your favorite anyway."

"No. Tasting you has become my new favorite."

"Oh... that's nice, but your new favorite is sleepy."

"Okay. Get some sleep." He kissed her temple and watched her until she fell back asleep.

"SO, TELL ME AGAIN WHAT this 'Lunching before Ming' thing is," Chase asked as he carried a crate of pineapples to the main tent where they were all having lunch.

"It started with Grandpa's family in Hawaii. They would have family get togethers where they would all have lunch and play games. The whole family is crazy competitive and play to win. The games used to be done while they were eating, but then one time Uncle Keanu punched Uncle Kona while he was eating chicken and nearly choked to death. So Great Grandma made a rule that it would always be lunching before punching and no games were allowed until everyone was done eating."

"And we are eating a million pineapples with lunch?"

"Nope that is one of the games."

"Right. I should have known that. And why are we bringing Ansel," he asked as the rodent tried to climb up his chest from out of the basket.

"He needs more interaction time. If I don't constantly socialize him, he becomes a terror and everyone loves playing with him at the studio."

They were greeted at the opening by Akoni, his wife, Jenny, and their two children Mike and Leah. Akoni took the basket from Chase and walked it over to the side of the tent where other supplies were stacked for the games.

The two children gaped as they saw Ansel resting on Chase's shoulder. Mike was the first to speak. "Is that a porcupine?"

Chase laughed. "No, he is a hedgehog. Do you want to hold him?"

They both nodded their heads with quick motions and wide eyes looking like one of those bobbleheads. Chase showed them how to hold Ansel properly and keep him calm. They sat on one of the chairs while they gently played with him.

Chase looked over at Dixie who was talking to Jenny with a wide smile and laughing with such ease and joy, it made his heart swell in his chest. He felt a hand on his shoulder and turned to see Akoni looking at their women. "There isn't anything like seeing the woman you love happy and laughing is there?"

Chase shook his head. "Nope."

"So, have you ever been to one of our game day events?"

"No, this is the first time."

"Well just so you know, anytime you see eyes narrowing and teeth gritting, put your guard up and duck, because there is probably a fist coming your way. And none of this you can't hit a cop bullshit. You're family now so that doesn't count."

"Good to know."

As it turned out there were several games set up after lunch and there was some kind of complicated sign up system using an app on Dixie's phone to schedule it all. Their first game was a version of the Newlywed Game. It consisted of four couples. Rose and Hale who represented the "long-lasting marriage," Bronc's parents were the "middle length marriage," Bronc and Anne were the "newlyweds," while Chase and Dixie were the "new couple."

Maleko was playing the game show host to ask the questions and seemed to love the spotlight. He opened the game with jokes and dismissed the men while he got the women to answer the questions and write the answers on poster boards. When Chase came back Dixie was biting her lower lip nervously. He held her hand and whispered, "We've got this. We are going to kick their asses."

Maleko cleared his throat. "Okay men, let's see how you do. How many dates did you go on before you got your first kiss?"

Going in order of longest together to the newest couple, Chase watched as each provided their response ranging from four dates to one. When it came his turn to answer, he looked at Dixie who was blushing. Scratching the back of his neck he thought for a minute. "Well, I would have to say zero. I kissed her first and then got her to go out with me."

Dixie smiled and pulled up the poster that indeed confirmed "Zero." She kissed him and bounced on her seat.

Whispering she said, "I wasn't quite sure how to answer that one."

The next question was easy, asking if they were to go on a double date who would he want to go with. Seeing that they both had the same friends and the only ones paired up were Zoey and Tyler, that was an easy point. The last question that Dixie had to answer made him smile brighter than the sun. "For dessert would your man choose cake, pie, cookies or something else?"

"All of it. I want it all."

Giggling Dixie held up her card to show "all of them." After the round was over, they were tied with her grandparents for first place. The women had to leave, and the men had to answer. After the answers were collected Dixie came back practically glowing in her yellow dress. They gave each other a kiss and began the second round.

The first question was simple asking what her biggest fear was. She shuddered and answered with a grimace. "Clowns. They are creepy and just need to be taken off this earth."

He remembered watching the old 80s version of IT with her and Summer, and she had nightmares for a week. She stayed with Summer that whole week and he had to sleep on their floor to protect them from killer clowns. He held up his sign with a triumphant grin that showed he had the right answer.

The second question was way too simple asking if she was texting someone who would it be. With a simple one-word answer she replied "Ariel" for another point.

It was the last question and her grandparents were still tied with them at a perfect score. "When did your man first fall in love with you?" Chase looked at Dixie. She looked nervous and was fidgeting with her fingers. He realized that he had not actually said the words yet. He needed to say the words, but he didn't want to just whisper them to her now. This was it. He was going to have to pour his heart out into this answer.

Clearing his throat, he looked into her wide eyes and began. "She was sixteen. I was too old for her. I had come home from my first year in college, still a complete idiot. I was getting out of my car when I saw her sitting on her front porch railing perfectly balanced on that narrow ledge wearing cut-off shorts and a tank top. She was drawing on her sketch pad with some charcoal. She was mesmerizing, and I realized just how much I missed seeing her, how much I just wanted to be near her again. I almost started walking towards her, drawn to her like a magnet. I was holding my breath wanting to sweep her up off that railing and never let her go, but I heard my sister's voice behind me. She asked me to wait, that it wasn't the right time and I would know when it was. It took me longer to know what was the right time than it should have, but it is our time now."

Everyone was staring at him. The whole room was drowning in silence. Dixie just stared at him blinking a few times. Finally, she looked over at Maleko and said, "Grams and Gramps just won. I had it all wrong." With the words dangling in the air she threw the poster board over her shoulder and pulled Chase by the hand out of the tent and to the shoreline.

DIXIE'S HEAD WAS SWIMMING as she pulled Chase along with her to get some privacy. Once their feet touched the place where the water barely grazed their toes, she pulled him into her and crashed her lips onto his. All this time this crazy man loved her and she had no idea. She was over the moon happy about the words he just told her whole family, but there was also a small part of her that was completely frustrated about all this time they wasted apart from each other. Maybe they needed the time in the beginning. But all these years later? That was more than a little frustrating. She broke the kiss and put her hands on his cheeks. "Okay Montgomery, I've got some things to say to you now."

Chase looked a little confused and just said, "Okay."

"First, that was the most amazing speech I have ever heard, and before I forget I just want to say, God, I love you too. There isn't a place on my heart that isn't owned by you. You have been my best friend, my protector and now my lover. I can't picture my life without you in it." Chase started to speak, but she covered his mouth with her hand. "I'm not done. Second, I have questions. Why did you wait so long? What finally made you take that step?" Chase started to talk, but she still pressed firmly on his mouth. "One more thing. My heart is fragile. If we break up, I won't survive. So, you are stuck with me. Got it?"

Dixie could see his eyes smiling at her as he nodded. She finally released her hold over his mouth and he took a second before speaking. "My turn?"

"Yes."

"I love you too. I know I said it up there in that big probably overdramatic answer, but I love you. And to answer your questions, I waited so long because I thought I wasn't good enough for you. I blamed myself for the accident because Mom picked you guys up instead of me. You had to work so hard to rehab your hip and I had to deal with my guilt. Then you started dating, and I figured you were better off with someone else. I realized that you were dating idiots that wouldn't last. At least until Jay. I started to panic. I was really going to lose you but you seemed happy, and I thought that I could live with that. I could live watching you be happy with someone else that wasn't me. As it turns out, it just turned me into a grumpy asshole. But this asshole wasn't going to confess his feelings and then put you into a position to make you choose. I swear when I saw you sitting in that gazebo and you told me that you and Jay broke up, I damn near did a happy dance in the courtyard. I was going to give you some time and then claim you like I should have done years ago, but then this whole family reunion thing came up and I saw my opportunity and grabbed it. I was going to do everything in my power to make sure you would know that it will always be me and you from now on."

That pretty much left her speechless. There really wasn't anything more that needed to be said. There was no doubt in her mind anymore. She wrapped her arms around his neck and said, "Those are some damn good answers."

Their kissing session was interrupted by the sounds of her phone reminder chimes and then Chase's went off as well. Groaning, Dixie pulled out her phone. "We are due at the next games. You are supposed to be at the pineapple bowling with Bronc, Akoni, and Lonan. I am off to the limbo."

"What if we just skipped it?"

"Not an option. Forfeits also result in a punch. They don't like winning by default."

"Violent family."

"You have no idea."

DIXIE KNEW BETTER THAN to try and limbo with her hip. While the mild exercise she had been doing in the water and sand all week hadn't put too much stress on her hip, trying to bend over backwards under a low bar proved to be too much. She crashed down hard and felt a stabbing pain rush down her hip and into her thigh. Her whole leg on the right side froze up, and it took her rolling over onto her side before she could extend it back out normally.

Anne helped her up, while Dixie's mom went to go get an ice bag. It struck her now just how little time she had spent with her parents so far and began to feel a little guilty. She didn't have a great relationship with them but she needed to try to connect with them a little more on this trip. She sat on the chair as her mom placed the bag of ice on her hip.

"Are you still going to physical therapy?" her mom asked as she worriedly scanned her daughter's leg that was still slightly spasming from the overstretch.

"No Mom, I was discharged from that a long time ago." *When I was twenty*, she thought. "They gave me exercises to keep my range of motion, which I do as they ordered."

"Good. Make sure you keep a healthy diet as well. That will keep your body functioning at a higher level to compensate for your limitations."

Dixie knew that her mom was trying to show concern for her daughter and she really should be grateful. This was the most they had talked in months. Dixie rested her head back on the chair and struggled to find another topic. "How is dad doing?"

"Oh, you know your father. He is presenting his findings at the conference next week in Paris, while I will be giving a lecture in Italy."

"It's a shame you both can't enjoy Europe together."

"We will have time for that after we retire."

"Yeah, but shouldn't you both enjoy and explore together now? Don't you miss him when he is gone?"

Dixie's mom gave a small smile as she patted her arm. "Your father and I don't connect the same way you and Chase do dear. We are more intellectually connected. I feel closest to him when we talk about our work. We don't need that physical connection like others do."

That had to be the saddest thing she ever heard. Maybe it was enough for her mom, but it wasn't enough for her, and if she had to bet, not enough for Elena either. After seeing her sister and Charles in their passionate escapade at the tent, she knew there was hope for her sister.

She heard Chase's voice before she saw him. His quick footsteps and booming voice rose over the surrounding people. "What happened?"

Dixie turned her head and smiled as he dropped to his knees beside her. He was sporting a bruise on his left cheek and was staring at her ice bag. "Calm down. It just flared up because I was trying to limbo like a dumbass. Apparently, my hip does not like to have me bend backwards while walking."

Chase gave a frustrated grunt. "I should have known better after you told me you were going to limbo."

"Stop right there, Montgomery. I am a big girl who can make her own decisions and should know her own limitations. This is my fault, and I will be fine in about an hour. It just needs to calm down."

Before she could protest Chase scooped her up in his arms and began carrying her to the bungalow.

"Put me down you big caveman."

"Nope. You are going to rest that hip and I am going to wait on you until you get better."

While she didn't appreciate Chase causing a scene by carrying her out like an invalid, the idea of him spoiling her the rest of the night and having some quiet time did have its appeal.

TRUE TO HIS WORD CHASE hovered over Dixie the rest of the day. He even treated her to a round of orgasms when he went down on her for what he called his appetizer. Dixie had fallen asleep sated and content early in the evening. It was around 11:30 pm when they heard Chase's cell phone ring.

Dixie groaned as she rolled over and tried to listen into his side of the conversation. She heard a bunch of "uh-huhs" and "okays" with a few curse words until he finally said, "Okay I'll be there soon."

He disconnected the call and sighed. "I have to go back home."

Sitting upright now she asked, "What happened? Is your dad okay?"

"Yeah. It's not him. The mayor was attacked and stabbed in his home. He is okay, but he is insisting on having me handle things. He said he doesn't want 'Tweedle-Dee and Tweedle-Dum' working on his case."

"So, I guess he is going to be okay?" Dixie knew that the mayor could be demanding, but in general he was a kind and decent man who was good to his family and his city.

"Well, he called me from the hospital so I think so."

"I'll come home too. Just give me enough time to pack."

Chase leaned over and kissed her on her forehead. "No. Stay here. Spend time with your family. If I can wrap this up quick, I will come back. I promise."

"Okay. Take my car. I can get a ride with someone else back home."

"Alright, but if you need me to come back here to get you, just call me."

Dixie nodded and watched Chase pack up. As he was putting the last of his clothes in his duffel, they heard a knock at their door. He looked at Dixie who just shrugged. He opened the door to find Bronc holding two Styrofoam containers. He looked at Chase's bag and frowned. "Everything okay?"

Chase shook his head. "No, I have to go back home for work. The mayor got stabbed and wants me there to deal with it."

"Oh. Shit. Do you have a car here?"

"We just have Dixie's car. I am taking it back home and will come back to get her if needed."

Bronc handed the containers to Chase. "Here take these with you. It is cupcakes and cookies that Aunt Rose insisted I bring over for you. And here, take my truck. We can ride back with Dixie, get the truck from you and then drive back home. Blossom Hills is on our way."

"I don't want to leave you guys stranded."

"Don't worry about it. We'll be fine. We can use Dixie's car if needed."

Chase took the keys and said a word of thanks as gave a kiss to Dixie and left.

CHASE WAS ALMOST SPRINTING to Bronc's truck and barely noticed when he saw Wilbert out of the corner of his eye. He heard him yell at him on his way to the truck. "Trouble in paradise asshole?"

Chase wasn't even going to acknowledge him. The man was obviously on his way to get drunk, probably with some woman he just met since he was carrying two bottles of wine with him. He had more important things to do then to placate a man acting like a child.

He turned the corner of the lot and ran into someone. After shaking off the unexpected bump he looked down to see Lucy laying on the ground. Shit. He knocked her over in his haste to leave. He bent down, helped her get back up and she tried to give a coy smile that just looked all wrong. "Sorry, I didn't see you. Are you okay?"

She looked at the duffel bag and widened her smile even more. Balanced back on her too high stilettos, she glided her hands up his chest and leaned in. "Maybe I should be asking you that question."

"I'm fine, but I'm sorry Lucy, I have to go." He made a quick turn around the corner and could see the truck just ahead. He heard Lucy's footsteps clicking behind him. He didn't have time for this. He opened the door and threw in the bag. He felt a small hand on his shoulder try to turn him around. He allowed himself to turn and face her. She grabbed him by the crotch and squeezed. "If you left the little picture bitch why can't we have some fun?"

Chase wrapped his hand around her wrist and pulled her off of him. "If you do not let go and leave me and Dixie alone, I will arrest you for sexual assault."

Lucy huffed in disbelief. "You wouldn't dare. My family would crucify you."

Chase gave a shrug. "Maybe, maybe not. Do you really want to take that risk? It would be my word against yours, and last I heard your family doesn't like to make the headlines."

Lucy left looking more pissed off than he had ever seen any woman, but that wasn't his problem. She could go take her anger out on someone else.

After getting in the car and making it to the edge of town Chase tried to shake off the encounter, but something in his gut was pulling from the inside. There was a spark of something in Lucy's eyes as she left him. It was almost that same spark he would see when a criminal would decide to make a last-ditch effort to escape arrest.

He pulled over into the gas station to fill up the car and called Dixie. He grimaced as he got her voicemail. "Hey Dix. I just wanted to call to say I'm sorry that I had to go so quickly and hopefully I can get this straightened out and come back to you before you have to leave. Nothing would make me happier than wrapping my arms around you and watch the sunrise on the beach together. Also, I wanted to let you know that Lucy came on to me pretty strong in the garage. I told her to leave both of us alone, so if she gives you any problems let me know. If I can't come fix it right away, maybe send Josie down to torture her. Okay, well I gotta go. Love you."

Chase plugged his phone back into the charger and watched the screen dim as he drove back onto the road. He was a bit disappointed that he didn't get to hear Dixie's voice, but was looking forward to the future when they would be back home and together.

Chapter 15

Dixie awoke the next morning reaching over to Chase's side of the bed and felt the cold emptiness greet her searching hand. She had almost forgotten about Chase's late night call that pulled him away from her. She went to reach for her phone and didn't find it on her nightstand. When was the last time she had it? Rewinding the previous day's events, the last time she remembered having it was just before the limbo game. Mumbling in frustration, she realized that when she fell and aggravated her hip that she did not bother to grab her phone. She would have to check with the front desk or her family to see if they had her phone.

Hoping against hope she called her phone from the bungalow's desk phone first. It just continued to ring until her voicemail picked up. She knew that she was overdue to get a new phone since it never made it through a whole day without charging it in the afternoon, but she kept telling herself it was never a big deal since she usually charged it while she worked most of the day.

Annoyed with herself, she grabbed some clothes and stepped into the shower to get ready for the day. She had only been under the relaxing spray of water for a few minutes when she felt a draft with the door opening. With a huge smile on her face she stuck her head out of the shower ready to greet Chase, only to squeak in surprise and hide back in the shower after seeing her sister leaning against the counter.

With a bored tone Elena said, "There is no need to be all jumpy. It's just me."

Is she kidding? Who just walks in on someone taking a shower without any consideration to that person's privacy? Oh yeah... her sister. "Elena, what are you doing in my bathroom?"

"You were late so Mom sent me over to check on you."

"Late? Late for what?"

"The bike trails. The ones you scheduled us for. Mom, Dad, Charles, you and Chase." After a moments pause, she continued, "Where is Chase anyway?"

Dixie turned off the water and grabbed a towel. "He had to go back home for work. The mayor insisted on him handling something personally."

Elena tilted her head and studied Dixie. "Are you going to be okay living your life like this?"

"Like what?"

"The life of an officer's wife."

Dixie lifted her chin with more confidence than she ever felt before. "I would be lucky to be his wife. He may have an unpredictable schedule with his career, but if he made that commitment to me, I know I would come first in his life, always."

Elena nodded. "As long as you know this is what you both want, I believe you both will be happy."

Dixie was ready to argue but then stopped. Was this her weird way of giving her blessing for the relationship? She was so confused, but she didn't have time to dwell on it because Elena made a hurry up motion with her hands and walked out of the room.

Once Dixie was ready, she walked with her sister back to the resort and checked with the front desk about her phone. Dixie was thankful that Elena bit back her lecture about being responsible with possessions. Dixie could see that she was dying to say something about the missing phone, but for once kept her opinions to herself. The resort staff advised they had not seen her phone, but assured her that they would check with the other staff and let her know If it showed up.

A short time later, Dixie's parents and Charles joined them in the lobby ready to board the bus. When Dixie asked about Martin, Elena informed her that their grandparents wanted to spend the afternoon with him and were taking him to the pool.

Much to the delight of Dixie, the bike trails were a good mix of scenery with light difficulty to satisfy her sister and parents desire for exercise. She was afraid that her leg might give her trouble with the bike, but she was pleasantly surprised that the time she spent in the hot tub helped to provide some relief for today.

At the end of the bike path there was a beautiful creek with a waterfall. Dixie wished she had her camera. She would have been able to adjust to a slow shutter speed and increase the aperture to capture the images where the water would appear almost as a sheet of ice over the rocks. Dixie twitched her fingers wishing she had ignored Gram's command just once.

Charles approached with Elena. "It's beautiful isn't it?"

"It is absolutely amazing."

"Wish you had your camera?"

Dixie sighed. "With every fiber of my being."

Charles pulled out his camera and handed it to Dixie. "Elena told me about your grandmother's wish for you to not be behind a camera this trip, but my phone has a good camera and I am sure you could change the settings as you see fit to get a picture."

Dixie resisted clutching it to her chest and calling it `precious' like the creepy bald guy from *Lord of the Rings*. Wow. Zoey and Tyler were having too much influence on her. They kept making her watch all those weird nerd movies. Relaxing her grip on the phone she smiled warmly and thanked Charles who now had his other arm wrapped around Elena.

Dixie spent a few minutes adjusting the settings and then using the bike to stabilize the phone while she took several pictures. Elena looked over her shoulder at the pictures. "That is actually impressive, Dixie. We just usually point and press the button to capture images of Martin."

Dixie turned up the corner of her mouth. Her sister gave her a compliment about her career. Sure, it was about simple cell phone pictures, but this was a big deal. "Thanks, Elena. You know I would be more than happy to get some pictures of you, Charles and Martin together while you are here. I could even print, frame and send them to you."

Elena placed her hand on Dixie's arm and then looked at her husband. "That would be nice. We would love that, thank you."

Charles waved her parents over so that he could take a picture of her with her parents and sister. This was probably the first picture with the four of them in years. There was a pain in her chest rising up from this realization. She made a silent promise that she wouldn't allow so much time to go by before seeing her family again. Having that connection would help maintain this bond they seem to have found this week. She realized that her family loved her; they just had difficulties showing it.

Riding the bus back to the resort she had a rare moment of calm peace as she watched her sister and mom talking about normal everyday things like husbands and children. She felt like she was catching a glimpse of a shooting star and if she didn't soak it all in, she may never see it again. Her eyes drooped in contentment as she rested her head on her dad's shoulder. Her dad squeezed her hand in response as she fought to keep a tear of happiness from falling down her cheek before she fell asleep.

CHASE SCRUBBED A HAND down his face while sitting behind his desk. It had been an excruciatingly long day. It all started with interviewing the mayor and his wife. The mayor, Howard Snowden, and his wife, Susan, had stumbled onto a masked intruder in their home after coming back home from dinner. The intruder got startled, and he drew out a weapon. During the altercation the mayor suffered a couple lacerations, and the intruder ended up holding his wife at knifepoint while backing his way out the door with his backpack. Susan was struck over her head with the butt of the knife before the man had made a getaway in a dark sedan.

By the time Chase had made it back to town, Susan was just regaining consciousness at the hospital. Mr. Snowden was standing guard beside her and gave Chase the details of the break in. Nothing that Howard provided was of any assistance until Susan had given a description of the man's weird shoes. They were bright orange with white soles and what looked like drawings in black ink. She said they stuck out in bright contrast with all his other black clothing like a beacon.

That description was enough to lead Chase to Johnny Hill. He was often in trouble with the police for stolen possessions, drunken disorderly, and various drug charges. The last time he was arrested the deputy didn't realize that somehow a sharpie was left on the back seat of the cruiser. Johnny decided to take some liberties to doodle on the seats and his bright orange shoes. Chase nearly lost his temper when they returned and the deputy told him about the damages. How could you not realize a man was drawing on the car and himself while you drove him twenty minutes back to the station? The station had tried to recoup some of the costs for the damages from Johnny, but even though the court ordered the payment, they still hadn't seen a dime from that costly stunt.

Having enough information to make an arrest, he took two deputies with him to arrest Johnny. One of his deputies, Duncan Guthrie, had forgotten to quiet his radio while they took their positions and alerted Johnny to the approaching police. Johnny had made a sprint for the back door as the officers followed him around the house. Duncan was the first to be able to tackle him to the ground but not before Johnny had used the same knife from the attack earlier to lodge in Duncan's leg. Chase was easily able to catch up to Johnny and tackled him face down into the ground. He quickly handcuffed him and started to read him his rights. He could tell he was heavily under the influence of narcotics again and would be a pain in the ass getting processed.

Deputy Guthrie was sent to the hospital to have his wound tended to and would be off work for a few days. Chase knew he wasn't going to be able to make it back to Dixie before she left the resort. He texted her to give her an update that everything was okay and had some things to clear up at the office and would be back later. It was a little disappointing that she hadn't texted back or called, but he figured she was busy with the family and didn't want to disturb her. If he didn't hear from her after the family dinner, he would try her again, or maybe Bronc just to make sure she was okay.

Chase was still rubbing his temples trying to ease his headache when he saw Tyler and Kyle standing in the doorway with a bag from McKenna's pub and a box from Zoey's bakery. Removing one hand from his temple he reached out with the child like grasping motion. "Gimme."

Tyler tilted his head and smirked. "Is that anyway to ask for delicious food brought to you by your friends?"

With a deep low feral growl, he responded, "Gimme... now."

Kyle was chuckling and said, "Maybe we should feed him like they do at the zoo. Drop it on the floor and slowly back away, not turning our back on the bear."

Chase dropped his head. "You guys are assholes. Food. Now... Please."

Tyler immediately dropped the bakery box on Chase's desk while Kyle was still withholding the food from McKenna's. "I am still holding onto the food in exchange for your press release statement."

Chase reached over to a piece of paper beside his computer and handed it over. "Here jackass, I knew you were coming and expected you a couple of hours ago. You are getting slow in your old age."

Kyle gave one shrug of his shoulder and said, "Whatever, you are older than me old man." Kyle continued to read over the press release and nodded. "You are getting better at this. I see you must have used spell check this time."

Tearing off the meat from a buffalo wing Chase glared at his friend. "Seriously, why are we friends?"

"You picked Tyler as a best friend. Being his brother, I became your friend by default, it was just one of the perks."

Chase looked at Tyler and said, "You have crappy perks."

"Hey, my perks are awesome. I am marrying the town baker, and you get free desserts as my best friend."

Chase lifted the bakery box and inhaled the sweet scent of peach pie. "I do love her baking."

The three friends talked about the events surrounding the break in and subsequent arrest of Johnny Hill. Kyle left to update the paper and its website, leaving Tyler and Chase alone.

Tyler thumped his fist on the arm of the chair and got straight to the point. "Are you going to tell me what is up with you and Dixie?"

"We're together."

Tyler quietly looked at his friend seemingly waiting for more. When Chase didn't elaborate, Tyler sighed. "Are you going to give me a little more detail, or do I have to get Josie to pry it out of you? I think her interrogation skills could rival yours."

"Shit. Don't bring her into this, I already have a headache. She will pulverize my brain into mincemeat. I put it all out there. I told her that I loved her and I have since we were kids. It took a little convincing to make her believe this was all for real, but once I did... it was amazing. I just hate that I had to leave her there alone. Her cousin is a douche, but at least it seemed like her and Elena were making progress on their relationship. Having her nephew there helped."

"Shit, that's right. I forgot Elena had a son."

"Yeah she warms up around her husband and son. It's good to see."

"Are you going to take it slow with Dixie?"

"Like you did with Zoey?"

Tyler just shrugged and took one of the leftover wings.

"I am going to go as fast as she will let me, without getting freaked out. I would move her into my house today if I didn't think she would get pissed off at me."

"Wow, and to think Zoey and I still have our two apartments."

"Don't kid yourself, if you both didn't have your leases with the Glovers you would be in the same place now. Have you even spent a night apart since you proposed?"

"No."

Chase pointed at Tyler. "Exactly!"

DIXIE WAS ABLE TO ENJOY the rest of her afternoon at the bungalow. She rested in the hot tub letting the pulsating jets ease her back and legs from the morning bike ride. Ansel was making laps around the hot tub occasionally sticking his face over the edge to feel the steam. She missed Chase and wished he was there with her to enjoy the hot water and warm breeze coming out from the ocean. They had one more big dinner tonight as a family and then many of them were going to start heading back home that did not live as close as Dixie and her Grandparents to the beach.

As she was getting ready, she was still a bit concerned that she wasn't able to find her phone. She made another call to the front desk again to see if anyone had returned it. After advising that they hadn't found her phone she went to finish getting ready for dinner. If it wasn't found by tonight, she was going to have find a store in town and buy a new one.

Entering the banquet hall, she admired the vast spread of food and the cake that replicated her grandparents' wedding cake with her glass blown flowered picture frame on top. This was it. All of her hard work to organize the week was complete. After tonight, everyone was on their own for however many days they stayed beyond this. It was a huge relief.

She found Bronc and Anne sitting at one table alone and decided to join them. As she was talking to Anne about her pregnancy, the banquet manager came over to confirm that they received the updated slideshow and had it all set up with the DJ to be shown after dinner. Dixie stopped for a moment pausing on the man's use of the word "updated" but shook it off as a miscommunication and thanked him for his time. Bronc's parents and grandparents joined them at the table and Dixie enjoyed the time reconnecting with them. They lavished her with praise about the resort, events and her now missing boyfriend. Chase had charmed nearly every single person in her family and they were disappointed he was not there with her at the last dinner. Dixie explained about Chase's position as the sheriff and that there was an emergency that took him away with the mayor.

Elena walked in with Charles who was holding a sleeping Martin who was nearly swallowed by his backpack with a cartoon Einstein saying his famous equation of $E=MC^2$. Dixie nearly melted into a puddle watching the cuteness of her nephew sleeping with his mouth open and a bit of drool on Charles' shoulder. Elena nodded to her sister and sat with their parents. Once the meals were being served, Martin waved ferociously to Dixie and appeared as if he was going to leave the table but Elena whispered something into his ear that made him sit back down and give her a small wave again. Dixie gave a wave back at her nephew, with a sly wink that made him giggle.

The lights dimmed and warm piano tones started with Ella Fitzgerald singing Sentimental Journey. The screen lit up with a series of photos throughout the lives of her grandparents. When Dixie looked over at them, Grams had a wide grin and watering eyes as she watched the photos glide past, each one showing how their lives had grown with the people they loved around them.

As the slide show ended, it broke into a grainy video of two people and what looked like security camera footage of a parking area. It appeared to be a man and a woman who were in a hurry and were picking things off the ground. As Dixie stood up straighter, she took a more focused look at the woman. That was Lucy. There was no mistaking the too short skirt and perfectly styled hair she had seen her wearing the day before. Dixie's eyes couldn't leave the screen as Lucy ran her hand up the man's chest and then the two people quickly walked to a truck... Bronc's truck. Dixie heard Bronc curse as the footage continued. As if in slow motion she saw Lucy grabbing Chase's crotch. She was mortified. She wanted to throw up. She needed to look away and yet she couldn't stop watching the screen as it kept looping on repeat. The short thirty second clip just kept playing over and over and she could hear the whispers and feel the stares all pointed at her.

What just happened? She couldn't believe it. Chase wouldn't do this to her. And why did the video stop so suddenly? Why couldn't she see what happened after she touched him? Did he rebuff her advances? Did he take her with him? No that couldn't be it. He would never do that to her. Would he? Her heart was racing and the bile in her stomach kept churning. The voices grew louder and the stares and concerned looks that Dixie could feel on her were too overwhelming. She felt a strong hand on her shoulder and turned to see Bronc had approached her from behind showing a protective stance trying to block everyone's view from her. Everyone was still quiet, while it seemed like they were waiting for her to do something.

Dixie scanned the room and finally found what she was looking for. Lucy. The woman had the audacity to stand in the corner with her arms crossed and a cold smirk across her face. Of course she did this. Dixie took a deep breath and knew what she had to do. Standing up she looked at her family and realized she should have been honest from the beginning. She cleared her throat and stood straight and proud as she walked over to the DJ. She asked him to turn off the projector and to give her the microphone. She looked at her grandparents with a sad smile and mouthed the words "I'm sorry" before she began.

"First, I want to say that I owe each of you an apology. Up until a few weeks ago I was dating a different man other than Chase. He was a good man, but I couldn't let him in enough to give him what he needed so he dumped me. The worst part was that I was more upset that I wouldn't have a boyfriend like you all were expecting for this trip. I have never felt good enough for most of you, and that is my issue that I need to work on and not really any of your fault. Chase was kind enough to step in and make this easier for me. He has been one of my best friends since we were kids and he never wants to see me upset."

She briefly looked around the room to find Elena and her parents. "I wish I could be the person you expect of me, but I love my simple life, my friends and my photography." Dixie's mom shook her head and put her hands to her mouth in what looked like an expression of concern and disappointment. "At this point I don't know what was fake and when it turned real with Chase, and we will figure that out. But I can tell you this. That video is a twisted version of the truth. We don't know what happened after the video was cut and I have to believe that he would never hurt me like that. So, please don't be mad at him. You can be disappointed with me that I felt that I had to deceive all of you, but he is and will always be the best man I've ever known. If you all don't mind, I have some things to take care of and I am sorry but I... I just have to go now." Dixie dropped the microphone back on the table and quickly went back to the table for her purse. She felt a small tug on her dress and looked down to see Martin.

Martin's eyes were big and looked concerned. He extended his hand to Dixie holding her phone. "I wanted to give this back to you. Mom said if I ever find something, I should always give it back to the person who lost it. And don't worry, I'm not mad at Mr. Chase."

This little boy had Dixie's heart in his hands. She hoped that he would always stay this sweet and kind. Dixie knelt down and took the phone from him. "You were holding this just for me?"

Martin nodded. "Uh-huh. I found it yesterday by the chairs at the games. I knew it was yours from the sunflower on the back."

Dixie's heart just bubbled over at her nephew. "You are such a smart and good boy."

Martin beamed.

Dixie turned to leave as she saw her sister and parents' approach. She turned to Anne. "Can you stall and get me a head start?"

Anne nodded and whispered, "Go."

Dixie made fast strides out of the hall and began her trip back to the bungalow. Once she made it through the doorway, she was making a mad dash to pack her bags. Tears were streaming down her face as she gathered her things tossing them into suitcases and bags. She was embarrassed and freaked out at seeing another woman's hands all over Chase. She needed to hurry up and get out of there. At least there was a lot less to pack up on the way home. She heard a loud knock coming from the door and she chose to ignore it. Only a minute went buy until she heard it again. This time her sister's voice came through loud and clear. "Open the door Dixie."

Sighing, she knew her sister would not take a hint so she opened the door only to see not only Elena but Wilbert too. Only instead of his usual smug nature his head was hung down low and was looking at the floor. Since no one was moving, Elena roughly shoved him through the doorway. She followed him in and had her arms crossed staring a hole through Wilbert. "Speak. Now."

He still wasn't speaking. His eyes were just focusing on the floor.

Obviously annoyed, Elena decided to talk first. "Dixie, I am sorry about the video, but I wish you would have been honest with all of us in the beginning." It was the strangest thing. It seemed like she was trying to comfort Dixie, but she didn't know quite how to console someone without being direct and abrupt. "Anyway, while everyone was watching the video or watching your reaction, I decide to watch everyone else. Of course we know that skinny bitch was involved with her smug look of satisfaction on her face, but then I saw this idiot. He wasn't watching the video or you. He was sitting at the table with the same sad guilty face he has now." She arched an eyebrow at Wilbert and was obviously waiting for him to talk.

"I gave Lucy the presentation drive to add to the video."

Dixie felt like she had been slapped. "What? Why? Why would you do that?"

"I was in the garage that night. I saw her making a move on Chase." He lifted his head and looked Dixie in the eyes. "It was all her. He didn't want her. He kept taking her hands off of him and he left without her."

Dixie felt like she was missing an important part of the story. "I don't understand. How did that lead to you giving her the USB drive?"

When Wilbert didn't continue Elena gave him a pretty hefty push on his arm. He turned and glowered at her. Dixie was looking at her sister in a new light. She was suddenly missing her friend Josie. They seemed to be quite similar, strong women without a fear of physical force. He rubbed his arm where Elena pushed him and said, "I was also carrying two wine bottles out to my car that I got from the bar... that I didn't pay for... and apparently they were very expensive. She said that if I didn't get her the slideshow drive that she would report me to the police for theft and that she was sure there was enough video evidence for the arrest."

Dixie's head was spinning. She rubbed her temple to try and refocus. "Just how expensive was the wine?"

"About eight thousand dollars."

"I'm sorry did you say eight thousand?"

"Yeah," he shrugged. "Per bottle."

"Have you lost your damned mind?"

Elena had a smirk on her face. "He never had one to begin with. He thought that he was swiping twenty-dollar wine and was going to get drunk off of it."

"Hey! You get your balls swollen five times their size and let me know just how you deal with it." He sighed. "I'm sorry Dixie. I couldn't get arrested again. I thought she was just going to erase it or something. I didn't realize she was going to hurt you. Look I know I am an asshole but I am not a complete asshole, and I think you deserve to know he didn't cheat on you."

"Thank you. I appreciate that."

Before Dixie could say anything else, Elena was shoving Wilbert back out the door again. "We are done with you. Get out now."

Dixie sat with her mouth wide open like a guppy as Elena shut the door and started back to where Dixie was standing. "What? Close your mouth."

"Geez. You have no filter."

"Life is too short to filter your words. Speak your mind and speak it clearly." She looked at the bags all packed on Dixie's bed and frowned. "Are you really going to let that woman drive you away from your family?"

"No. That isn't really it. At least not all of it. I am exhausted. I just want to clear my head. I shouldn't have lied to everyone."

"I assume that our grandparents were in on your deception?"

Now she felt really bad. All she could do was nod. "But here is the thing. It was a lie, but it also wasn't."

"I know you love him. That is clear to everyone."

"Yes, I do. I told him I didn't want to pretend to be together and so he said we should be together for real and just fudge the time line a little. All of a sudden I went from being his friend to being something more, and now I can't see my life without him in it."

"So, why not just tell us that you broke up with the other guy and now you were with him?"

Dixie began to trace the pattern of flowers in her dress before replying. "I don't know. I just had so many failed relationships that I didn't want you or Mom and Dad's judgement about being dumped again."

"It isn't really being dumped if you didn't want to be in that relationship anyway."

Dixie gave a small laugh. "That is the most illogical thing you have ever said."

"Yes, well... that illogical thought got me through a lot of dating disasters."

Dixie searched her sister's eyes and found a bit of sadness behind them. "I didn't think you dated at all until Charles."

"I am a scientist Dixie, not a nun."

A weight seemed to lift off her chest and Dixie began to laugh. At first Elena didn't change her facial expression at all, but finally seemed to crack and smiled as Dixie calmed down enough to wipe tears from her eyes.

Elena looked at the bags and asked, "Are you still going to leave?"

"Yes. I want to get some space and talk to Chase. I need to at least give him a heads up about what is going on. Grams and Gramps will still be here a couple more days, and a lot of the family will be leaving in the morning anyway. I will come back for them when it is time to check out. Oh... please also tell Bronc and Anne I will be back for them too, or if I don't make it back can you help them get back to Blossom Hills?"

"Yes. Alright then." Elena reached the door and finally turned with glistening eyes. "Dixie, please come for a visit soon. I know Martin would love to see you. He has grown quite attached to you on this trip."

"Is it just Martin who would love to see me?"

Elena only slightly lifted one corner of her mouth. "No. Not just Martin." And with that small admission she turned and quietly closed the door.

Chapter 16

Dixie was almost home. Her phone had charged enough after she left the city limits to listen to her voicemail and heard Chase tell her about Lucy. She was so relieved knowing that he was always upfront and honest with her. She had tried to call him back a few times but only received his voicemail and knew that he must have been busy. She was singing along to some music when her radio started fading in and out and then the car lights dimmed and brightened several times. She only made it a couple more miles before she rounded a curve in the road and the car just died.

Dixie tried to restart the car several times but decided it was useless. Darkness surrounded her and it only took a moment for her to realize where she was. She was at the sunflower fields. The white picket fence was to her right while a steep hill was on the other side of the road. She pulled the car over as much as she could by the fields and called the tow service. The tow service asked if she was in a safe location and Dixie described her surroundings to the woman.

"Do you have your emergency flashers on?" asked the woman.

"No. Nothing is working."

"Okay Miss. We recommend that you wait outside of the vehicle away from the edge of the road until we can have a service truck reach you."

"Do you know how long that might be?"

"It looks like he is on another call so it may be one to two hours before he can reach you. It looks like we will be sending you a tow from Tank's Garage."

Of course, it would be Tank's Garage. She just hoped that it wouldn't be Jay covering for someone's tow shift tonight. That would just be the perfect ending to her night. Dixie thanked the dispatcher and looked at Ansel. "Well buddy, it looks like we are going to stretch our legs."

Dixie got out of the car and ducked under the picket fence to look at the sunflowers. She used to love this place. She had gotten so many amazing pictures of the fields when the sun was barely kissing the sky. Even when they were young Grams would bring her and Summer up here to play in the fields and get a few pictures. After playing with Ansel in the dirt for about forty-five minutes she scooped him up and made their way back to the front where the iron butterfly bench was on the edge of the field.

As she sat down, she remembered the numerous times her and Summer would sit on this bench and talk about school and boys. Their last conversation echoed in her mind as the warm breeze caressed her face.

"You know I would be okay if you dated my brother," Summer said with a sly smile.

"What? No. We would never."

"Hmm... maybe not now, but I know in the end it will be the two of you. I just know."

There was such a seriousness to Summer's tone. Summer had this way of knowing things that always kind of freaked Dixie out. Actually, it freaked out a lot of people. Summer became more reserved around others. It was never anything helpful like answers to an exam or lottery numbers, but instead she could almost see when someone was sick before they could, or she even knew when someone was close to dying. She didn't like going to the retirement village because she always said it was too sad and made her feel queasy. Grams called her an empath, saying that she could feel what others felt, not just sickness, but happiness and love too.

Dixie had wanted to shake Summer's mood, so she lightly pushed her with her shoulder. "Actually, it will be the four of us. Me and Chase and you and Austin." Dixie knew how much Summer liked Austin, and she had caught Austin looking at her a little too long sometimes.

A sad smile went across Summer's face and she said, "You have no idea how much I wish you were right."

Breaking her memories, Dixie felt Ansel nuzzle her and bring her back to the present. She nuzzled her nose to his. "Thanks. You knew I was getting sad, huh?"

He didn't reply. He just made faster breathing noises like he was getting excited. Dixie closed her eyes and breathed in the sweet aroma of the flowers. "You knew you were going to die, didn't you? I can't believe I forgot our talk from that day. I know you never knew how it would have happened, but I sure wish you could have warned us."

In response a stronger breeze lifted strands of her hair. "Well, I think you were right. It will be me and Chase, but we are not alone. We still have some great friends and family who will support us."

Holding Ansel enjoying the summer night, she sat quietly for a few more minutes as they waited for their rescue. It wasn't long before she heard what sounded like footsteps in the field behind her. She picked up Ansel and went to check it out. "Hello? Is anyone there?"

Only making it a few steps away, she heard a high-pitched squealing noise that she suddenly recognized as tires trying to stop too quickly. Someone was going to wreck. There was no mistaking that sound. Then the loud crunching of metal on metal could be heard, and she turned to see a beam of light approaching her. She froze unable to scream and felt something force her down to the ground with a blinding pain tearing into her skull, and then total darkness.

THIS DAY WOULD JUST not end. Chase was working extra hours to cover for his deputy's injury and he just wanted to get some sleep. It was bad enough that Dixie would not be in his bed, and now his body ached in protest at still being awake. His new officer, Oliver Michaels, was now following him for the day as well since he was originally assigned to the injured deputy for his first week.

Chase's secretary popped her head in. "Tank's garage called. There is a disabled car on highway 421 by the sunflower fields. They are not going to make it out there for almost an hour or two and there is no power for the flashers on the disabled car."

Groaning Chase picked up his hat and keys. "Okay, we will go put out flares and direct cars until they can get there."

Chase nodded to Oliver, and the two headed out to the cruiser. Oliver did not seem to run out of questions. He was so eager to perform well and he never stopped talking. At least the incessant chatter would help keep Chase awake even if it was annoying as hell. Every so often he would get a whiff of the onion rings Oliver had from Daisy's Diner for dinner. He wished he had mints, or gum, or god anything to lessen the smell. Grimacing, Chase rolled down the window to let in some fresh air.

They were almost there, maybe a mile, maybe two at the most when Oliver finally stopped talking and began waving his hand up and down in the air like a child. Chase could just picture a video on the internet showing a cruiser with the hand waving up and down the road like a bunch of dumbasses. "Could you not do that?"

"Do what?"

The question was barely leaving Oliver's lips when the unmistakable ear-piercing sound of squealing tires echoed through the canyon of the road. Then the loud crash of metal upon metal overtook the tire sounds. "Shit!" And it didn't stop with just one crash he could hear the second and third booms, that were probably ricochets off guardrails or the second car moving and hitting something else. He straightened up in his seat and flipped the switch for sirens and lights. At least they were close. He just hoped that there were not any fatalities.

It took less than a minute before they saw debris in the road and a truck wedged into the guardrail and side of the hill. The other car was in pieces. Chase jumped out of the cruiser and ran to the heavily damaged car. Oliver approached the pickup truck where the driver had gotten out and had blood trails going down his face. Chase's steps faltered as he got closer to the car in the sunflower field. Then once he rounded the side where he could see the trunk there was the unmistakable sign that this was Dixie's car. The black sticker of a camera with the words Capture Life boldly stood out against her little white car. Chase could have sworn his heart was breaking into a million little pieces as he ran to the front of the car where the driver should have been. He was screaming her name over and over praying that she was okay.

The car was lying on its driver side so he looked through the front windshield to see if she was in there. He tried to inhale and get some oxygen because it seemed as if all the oxygen from the earth had disappeared and he couldn't breathe. He stood up looking around and continually calling her name. "Dixie! God dammit. Dixie!"

Oliver made it to Chase's side. "Where's the driver?"

"I don't know. There isn't blood in the car so she might not have been here, but we have to find her. Dixie!"

Oliver took a second look at the car and his face was clear that he finally realized who they were talking about. "Shit, sir. We'll find her."

The driver had made it over to the two of them and Oliver asked if he saw a woman in the car.

"No. Sorry. I just turned the corner, and the car was in the road. I couldn't stop. Oh god, I'm so sorry."

"Okay. If you are feeling good enough help us find her."

Then a loud growl came from Chase's throat. "The bench is gone."

"What," Oliver asked turning around.

"The iron butterfly bench is gone." Chase's throat was beginning to close, and he thought he was going to throw up. "If she was sitting on that bench..."

Looking to the side where the bench was supposed to be, there were broken flowers on the ground. Chase ran over and found Dixie lying unconscious with blood on her head and abrasions on her legs and arms.

Chase could hear Oliver in the background radioing for a second ambulance. He knew that he couldn't move her head for fear of making things worse, but he was continually scanning for other injuries. She could be bleeding internally or have other injuries that he couldn't see. His whole world was crashing around him. He couldn't lose her too. They just started allowing themselves to be happy together. "Dixie, babe. Wake up for me okay? I need you to wake up and tell me I am being an idiot, or shove food in my mouth to shut me up when I say something stupid. Babe, please. I need you."

A shadow loomed over Dixie and Chase heard a man behind him. "I'm sorry. I didn't see the car."

Chase's hand itched to reach for his gun and shoot the guy who may be responsible for taking his Dixie away. He immediately stood to his full height and glared at the man. "You need to go. You have done enough fucking damage and need to get the fuck out of my sight!"

The gangly little man took some steps back and Oliver gently guided him back to the edge of the road. Chase was back on the ground kneeling next to Dixie. He finally took a moment to look around and he could see the mangled bench off to the side with blood on it along with some of the posts from the picket fence around the fields. He felt little pricks across his ankle like thorns from a flower and went to remove whatever it was but found Ansel trying to crawl up his pant leg for comfort and a hiding place. He gently picked up the hedgehog and stuffed him in between his shirt and vest so he could hide and the vest would stop his quills from poking through.

"I've got Ansel babe. He is going to be all upset until you wake up. We both need you."

Finally, the distant sound of the sirens could be heard from the ambulance. Thank god help was on the way. He wasn't sure just how much more he could take feeling so goddamned helpless. Once the first medic made his way over to Chase, he took one look at Dixie and gasped. "Shit, Sheriff. Dixie."

All Chase could do was nod at this point. Chase gave a brief description of how she was hit with the bench and possibly a post and was not in the vehicle at the time of impact. He answered the medics questions about her injuries and medical history, and stood back as they applied a neck brace and loaded her on the back board.

He followed the medics and informed them that he was going with her. He tossed the keys to the cruiser to Oliver and told him to finish up here.

"You're just going to leave me here?"

"Yes, I'm leaving you here and I am going to go with my fucking wife in the ambulance."

Oliver stood blinking for a moment and said, "Your wife, sir?"

"Yes. Or at least she will be as soon as she fucking wakes up, now take care of this shit. I've gotta go."

Chase watched as the medic hooked up an IV and continued to take vitals. Chase held her hand and tried to stay out of the way.

What was probably only about ten minutes felt like an eternity when they reached the ambulance bay at the hospital. Dixie was rushed back and Chase was ordered to stay in the waiting area until they found out more. It was when Chase was alone in a room full of chairs and a TV on with a horrible sitcom rerun playing that he finally broke down. His anger, frustration and fear gathered into one big guttural cry as he dropped to his knees.

He wasn't sure how long he stayed there before he felt a small hand on his shoulder. He popped up on his feet quickly to see Zoey and Tyler standing next to him. He didn't remember calling anyone. He ran his thoughts back through his mind again and was sure he hasn't functioned on any level since he got to the hospital. His confusion must have been obvious on his face because Tyler began to speak. "Kyle heard on the dispatch about the accident. Then he heard Dixie's name and that she was being transported to the hospital. He called me and we came right over."

Chase looked at his friends, so grateful that they cared so much about him. So much about her. "She wouldn't wake up. Her car broke down and she was waiting for the tow truck at the sunflower fields. Then this idiot hit her car, and then it went through the fence and forced the bench and some posts into the field where it hit Dixie. We couldn't find her at first, and when we did, she so fucking bruised and bloodied, and she wouldn't wake up for me."

He watched Zoey as her eyes welled up with tears and she touched her lips with her fingertips. It wasn't that long ago when Zoey was in this same hospital being treated for a gunshot wound that she got from her ex-boyfriend. Tyler thought he was going to lose her then, and now Chase was suffering that same agonizing feeling. That feeling of utter helplessness and devastation and not knowing what was going to happen.

It wasn't long before more people flooded the room including Ariel, Derek, Josie, Kyle and Chase's dad. A doctor finally approached and Chase held his breath as the doctor began to speak. "We have run several tests including a CT scan. She has had a traumatic brain injury caused by the debris hitting her on the back of her skull. It resulted in her brain jolting back and forth causing swelling. There is a linear skull fracture, but we do not see any hematomas occurring in that area. At this point we are most concerned about getting the swelling under control. She is still unconscious and we are monitoring her vitals."

"Can I see her now?"

"We can allow two people at a time for now."

Ariel quickly stood up behind Chase and grabbed his hand. He looked down at her and nodded. They walked in silence as they meandered down the maze of corridors to get to Dixie's room. She looked so pale, as if her blood had been drained and she was desperately cold. Her face and arm had bandages and he could see where she had gotten a couple of stitches. Chase took the seat beside her and took her hand to gently bring it up to his lips. "That's enough of a nap now babe. You have to wake up. We are all here waiting to talk to you."

There was no response, just that beep beep-beep of the monitor that provided the proof Chase needed that she was still there with him. Ariel pulled over a chair and sat on Dixie's other side. She gently brushed one of Dixie's curls away from her face and began talking to her friend. Ariel's soft melodic voice was almost like a lullaby. She just kept talking in soft tones and Chase watched Dixie's face for any response.

He had tuned out the specifics of Ariel's one-sided conversation until she repeated his name a few times. "Huh?" he finally asked.

"I called Grams and Gramps. They have left the resort and are on their way."

"Shit. I didn't even think..."

Ariel started to have a tear fall and said, "It's okay. Nobody expected you to. We are here for you. For both of you."

Looking at Dixie he nodded and said thanks. They were both waiting quietly as Chase stood up to stretch his legs when small little huffing noises broke the silence. Ariel's head quickly looked up at him and focused on his abdomen. "What the hell is wrong with your stomach?"

Chase looked down and saw his shirt moving around as if a baby was stretching for room. "Oh. Ansel. I completely forgot I shoved him in there." He opened his shirt to only have a little nose and beady eyes poke out sniffing around the room. "He was on the ground next to Dixie when we found her. He was crawling up my leg when I squatted down to help her."

"Give him here. I have a little pouch in my purse he can snuggle in."

"You keep a pouch just for him?"

"Of course. She visits me with him sometimes and when we are slow, he keeps me company if she has errands. We've bonded." She reached out her hands and Chase handed Ansel over to her. "I am going to go out to the waiting room to let the next person in. I think I have taken up enough time."

Chase nodded and went back to the bed clasping her hand with his two hands as he leaned forward and bowed his head. "Mom, Summer... I don't know if you can hear me but if you could put in a good word to the big man up there to help us that would be great. I need her. She may not need me, but so help me I can't do this without her. I'll do anything if you let her stay here with me."

"Then how about this time you don't push her away when she recovers."

Chase's head popped up to find Elena standing in the door. "Elena. When did you get here?"

She walked in with every bit of calm composure and sat down. "Only a few minutes ago. Charles knows how to drive quickly when needed."

"When you say quickly..."

"If you would have caught us, I am sure that it would have been a hefty fine, or possibly jail."

"Okay," Chase said drawing out the word.

"Some of the rest of the family are here already too. Mom and Dad are still on their way with my Grandparents."

Still holding Dixie's hand, he just nodded.

Elena looked at him and then Dixie. "We got the details of what happened from the woman with icing on her face."

Chase gave a small lift of the corner of his mouth. "That had to be Zoey."

"Yes. I believe that was her name. Anyway, it sounds like we were lucky."

"Lucky?"

"Yes. If she was in that car at the time of the accident it could have been much worse, or if the car had struck her instead of just a bench and post."

"We were lucky she wasn't sitting on that bench while waiting for the tow truck."

"Agreed." Elena looked into Chases eyes and for the first time he saw a crack on her wall that she always put up. "You aren't going to push her away again, are you?"

"Again?"

"Dixie told me about how you both had gotten close when she recovered from the last accident. Even though I wasn't there she still called and talked to me every couple days to give me updates, did you know that?"

Chase was surprised. He didn't think they were close at all. He thought the only people she confided in back then were Ariel and him. "No, I didn't know that."

"I know people think that I am cold and don't love her, but they are wrong. I spent hours researching the best way for her to regain her strength and get a full recovery. All those exercises she was doing with you every day; they certainly did not come from her physical therapist. That man didn't devote the time and energy she deserved. She told me all about how you both were getting close and that she was falling for you. Then when she tried to show you her affection, you rejected her. She was just getting strong again, and you didn't want her. I told her that you were not worth it and to find better friends. She defended you down to her very core. I wasn't here, I didn't know what it was like for the both of you. I assumed ultimately that you blamed her for the death of your mom and sister, and that you would never accept her."

Chase rubbed tiny circles on the back of Dixie's hand and looked her sister in the eye hoping to convey the honesty in what he was going to say. "I never blamed her. Myself, yes, but never her. I was supposed to be the one to pick her up that day, not Mom. She told me not to carry that blame, but it was always there, and watching her struggle to walk just compounded that guilt. It took a long time for me to accept what happened, and during that time I tried to let her find happiness with someone else, but I couldn't do it anymore. She was always meant to be with me, and I will spend the rest of my life showing her that."

"Good, I believe you."

Elena's phone buzzed, and she stood up extending her hand. "Come on. My grandparents and parents are here. Let's get a drink and let them come in."

"I don't want to..."

"You have to take care of yourself too. Dixie would be upset with me if I allowed you to starve or dehydrate yourself. Come on."

Chase followed Elena to the waiting room where it was overflowing with people. Most of Dixie's family was there with concerned looks on their faces. Dixie's mom walked past him with her grandmother as they made their way to her room. Tyler handed Chase a bottle of water and guided him to the chair. The room was mostly silent the remainder of the night with occasional soft conversations as they all waited for Dixie to wake up.

IT WAS THE NEXT MORNING when Chase woke up next to Dixie's bed stuck in a slumped over position. His back was killing him. He sat up to see Bronc in the other chair. He cleared his throat. "Anything from the doctors while I was passed out?"

"No. I sent most of the family over to the B&B. Elena, Charles and Martin are at Dixie's. Some of your friends were still in the waiting room and Anne is with most of the girls in the cafeteria."

"You all got here quickly."

"Well thanks to Lucy's stunt, we all checked out of the hotel with the understanding that everyone's things that were not packed would be driven here and delivered to the B&B. We all crammed into cars together and the passenger van from the resort drove some of us who didn't have cars."

"How did you swing all that?"

"I have resourceful friends who got in touch with her father and threatened to expose her little stunt if they didn't help all of us get to Dixie."

"Do I want to ask?"

"As an officer of the law, I wouldn't recommend it."

"Noted."

The two men chatted and sat by her side when Chase finally felt a flutter of movement from her hand. He stood quickly as the chair scraped the floor.

"Dixie, babe. Wake up honey. It is time to show me those beautiful brown eyes of yours." Her hand squeezed a little hard as he kept talking. "There you are. Come on. Wake up. I kind of need you conscious so we can hurry up and get married. Come on babe."

Dixie gave a slight groan and started to open her eyes.

"Bronc go get the doctor."

Bronc quickly left the room and Chase's view from the doorway.

"Hi babe. Let me see those eyes again. You almost had it."

Dixie finally opened her eyes fully and a soft smile fell across her lips. She tried to raise her other hand, but it quickly fell down and she just gave a small squeaky "Hi" before closing her eyes again.

The doctor arrived with Bronc who seemed to be trying to catch his breath. Chase quickly stood away from the bed so the doctor could perform a check. "She completely woke up?"

Chase nodded. "Yes. It was only for about ten seconds. She said hi and closed her eyes again."

"This is a good sign. Sometimes it may take a few times before she will stay conscious for an extended period, but it is good that she woke up. I will come back again and check on her in about an hour."

Anne, Ariel, Josie and Zoey stood in the doorway as the doctor left. Bronc excused himself and took Anne with him. The three girls entered as Josie raised an expectant eyebrow.

"She woke up for only for a few seconds, but then went back to sleep. The doctor said that is still a good sign though."

The girls surrounded Dixie and insisted that Chase get some fresh air. Zoey informed him that Tyler had food from McKenna's waiting on him outside. When he didn't budge, Josie pulled him up and pushed him out the door.

"You are no good to her if you are not taking care of yourself. Now go."

It was only about thirty minutes before Chase made it back to the hospital room to see Dixie wide awake and listening to the girls talking about a mile a minute about everything that had happened since the accident. Dixie's eyes locked on Chase's and she gave a small weak smile that nearly made his heart pound out of his chest. For the first time he was allowing himself to breathe with the knowledge that she was going to be okay.

Ariel looked between the two of them and stood up. "Come on girls. Let's give them some time alone."

Chase made his way over to the bed and bent over to give her a kiss. He kissed her softly not wanting to aggravate her injuries, but she clenched her fists in his shirt and pulled him closer. This kiss was everything he felt down to his soul. He was not ever going to let her go. He needed her humor and spirit in his life always. When Dixie finally broke their kiss, she looked at Chase with questions in her eyes. He awkwardly sat on the edge of the bed and brushed some stray locks from her face.

"What's wrong babe?"

Dixie bit on her lower lip and slowly released it. "Did you really propose to me by saying you need me awake so we could hurry up and get married? And really Montgomery, that sounded like an order and not a question."

Chase wanted to laugh. He actually had to clear his throat to prevent it from bursting out from his chest. Holding her hand, he studied her face. "Let me first say that was the first time you woke up and I was a bit excited, and just kind of blurted it out."

"So, you don't want to marry me?" Dixie asked with a frown.

"No babe. I want to marry you to with every ounce of my soul. That is not what I had in mind when I would ask you to be mine, so let's try this again." Chase eased off the bed and bent on one knee. "Dixie, I knew you were meant to be mine from the time we were young. But then life happened, and we took a bit of a detour and developed this amazing friendship that I wouldn't have traded for the world. It took me way too long to realize that the detour was just that, a detour. We still belonged together, and I had to step up to be the man you deserved. I promise to always make you first in everything and that you have my heart completely. Will you please marry me?"

Dixie put her hand on his cheek and smiled so brightly as she said, "Yes. God yes."

Chase stood and kissed her all over not wanting to leave an inch of her face untouched. "Can we get married as soon as we spring you from here? I don't want to lose another day with you."

"Oh, I don't know, that seems a bit too fast. How about two days after I get my freedom?"

"You drive a hard bargain, but deal."

Epilogue

True to their words it was two days after Dixie was released from the hospital that she was standing in front of a mirror wearing Chase's mother's wedding gown. It was a beautiful simple satin A-line gown with beads that traced down the chest and then crisscrossed around the waist.

The idea to use his mom's wedding dress came from Chase's dad while they were planning the wedding at the hospital. When Dixie tried to object his father simply shook his head. "Carrie loved you like her own daughter, and she would have been thrilled to have known you were marrying our son. Chase told me about your grandmother's gown and I know Carrie would have wanted you to have this."

Dixie gently traced her fingers on the gown, gave a warm smile and accepted the gown from Jeff's extended hands. "Thank you. This means so much to me. The dress... and that you are being so nice to me."

"Sweetheart, I am so sorry if you thought I didn't care for you anymore. I just have been living in my own little world since they died, and kind of ignored everyone. I was never mad at you, and I couldn't have chosen someone better for my son."

A gust of wind blew in from the door opening to the bedroom breaking Dixie away from her thoughts from the previous day with Jeff. Ariel swept in with a light blue chiffon dress similar to the A-line dress that Dixie was wearing followed by Josie who wore her traditional pencil skirt but this time instead of her button-up shirt, she wore a softer beige blouse that gently flared at her waist. Ariel's soft voice squealed with excitement. "I can't believe you are getting married already. The big bear couldn't wait for us to plan a big proper wedding?"

Dixie laughed. "No, but neither of us wanted that. Plus, most of my family extended their stay since I got hurt and it just seemed like the perfect time." She wasn't kidding either. Most of the family descended on the town in swarm after she got hurt. Even some of her grandfather's side from Hawaii stayed. The bed-and-breakfast was booked solid, and they had family staying with several of Chase and Dixie's friends.

Josie set her make up case on the dresser table and brought over the floor lamp as she removed the shade. "Sit," she said in her usual commanding tone. Dixie sat quickly and obediently.

"No fancy makeup Josie Stabenow! Keep it simple."

Ariel immediately stopped what she was doing and looked at Dixie. "You knew Josie's last name and didn't tell me?" She glared at Josie. "I have asked you like a dozen times and you would never tell me."

Narrowing her eyes on Dixie she replied, "You are so lucky you are the bride or you would be walking out of here looking like that damn clown from that one movie with the red balloon." Josie turned and looked at Ariel. "I had to give my full name when I was visiting Zoey when she got shot, and little Miss Nosy over here was creeping over my shoulder when I filled out my paperwork. I don't like my last name and I just haven't gotten around to changing it yet."

Ariel rolled her eyes. "Okay, geez." She paused. "You don't have to get all *stabby* about it."

Josie slammed down the foundation on the dresser looking as if she would torture Ariel, but the little blonde princess took off for the door before Josie could get her clutches on her. Ariel's stumbling steps could be heard throughout the house as she hurried down the stairs laughing. Josie gave a slight growl as she sat down next to Dixie to start applying the makeup.

Before the first layer of foundation was complete, Kyle poked his head in. "Is there a reason Ariel ran out of here like her life depended on it?"

Josie put the foundation away and calmly picked up the eyeshadow. "You may want to keep the little princess away from me if you want her to live long enough to be in the wedding."

Kyle scratched at his chin and watched them for a minute before asking, "And how am I supposed to do that?"

Pausing with a brush in her hand, Josie turned and stared at Kyle who now looked extremely uncomfortable standing in the doorway in his button-down shirt and dress pants. "Oh, I don't know Kyle, how about you do what you should have done years ago and go kiss the woman senseless. Or better yet pick her little pip squeak ass up and bang her on the nearest wall."

Kyle stood there with his eyes wide and mouth slightly open. He started to say something and then closed his mouth again. Dixie watched as he struggled for words and Josie waited with an expectant eye. Finally, he cleared his throat. "I can't... I mean... Ariel and I..."

Josie shook her head. "Kyle, one of these days you are going to realize what you are missing and it will be too late. Chase woke up and grabbed what he wanted. When are you going to do the same?"

Kyle's shoulders drooped and his eyes fell to the floor as he shook his head. "I just can't." He turned to leave and Dixie heard him say to the empty hallway. "I already know what I am missing."

Dixie closed her eyes as Josie returned to finishing her eye makeup. "That was a little harsh."

Without missing a beat Josie tapped Dixie's temple. "Look up." She began putting on her eyeliner. "He needs someone to be harsh with him. I am tired of seeing Ariel so tied up in knots over him, and he keeps her so close that she'll never move on."

"We have all tried to talk to him, Derek and Tyler especially, but he won't budge."

Josie started with the mascara. "Mmm... maybe, but it is probably using man logic, so it is inherently flawed." Josie grabbed the handheld mirror and held it out to Dixie. "So, what do you think?"

"Josie you are amazing. I look like I have perfect skin," Dixie said in awe as she turned her head from side to side.

"Yeah that would be the spackle."

Dixie's eyes widened. "You put spackle on my face?"

"Calm down. Face cream spackle. It works the same as wall spackle. It fills the holes in your face and then I get to cover it up with the foundation."

Dixie frowned. "Sounds like a lot of work."

"Darling looking this perfect takes a lot of work," she said as she moved her hand around her face. "I don't wake up looking like this."

"Humph. We all just thought you sprang out of bed with perfect hair and wearing your perfectly pressed blouses and skirts."

"I love that I have all of you fooled." She winked and gave Dixie a small squeeze on her shoulder. "I am going to give you a few quiet minutes before you go downstairs into the craziness. Do you want me to send anyone up?"

"Yeah. Will you send my matron of honor up?"

Josie nodded and quietly walked out of the room closing the door behind her. Dixie looked around at what used to be Summer's bedroom. Her dad didn't change much. He had finally donated her clothes a few years ago and took down the boy band pictures from the walls, but the furniture and bedding were still the same. On a shelf was a picture of Summer and Dixie wearing t-shirts and cutoff jean shorts leaning with their heads together while sitting on her grandmother's porch railing. It was the first picture taken with Dixie's new professional camera. She had learned how to set the timer and use the tripod to get the perfect shot. She remembered Chase teasing her that he could just take the picture for her, but she had refused saying that if she was going to be a photographer, she needed to learn things on her own. When Dixie had gotten back on the railing to be in the picture Chase said she wasn't smiling big enough. Summer told him to hush, and he started making faces behind the camera. The girls had finally cracked up with laughter and that was when the camera finally clicked.

Dixie picked up the picture and placed a small kiss to her fingers and then to the image of her friend.

"She was very pretty."

Dixie turned to see her sister looking at her with her head tilted. "She was very pretty, and one of the best people I have ever known."

"Dixie, I know I never said this before, but I am sorry about Summer. I know she meant the world to you."

"She did, but I have amazing friends now too." Dixie reached for Elena's hand. "And I hope that we can start to build a friendship too. You have been my sister, but I missed that thing about sisterhood where we are friends too."

Elena's spine straightened. "I promise I will try."

Dixie hugged her sister tight. "Thank you."

Elena let her hug her for a few seconds and pulled her away to look at her. "You look beautiful. Now let's go and get you married to the big grumpy man."

"He's grumpy?"

"He was. He seemed to calm down when your little baker friend pelted him in the head with some kind of muffin."

Dixie laughed. "Oh. Yeah, you have to keep him fed, or he is the worst. Wait did you say she hit him in the head with a muffin?"

A smile quirked at the corner of Elena's lips. "Yes. He had just finished eating one, and he was griping about how he was starving, and your friend got annoyed and threw one of the muffins from a nearby table."

"Well then, we better hurry before my ceremony gets shorted to us just saying 'I do' with a kiss so he can eat."

Dixie left with her sister to make the short walk across the street to get married. Chase wanted to marry her on the steps of the porch where he first knew he was in love with her. Dixie's grandparents had long ago sold the house, but a nice middle-aged couple lived there now who agreed to allow the ceremony on their front porch. Chase had told Dixie how he had knocked on their door and spewed out the story about how he grew up in the house across the street and fell in love with the girl who used to live there. He continued to explain to them how he almost lost her twice, that he couldn't live without her and begged to be able to marry her on that porch. He confessed how he nearly passed out from telling the story in almost one breath. The wife had misty eyes, and the husband wrapped his arm around her as he told Chase they would be happy to have them here. The wife said her only condition was that they would be invited to watch them get married. Chase was so happy and excited he wrapped both of them in a bear hug, lifted them up off the ground and thanked them over and over again.

As Dixie approached the front door to take the steps to become Chase's wife, she took a deep breath. Ariel stood with Derek who was walking with her as a groomsman. Elena met up with Tyler who was walking as the best man. Kyle was taking pictures of everyone with Dixie's camera. She had been teaching him for a few months how to use it and how to take professional pictures for the paper when she couldn't help him. Once the wedding was planned, Kyle volunteered to take the pictures.

In pairs, the wedding party walked across the street to the other house's improvised altar. Dixie walked up and met her dad and grandfather to walk her down the aisle. She didn't want to choose between her dad and her grandfather who had such an important role in raising her, so she asked both of them to give her away. The two men had silly grins as they took her arm and walked her out of the house.

Dixie thought she was going to ruin her makeup and let some tears fall until she looked at the street and started laughing. Chase had blocked off the whole block with the cruisers so no traffic could come through. He must have bought the whole flower shop because the entire path on the street between the two houses had been lined with flowers for a makeshift aisle and petals were all on the street for her to walk across. She couldn't dare to take a peek at the steps of the porch yet. They had just reached the curb, and she looked down to step onto the pavement when the string quartet started playing the wedding march. Where on earth did he get the musicians on such short notice?

She finally lifted her head up and saw Chase standing next to the mayor who had agreed to perform the ceremony. Her eyes locked with his and she felt like she was floating, being magnetically drawn to him. She wasn't even sure how it happened, but they reached the altar and they stopped. The mayor said something and then she heard her Dad and Grandfather say, "We do." She felt their kisses on her cheek and she still hadn't broken her gaze with Chase. She knew there were other people there, but she didn't look at anyone but him. She watched as he dropped down a step and took her hand.

"Are you ready to start our life together?" he asked in her ear.

She beamed. "Absolutely."

THE WEDDING HAD BEEN beautiful. Chase couldn't believe how smoothly everything had gone. His wife was perfect. His wife. That word was probably the best word he had ever known. He knew it was such a small word but held so much power. When he first saw Dixie in his mother's dress, he thought his heart would burst right out and fall onto the floor. She was amazing and he would never stop showing her that he knew just how lucky he was.

Dixie had even surprised him by adding in her vows that she would always make sure that he was fed properly to ensure the town's safety. The Mayor had even laughed and said that the whole town would thank her for that. Chase knew that she would always make him laugh and they would support each other in whatever they chose to do. He held her closer as they danced their last dance for the night.

"I have another surprise for you. Are you ready to see it?"

"This amazing wedding wasn't surprise enough?"

He kissed the crown of her head. "I have to admit your sister and Josie did most of the planning for this. You put two type A personalities in charge and they can plan a wedding in twelve hours, but this present is all me."

"Awe. You got us a giant-sized tower of donuts."

"You get one donut cop joke a day woman, and you just used it up."

"I'm sorry. I would love to see my present now."

They said their goodbyes to the remaining guests as they made their way to one of the cruisers. Dixie paused as they got closer. "Are you arresting your wife on our first night together?"

Chase chuckled and opened the passenger side door. "Get in the car woman."

As they drove to their destination Chase held her hand and toyed with the newly placed wedding band on her hand. He loved that he had tangible proof that she would always be his. They only drove a few blocks to the edge of the residential area, when he pulled onto a gravel drive and into what appeared to be a small parking area. Turning he told Dixie to close her eyes. Thankfully she did so without argument.

Chase turned on the flood lights from the cruiser and rounded the car to help her out. He moved her to one side of the car and whispered in her ear. "Okay. Open."

She opened her eyes to find a giant field separated by a beautiful white and blue stone path. One side looked like it had been newly planted with rows of something new, while the other was obviously just landscaped with beautiful flowers, trees and alcoves with benches and archways. At the end of the path was a replica of the iron butterfly bench with an arbor surrounding it with twinkle lights.

Chase was now behind her and wrapped his arms around her middle. "This is all yours. You will be able to take pictures for couples in the garden over there. On the other side is going to be a sunflower field. I just planted that, so it will take some time to grow but it will be almost as big as the other one. I want you to have a safe place to take your pictures and somewhere you can come to escape when I annoy the shit out of you, because you know I will." He took her hand and continued. "Come on. I have one more thing to show you."

They approached the butterfly bench, and he pointed to small plaque that read "To my Dixie, my love and perfect image of devotion." Dixie read the small dedication and then pulled him down to have her lips touch his. They got lost in each other under the moonlit sky and the gentle lights twinkling from the arbor. Chase knew that they both had finally gotten it right.

Also by Kate Alexander

A Blossom Hills Romance
Images of Devotion

Watch for more at https://www.katealexanderauthor.com/.

Kate Alexander

About the Author

Kate grew up in the suburbs of Cincinnati, Ohio. While attending school, she participated in writing competitions and workshops for young adults. After college, she stayed in Cincinnati and chased her passion of helping others with her work in social services and volunteering in the community.

Shortly after marrying her husband, Tom, they moved to Phoenix, Arizona where she again found a love for reading and writing romance books. When she isn't writing new stories she can be found out with her husband taking in a movie, playing mini golf, shopping or cuddling with their dog Sally.

Read more at https://www.katealexanderauthor.com/.